A
HOUSE
DIVIDED

Other books

THE CURTAIN

THE SEER

TREE MEN

THE EXCHANGED

A
HOUSE
DIVIDED

By

ANDREW WOODS

I dedicate this story to my friend,

John F. Milchling.

You were my number one fan, supporter and the one that would continuously kick me in the backside to keep me going when I wanted to quit. Thank you…

First and foremost, I thank God for allowing me the time, determination and ability to endure for over fifteen months as I pieced this story together

I thank my friend John for believing in me and for not giving up on me. I can still hear him telling me "*You got this*".

I thank Jerry L. Lucky for his part in reading over the story while still in its raw form and for allowing me to add him to the story

I also thank David F. Minnick for taking his time and reading over my proof

Last, but not least,

I thank my wife Margaret for being there by my side

Table of contents

COURAGE

Ever have this burning desire inside
that you could almost scream?
It is something that you always wanted,
your real life dream.

The chance to be heard and
to somehow rise,
you want your life to be seen
through someone else's eyes.

You choke back your tears and
swallow your pride,
you stand up and walk out in front
because you realize that there is
nowhere else to hide.

You do all that is required in order
to continue on,
you find the strength no matter
how ripped, tattered or torn.

After many, many years you step
out into the light,
it's amazing, but it took many, many
years in order to feel right.

CHAPTER ONE

It was a beautiful spring day in April 1996 when Sergio Alverna once again set foot on U.S. soil for the first time in almost fifteen years. He dreamed of this day for many years and for many different reasons. From the time of his birth, he was bounced around every six months or so due to the nature of his father's employment. Sergio and his mom were the ones that were mainly kept in the shadows as his dad did his thing. By the time that he was sixteen, Serg, as most called him, was able to speak many languages and the dialects that came with them. He lived in many Eastern European countries and a few Middle Eastern countries as well. When he did make friends, they were usually the ones that were the outcast individuals in society. Not the kind that one would desire to bring home to mother. Each time, before he was to be swept away with his father, he and his comrades would make a pact that one day, they would all get together and do something that would forever change the world. Well, that day was coming soon.

As Serg exited the front doors of Dulles International Airport, he stopped, placed his bags on the ground, tilted his head back, closed his eyes and took a deep breath of the American air. As he exhaled, he gave a big smile and looked around, "Ah, the beginning of the American dream. Once I am with my comrades, we can begin a new life."

He hailed a taxi and handed the driver a piece of paper with an address on it for a secluded home in Chantilly, Virginia. The residence belonged to someone that was a regular customer of his father. The owner told Serg that if he ever got to the States, that he is to look him up and stay for as long as he sees fit. So, Serg took the man up on his offer and he made his way there.

When they reached the address on the paper, the driver stopped at the beginning of the driveway. He looked out the window and whistled, "Wow, sure looks like a nice place to be on a beautiful day like today." The driver looked around to see nothing but nothing. All that was visible was trees and grass. There was a slight breeze blowing and that added to the beauty as the grass swayed in the wind and the trees kept time swaying with the grass. Serg asked the driver to continue up the driveway.

The driveway was tree lined and at least three-quarter mile long with slight turns and an occasional dip that would rise over a crest. There was no way that anyone could see the residence from the road. Once they reached the main house, Serg asked the driver to remain here for a moment and that someone would be with him soon. He also asked him to keep the meter running. The driver looked at the fare so far and had no problem with keeping the meter on. "Hey Pal, take as long as you like, I'm not going anywhere."

Serg smiled, "I believe that with all my heart." The driver slumped down in the seat a little bit and stretched out his legs towards the other side.

About ten minutes later, there was a tap on the driver's door. As the driver sat up, he saw a man standing there pointing a gun in his face. "Turn off the engine and get out of the car." The driver had thoughts of throwing the car in gear and jamming the gas pedal. The man with the gun pulled the hammer back, "I will not say it again." With that said, he waved the gun for the man to exit.

The driver did as was told and exited the vehicle. The man motioned for the driver to start walking and he told another man to put the vehicle away. As the driver was walking and looking up while saying a little prayer, the man with the gun told him that he hopes that his prayers are answered. With those being the last words said, the man discharged the weapon into the back of the driver's skull. The man removed a radio from his belt and called for a cleanup crew. "Remove all traces of this man. All the way from his tire marks entering the driveway to his blood on the ground. We need this to be invisible."

The man that took the vehicle and drove it to a rather large garage that was a little way from the main house. As he backed the cab inside, he placed it in an elevator next to a DC city bus that had been acquired a few months back. There were four different levels to the garage. The man got out of the vehicle and pressed the down button located outside the elevator. Two levels down, there was another man waiting to take control of the vehicle. He gently placed the vehicle next to an acquired DC Police car. He removed the key and headed towards the stairs. Once on the top floor, he met up with the first man and they both filled out the log that was near the door.

The two men made their way back to the main house. Once there, they entered and joined the other seventeen individuals in the parlor, where drinks were poured, and hugs were given. For many, this was the first time that any of them have seen each other in years. They have all remained in contact, but never face to face as they are now.

Serg rose his glass and tapped on it with a coin. "Gentlemen, brothers in arms, I salute you all. This is a day to begin the celebrations, but the real celebrations will be many, many days down the road. We have years to build this so that all goes as we planned. Today, our cell wakes up, but, a few years from now, we will wake the giant. So, we need to be sure that we are one hundred percent ready when we wake this giant to slay it as David did with Goliath." They all rose their glasses and cheered loud.

After about an hour of celebration, Serg asked everyone to put their glasses down and listen to what he has to say. "Brothers, tomorrow, we begin our homework. I will pass out assignments and everyone will have their own assignment in life to fulfill. It has been years since we have seen each other and after today, it will be a few years until we all meet again. All that I ask of you all is that you all learn your new roles to the fullest. Once we rise, there will be no room for error. We need to be the best of the best."

MAY 2010

Just outside of Stafford, Virginia, thirty-seven-year-old, Francis Wayhome was driving back to her place of employment. Francis is owner and CEO of Premium Server, a software storage and cloud retrieval facility located outside of Langley, Virginia. Her business is probably more secure than Fort Knox and ten times more valuable. As she was driving, she heard a siren and looked in her rearview mirror to see that the police were pulling her over. Not sure why she was being pulled over. She knew that she always obeyed the traffic signals and the posted speed limits. Who knows, maybe she has a taillight out. As she pulled her BMW i8 Roadster off to the shoulder, she began to retrieve her license and registration.

The officer sat in his patrol car for about five minutes before Frances looked at her watch and decided that it had been enough time for him to have done his part and sent her on her way. As she opened her car door, the officer called over the loudspeaker for her to remain in the vehicle. A few minutes later, the officer emerged from his vehicle and headed towards hers. Frances observed him approaching and saw that he had his hat on and a pair of dark glasses. She rose her arm and waved her credentials for him to retrieve. "Here you go." The officer stopped beside the car and just stood there. Frances lowered her own sunglasses to the bridge of her nose and peered at the officer.

"Okay officer, if you do not mind, can we get this over with? I have to get back to work, I have a board meeting in thirty minutes, and I am…" She looked at her watch, "I am twenty minutes out. So, can we do this and get it over with?" The officer just stood there, no emotion, no expression change. Frances was getting a little perturbed, "Besides, may I inquire as to why you stopped me? I was not speeding, weaving nor was I impeding traffic. So, what is this about?"

The officer removed his phone and hit a few buttons, "Ma'am, may I have your license please?" Frances handed him her license and registration. "Just your license Ma'am."

She peered at him over her glasses again, "Okay, whatever you want, let's just get done here so that I can go." She handed him her license and he accepted it.

He looked at it, pressed a few buttons into his phone and then he began. "Ma'am, I need to ask you a series of questions, I hope that you do not mind."

She looked at him, "Questions? Questions about what?"

"Ma'am, I will explain if you are the one that I am looking for."

She looked at the officer with a quizzical stare, "Okay, if it will get me out of here any time sooner, fire away."

The officer kept the same emotionless stare. "Ma'am, are you Frances Elaine Wayhome from 23172 Hope Road in Stafford, Virginia?"

She looked at him and got a little ruffled, "Look moron, if you actually looked at my license, then I am pretty sure that you would be able to read that."

His expression never changed. "Are you the wife of Aaron, mother of Sean?"

She was not only getting a little upset, now she was getting worried, "What the hell is this all about? I want another officer here." She attempted to dial the phone when the officer grabbed it from her hand, and he placed his service weapon to her temple.

"Ma'am, just answer my questions truthfully and we can move on."

Frances started to shake and sob at that moment, "Look Officer, I do not know what this is all about, but please take that weapon off me. I will answer any questions." The officer asked the questions again and Frances answered each one.

After he was satisfied that he had the right person, the officer removed his phone and showed her a series of pictures. "What the hell is this? Why are you showing me pictures of my son?"

"Ma'am, you are the CEO of Premium Server, are you not?"

Frances was shaking from fear, "Yes, yes I am. But you already know that. But why? What is this all about?"

"Ma'am, I need you to calm down and to carefully listen to each and every word that I say. If you do so, then your son will be fine. If not, then I cannot guarantee the safety of your child."

6

Frances was beside herself as to what she was hearing. "Please tell me what this is all about. I want another officer here; I have that right."

The man was attempting to remain calm and expressionless, but she was about to push him over the line. "Ma'am, I need you to listen to what I am about to tell you. You have just become a part of something that is larger than you could ever comprehend. You have a talent that my organization is in need of. If you cooperate and provide us with the service that we need, then Ma'am, you will receive your son back. But, if you decide to take matters beyond what you have control of, then you will not like the consequences. Do I make myself perfectly clear?" Frances was numb, mad and scared all at the same time. "Ma'am, I need an answer right now."

Frances sat there a moment before she spoke up, "I do not know what you want, and I do not understand why you will not get another officer here. I have rights and I also have the right to refuse to answer any of your questions. Just tell me what you want so that I can go."

The man removed his phone, hit a few buttons, and then began. "Frances Wayhome is a positive and also an uncooperative." The man listened for a moment, "Yes. Yes, I understand. Terminate mission." The man reached inside of his jacket and removed a handgun with a silencer and placed it to Frances' temple. With no hesitation, he pulled the trigger, ending Frances' life and any part that she may have had in this operation. He removed the silencer before placing the handgun in her left hand. He reached into one of his pockets and removed a small can and sprayed a substance on Frances' left hand, the side of her head and body near where the gun discharged, her clothing and parts of the interior of her car around her left side. He gave Frances a little shove and she fell across the seat of her Roadster towards the passenger side. The man calmly returned to his vehicle and drove off, leaving Frances there to bleed out in her vehicle.

*****

"Good evening, everyone and thank you for tuning into WNEW Action News, I am Lenny Woods. Tonight, we have breaking news out of Stafford Virginia. The CEO of Premium Server has been found slumped over in her automobile in what appears to be an apparent suicide. On the scene, we have Vanessa Cole, she is with our sister station WASH-TV out of Washington, D.C." Lenny turns in his seat to the monitor over his left shoulder. "Vanessa, what can you tell us."

The screen goes to full picture with Vanessa. "Lenny, a call came in today just after one pm from a motorist that came upon a vehicle on the side of the road. The motorist said that he could not help but notice that the driver's window was down on the BMW as he was going past. He just thought that it was strange that an expensive vehicle would be open like that on the side of the road with no one in sight. He said that he pulled over and backed up to within a few feet of the vehicle and got out. As he approached the vehicle, he could see that there was in fact someone in the vehicle and it appeared that they were laying across the seat. As he neared the driver's door, that is when he saw the blood. Lenny, some of the pictures that you are about to see can be quite graphic." Still pictures came up on the screen.

"The motorist said that he did not attempt check for signs of life due to the amount of blood that was present. He then returned to his vehicle and called nine-one-one and waited for the police to arrive. The deceased driver was in fact identified as Frances Wayhome, she was the CEO and founder of Premium Server, a very secure server farm located outside of Langley, Virginia. At this present time, the preliminary examination and investigation has the cause of death listed as suicide. The body will be transported to the Washington Medical Examiner's Office for an autopsy. Due to the nature of whom this person was and the business that she had; the FBI has stepped in to perform their own investigation. For WASH-TV, I am Vanessa Cole. Back to you Lenny."

"Thanks Vanessa. As we get more on this investigation, we will pass it along."

CHAPTER TWO

"Good evening. We apologize for this interruption from WNEW Action News, but we bring you this special report." Lenny shuffles in his seat, "It has just been reported by Taiwan officials that an airliner of Taiwan Air, flight two-six-two has been lost somewhere over the Indian Ocean. Air Traffic Controllers confirmed that the flight departed Port Elizabeth and was en route to Singapore when it failed to contact Singapore after traveling through the eighteen-minute dead space over the Indian Ocean. Controllers waited a few minutes past the estimated contact time, and nothing was received. Both the Indian Government along with the Taiwan Government have dispatched ships and planes to search for the craft. At this present time, there is no additional information on the craft. As we get more information, we will pass it along. This is Lenny Woods reporting for WNEW Action News."

*****

Master Sergeant Timothy Webb just got off work at the Frances E. Warren Air Force Base, just outside of Cheyenne, Wyoming. Sergeant Webb was the head of the unit that steadily tracked and maintained the satellites that keep an eye on the secure boundaries of the United States. He had the highest clearance of any that worked in the room with him. His responsibilities were to ensure that the satellites remain secure and out of the reach of hackers.

He was not five minutes out of the main gate when he noticed that his vehicle was starting to overheat and create steam. He pulled off to the side of the road and shut the engine down. He got out and opened the hood. The steam was rising furiously. He waved his hands to get a clearer vision of the engine. As he waved, he heard a vehicle approaching. He stopped waving the steam and attempted to wave the vehicle down. To his surprise and good luck, it was a rollback truck coming his way.

The driver saw Sergeant Webb and he pulled over right in front of his vehicle. The driver got out and asked if he could possibly be of any assistance. Sergeant Webb never felt so appreciative in his life. He explained what had just happened and he told the driver that he could not believe his luck. The driver offered to load the vehicle and take it back to his shop. Sergeant Webb agreed, and the vehicle was loaded.

As they started along, Sergeant Webb introduced himself. "Oh, by the way, my name is Tim, Tim Webb." Tim stuck his hand out, but the driver did not accept it. Tim thought, 'Okay'. The driver did not say too much of anything for a few minutes.

Finally, he pulled the truck off to the side and he did speak. "Timothy Webb, husband of Lydia, father of Joanie?"

Tim looked at the driver, "What? What did you just say?"

The driver turned to Tim, "Timothy Webb, please remain calm. I have something to tell you and if you do not agree, then I cannot guarantee the safety of your child."

Tim was getting a little defensive. "What the hell is this? What is going on? Look, I don't know who you are, and you certainly do not know me. You ever mention anything about my child's safety again and pal, that will be it for you."

The man sat there a second before continuing. "Timothy Webb, we need your special skills, if you give us what we want, we will give you what you want."

Tim sat there for a moment. "Okay, I'll bite. What is this all about?"

"Timothy Webb, your specialty is satellite tracking, is it not?"

Tim looked a little confused. "Yes…and why do you have interest in that?"

"My organization needs your knowledge. When you fulfill your obligation, your child will be returned to you as healthy as she is now."

Tim chuckled a bit. "You are a little slow there, pal, what did I just tell you a moment ago? And what do you mean *returned*? My daughter is home."

The man removed his phone and pressed a few buttons before turning the phone towards Tim. "As you can see Mr. Webb, your daughter is in good hands." Tim was shocked and pissed at the same time. He was ready to lunge at the man. "Mr. Webb, please try to keep your composure and hear me out. I represent an organization that will stop at nothing in order to get what we have as our objective. Your child, along with a few others are just our way of guaranteeing that we will succeed in our mission."

"Mission? What mission?"

"Mr. Webb, that information is not for you to be concerned with. All that you are required to do is to fulfill what is asked of you and for you to not contact the authorities. If you do not cooperate and you contact the authorities, we will return your child, but just not as you desire."

Tim was starting to lose his cool. "If you harm my child, I will…"

The man cut him off. "Mr. Webb, the only one that can harm your child is you yourself. Your child will be given the utmost care while she is with us. Once you fulfill your obligation, you will be given your child and the amount of one million dollars cash for your services. Whether you accept and or report the payment, that is entirely up to you. Your child is fine. I need you to perform one other task for me."

Tim gave him the evil eye. "Yeah, and what will that be?"

"Mr. Webb, I need you to sit down with your wife, Lydia, and convince her to go along with this so that she can hold her child again. Can you do that?"

Tim sat there a moment. "Do I have a choice?"

The man smiled. "Of course, Mr. Webb, of course you do. Either one that you choose, that is the one that you will have to live with."

Two days later, just outside of Fort Benning, Georgia. Lieutenant Lawrence 'Larry' Rollins was jogging and keeping very good time with the audio book of TREE MEN bouncing in his head when he noticed a car was slowly keeping pace with him. He was on an isolated tree lined road that had little to no roads off it, just a few paths that he had beaten down so many times in his career as an Infantry Officer. He was just about to stop and turn to confront the driver when the vehicle swerved around him and accelerated off. The lieutenant stopped and stood there a few seconds wondering what was going on.

A few hours later, as he was about to run a few errands, Lieutenant Rollins heard a car pull up outside of his home and he saw two men in uniform start up his walk towards the house. Just as they arrived on the porch, Lieutenant Rollins opened the door. "Good afternoon, gentlemen, how may I help you?" The two men both sported captain bars. One was short, and sort of round and the other was large and muscular.

The portly one spoke up. "Lieutenant Rollins? Lieutenant Lawrence Joseph Rollins?"

Larry looked at them. "Yes, now how may I help you Gentlemen? Is something wrong?"

The men both looked at each other and then the larger one spoke up. "Sir, we need to discuss a situation with you in private, may we come in?"

Larry moved to the side and gestured for them to enter. "By all means, come on in."

As the men passed him, Larry noticed that the insignia on their uniforms were none that he had ever encountered. He asked them to have a seat and in unison, the two sat down. "May I get either one of you something to drink?"

They both waved off the offer. "Lieutenant, we are not here for a social call, may I see your I.D. please?"

Larry thought that this was a little strange of a request, but nonetheless, he offered it up. "Sure, let me grab my wallet." He retrieved his wallet from the mantle and removed his I.D. "Here you go. Now, can you tell me what this is all about?" The men looked at the I.D. and nodded in agreement.

"Lieutenant, I will be direct and to the point. You are the munitions supply officer, are you not?"

"Yes, yes, I am, why? Did something happen that I should be aware of?"

The bigger of the two spoke up. "Sir, our organization needs your assistance."

Larry chuckled, "Your organization? What organization?"

The bigger one continued. "Sir, our organization needs your assistance in acquiring the high explosive Semtex, lots of it, Sir. Approximately five thousand pounds, Sir."

Larry looked at them for a few seconds and he burst out in laughter. "Oh, that's a good one. Who put you guys up to this? Was it Smitty from the range?" The men were not laughing, and neither were they changing their mundane expressions.

The portly man took the control. "Lieutenant, this is not a joke. We, like yourself, have missions and orders to fulfill, ours is to get your cooperation in this matter, and yours is to fulfill what we ask for. Lieutenant, your daughter is Bella Marie, is it not?"

Larry jumped to his feet. "What the fuck? Why do you want to know that?!"

The bigger man stood up. "Lieutenant, your daughter is currently with us. She is being well cared for and we would like to keep it that way."

The look on Larry's face was of both shock and rage. "What the hell do you mean *currently with us*? Where is she?" The portly one removed his phone and pressed a few buttons. He turned the phone towards Larry. He could see Bella Marie on the floor playing with some other children.

She looked up, waved and called out. "Hi Daddy, I'm here playing with my new friends." The man hung the phone up and placed it back in his pocket.

"Lieutenant, I need you to calm down and listen closely to what we say. Like I previously told you, our organization has an objective, and we will do whatever we have to do in order to fulfill the requirements for that objective. The one way that we are sure that we can do such is by ensuring that there is a key ingredient in the objective. In this case, your daughter is the key ingredient. There are many that are needed to make this mission a success. Like you, the others that are needed also have a child that is being used as a way to ensure that we get what we need. Like the others, if you cooperate, then she is returned healthy. If you fight us by refusal or going to the authorities, then you will receive your daughter back, only in more pieces than we acquired her. Do I make myself perfectly clear, Lieutenant?"

"Yes, yes you do. I have one question though."

"Yes Lieutenant, what may that be?"

"What about when the school or Bella's friends or even the neighbors start asking about her whereabouts? What do I say for that?"

The portly man smiled. "Lieutenant, with your child and with all the others, that has been prearranged. Her school was given a letter from the Federal Government when she was picked up today by her aunt. The letter states that due to your position with the military that death threats were made against your family and the military thought that it would be best if Bella was relocated to a safe undisclosed place for a time being."

"You say that her aunt picked her up."

Larry laughed. "She has no one on her authorized pickup list besides me."

The big man smiled for once. "Lieutenant, that has all been taken care of for about a year now. She was picked up by her Aunt Sharon Kesson. You personally added her on the list last year. Well, as far as the school is concerned, it was you."

Larry sat there a moment just taking it all in until he had his thoughts together. "Okay, it appears that you currently have the upper hand, what now?"

The portly man finally attempted a smile. "Good Lieutenant, glad that I have your attention and your cooperation. Now...now we wait for our call. When we receive our orders to move forward, you in turn will receive yours. Once you fulfill your obligation, your daughter will be safely returned to you along with one million dollars cash for your services, all in unmarked, untraceable bills. You may do whatever you desire with the cash, that is not our concern. Our concern is to fulfill our mission."

Larry sat there a moment, then stood and began pacing. "You know, ever since my wife died, it has just been me and Bella. I do whatever it takes to make sure that she is safe. So..." Larry paused for a few seconds. "I am not looking to commit treason towards the United States, nor am I looking to spend the rest of my life in Leavenworth, but I will do what I must do to ensure that no harm comes to my daughter. Gentlemen, you have my full cooperation."

The men stood and the bigger of the two extended his hand, "Thank you Lieutenant, we will be in contact." Larry did not return the courtesy handshake, he just looked him in the eye.

"If the two of you would not mind me being totally honest for a moment, I would like to share something with you."

The portly man spoke. "By all means Lieutenant, please speak freely."

Larry got a blank cold expression on his face. "I would like you two to know that I too will have an objective. I want you two to know that when this is all over, that I will personally track the two of you down and I will kill you both. My objective will not stop there, I will attempt to find any of your family members, and I will butcher them. Do I make myself perfectly clear?"

The portly man smiled and spoke up. "Lieutenant, do as you see fit. Because the two of us will die in our mission anyway. There will be nothing of us for you to kill. Good day Lieutenant." The two men walked out the door and never looked back.

Fort Howard Park, Baltimore County, Maryland

Yuri Asimov was testing out a new drone with a new long-range program that would not have to depend on satellite assistance. If his design and program passed, he would submit it to the Central Intelligence Agency for use in the Middle East. The programs that the CIA currently has required a satellite to be present to send the signal. Yuri has spent the last three years coming up with this design. As he watched through his virtual visor, he saw that his range was well over eighty miles and that he could see Smith Island as he passed over. His goal on this trial run was to fly all the way to the Chesapeake Bay Bridge Tunnel, retrieve a small box with the claw and return it to him in Fort Howard Park.

As he continued, a man approached him. The man put his hand up to his eyes to shield the sun. "Good morning. Boy, that thing must be way out there, I don't even see it. Where is it?"

Without moving his head and with his hands steady on the controller that was attached to a harness around his neck, Yuri answered. "Yes, it is out there. Believe it or not, it is actually over the horizon and still going."

The man smiled. "Did you lose control of it, and it is still going?"

Yuri chuckled. "No. No, I very much have control of it. I am just testing out my new design. If all goes well, then it should be back here with its prize in less than thirty minutes."

"Wow! That must be some drone, huh Mr. Asimov?"

At the sound of his name mentioned and not recognizing the voice of the person saying it, Yuri got a little nervous. "Ah, yes, yes, it is. I'm sorry, I am a little busy at this moment, I am on a time test. Whom do I have the pleasure of not seeing at this moment?"

"Mr. Asimov, my name is not important, but what is important is that you listen to every word that I have to say. Can you do that?" Yuri did not have much choice. It was not like he could just set the drone down and have a conversation at this moment.

"Okay, what do you want? You want my drone? Is that it? If that is it, then you realize that I could send it into the bay, and you would never find it? So, what will it be?"

The man smiled. "Mr. Asimov, my organization does not desire your drone, but we do desire that technology that you have put into this version." Yuri turned his head a split second to look at the man. After a second, he realized that with both hands occupied and with the visor on, that he could not see the man and he turned his head back towards where he was looking.

"What do you mean, your *organization*?"

"Mr. Asimov, I need you to remain calm and focused as I tell you what I came here for. Can you do that?"

Yuri nodded. "I supposed so. Get on with it."

"Mr. Asimov, I represent an organization of people that will stop at nothing to get the results that they so much desire. We desire your skills at creating a program and the control ability to send a drone many miles without the need of satellites for tracking. We need your specialties."

"My specialties? And what do I get in return for my *specialties*?"

The man removed his phone and brought up a live feed, "Mr. Asimov, please take a peek at this phone. You may recognize someone." Yuri turned his head and used his arm to brush up the edge of the visor just a bit.

He looked at the screen. "Hi Daddy. Whatcha doin?" Yuri was numb and frozen at the moment.

He gathered enough strength to speak. "Honey, Daddy is a little busy at this moment. Daddy will call you back, okay?"

"Okay Daddy, love you."

"Love you too Sweetie." The man hung up the phone.

"Mr. Asimov, ready to hear me out?"

Yuri was without words or emotion at the moment. All that he could muster up was a slight, "Yes."

At about that time, the drone reached the center tower of the Bridge Tunnel and Yuri sat the drone down. He removed his visor and confronted the man. "What's going on here? Where is my daughter?"

"Mr. Asimov, may we have a seat on that bench, and I can tell you everything that you need to know?" The man motioned towards the bench, "Mr. Asimov, please."

Yuri obliged, and they sat down. "Mr. Asimov, Svetlana is safe and fine for the time being." Yuri did not like the sound of *time being*.

"What the hell have you done with my daughter? I should call the police and have you arrested."

"Mr. Asimov, that action would lead to dire consequences for Svetlana. And that is not something that I believe that you would desire to have. Here, let me show you something. We had an individual that decided to call the police, here is what he received in the mail." The man brought up a video that showed a small boy of about five years of age that was going to be returned to his parents. But before they got him back, the video shows a man with a mask on dismembering every part of the boy from fingers to toes to internal organs. "As you can see Mr. Asimov, the people that I am associated with are not too kind." Yuri sat there a moment frozen and sweating from fear.

"Okay, you have my attention, how do I get my little girl back safe and sound?"

"That's better Mr. Asimov. Much better. All you must do is what we instruct you to do, that is all. Nothing more, nothing less. In return for your services, you will be able to hug Svetlana and Svetlana will be able to hug you again for as long as you like. Also, you will receive one million dollars in cash that you can do with as you desire. Keep it or hand it in, that is up to you."

Yuri sat there a moment looking at the man. "So, what exactly am I to do and not to do?"

"What not to do is the easy part. You are not to contact the authorities nor are you to discuss this with anyone other than myself. The other part, well, the other part requires you to retrofit your program and your controls into a commercial airliner."

"What?! You serious? Not sure what you think that I do here but let me inform you. I build drones. 'D-R-O-N-E-S', drones. Not commercial aircraft. How in the hell am I to retrofit a commercial aircraft with something that is designed for a smaller unit?"

"Well Mr. Asimov, that question is for you to figure out. Because, as of today, you have about one year to come up with a working model."

Yuri looked at him. "You really are serious, aren't you?"

The man smiled. "Care to review the video again Mr. Asimov?"

Yuri stared him straight in the face. "No, no, I am good."

The man stood up. "Well then, Mr. Asimov, I will leave you here to continue on our work. I will be seeing you soon so that you can get started. Oh, you better pick up the package and get that drone back here before someone gets suspicious." The man walked away as smoothly as he appeared.

The weather for the day of the funeral for Frances Wayhome, was cool and damp. Though it was quite nasty out, there must have been over two hundred people that came out to pay their respects. One man in particular stood back away from all the rest. He continued to stand there after the service and watched as the people said their condolences. The man watched and waited for a certain individual that he knew would be there. As that person was done and headed towards his car, the man made his way to confront him. "Sure, is sad about what happened to Miss Wayhome, wouldn't you say so, Mr. Black?"

Jeremy Black elevated to the position of CEO of Premium Server after the apparent suicide of Frances. It was not a position that he was vying for any time soon, but as circumstances would have it, he did not have much choice. Jeremy stopped walking and turned towards the man. "Excuse me Sir, do we know each other?"

The man smiled. "No Mr. Black, we do not know each other, but I do know everything about you."

Jeremy looked at him, "Oh, and how so?"

"Mr. Black, may we have a seat in your vehicle? There is a lot that I need to inform you about."

Jeremy sort of laughed. "Sir, I do not know you and I do not believe that it would be a good idea to allow you in my vehicle."

Jeremy started to walk away, "Mr. Black, please listen to me or your wife Phoebe will never hold Mercedes again."

Jeremy stopped in his tracks. "What? What did you just say to me? You threaten me and my family?"

The man never changed his demeanor. "Mr. Black, you really need to hear me out. This is you last opportunity. Do not let what happened to Miss Wayhome happen to you."

Jeremy stood there, unsure what to say or do. After a moment. "Okay, okay, I'll listen, let's go to my car." The two of them proceeded to Jeremy's Town car.

Jeremy hit the key fob and started the vehicle remotely. He also hit the button to unlock the driver's door and he got in. The man walked around to the passenger side and pulled the handle...nothing. He tapped on the window and Jeremy looked at him. A few seconds later, Jeremy unlocked the passenger door and the man got in.

"Now, Mr. Black, I need you to listen to me."

Jeremy reached in a pocket on the side of his seat and quickly produced a handgun. With fire in his eyes and despair in his voice, he swung the handgun towards the man and began a rant. "No...No, you need to listen to me *asshole*, I am in charge here! Do you fuckin' get that?! I am in charge!" The man sat there with the same expression that he entered the initial conversation with.

Jeremy used his other hand to retrieve his phone. "Now asshole, you are going to jail!" Jeremy punched in 9-1-1.

The man spoke up. "Mr. Black, before you hit *send*, please hang up the phone before you regret your actions."

The man reached for his pocket and Jeremy jumped and thrusted the handgun in the man's face. "Slowly remove your hand from your pocket or I'll put a fuckin' bullet in your eye!"

"Okay, Mr. Black, I am removing my hand from my pocket." The man removed his hand and held something up. "Mr. Black, I do believe that your handgun would be a lot more effective with this." Jeremy looked, and he saw the man was holding the clip to his handgun.

Jeremy looked at the bottom of the gun butt and saw a hole where the clip should be. "Damn!"

The man reached his hand out and Jeremy placed the handgun in his hand. "Mr. Black, I will be totally honest with you. I have been well above the tolerance that I was allowed for who we need. But, if I was to dispatch you as I did Ms. Wayhome, then once again, I am back to the beginning. That is not one thing that I desire to keep repeating. I need you to listen to me and listen well." Jeremy agreed that he would listen.

"Mr. Black, my organization is in need of your expertise and your server farm."

"What? What exactly are you after?"

"Mr. Black, we are in need of a service that you can offer. If you cooperate, neither you nor your family will be harmed. You will be handsomely compensated for your time and trouble that we ask of you. Any questions?"

Jeremy sat there a second before answering. "What was that part about my wife possibly never holding my daughter again?"

The man removed his phone and punched in a few numbers and then turned the screen towards Jeremy. "Mr. Black, as you can see, Mercedes is fine. As long as you do what is asked of you, she will remain that way. If you feel as though you need to call the police, then you will not be happy with the final results. Do I make myself perfectly clear?"

"Where is my daughter now?"

"Mr. Black, she is being well cared for. Would you like to speak to her?"

"Yes, yes I would."

"Mr. Black, please do not do anything stupid, just act normal, okay?" Jeremy agreed, and the man had the phone placed near his daughter.

She looked up and saw the screen. "Hi Daddy!"

Jeremy attempted a smile. "Hi Sweetheart."

CHAPTER THREE

It took about two months for the organization to bring everyone together that they required. Along the way, there were a few that rejected the offer and decided to contact the authorities with the hope of busting this organization wide open and receiving their children back. All that those few received for going against the rules, were multiple packages in the mail that arrived with random body parts of their child. If only they had played along, their child would have eventually returned safe and healthy.

Every so often, someone from the organization would randomly show up out of the blue just to let the people know that things are still moving forward. When they would ask about their children, most times, there is a short phone conversation just to verify that their child is still okay. Most times, the parent will tell the child that they are away on a work assignment and that they will be back soon. Some of the children cry and tell them that they want to come home. That is the part that really gets to the parent and makes them want to cross the line. The man with the phone brings them back to reality quick. "Just a little while longer and everyone will be back where they belong."

*****

"Good evening, I am Lenny Woods, and this is WNEW Action News, thank you for joining us this evening. We begin this broadcast with a report coming out of the White House that states that the Department of the Army is currently looking into the alleged theft of a large cache of explosives. With the full story, we turn to Vanessa Cole with our sister station WASH-TV Washington." Lenny turned in his chair to look at the large monitor over his left shoulder. "Good evening, Vanessa. What can you tell us about the alleged theft?"

The screen goes full, with Vanessa at the center. "Good evening, Lenny. Reports are surfacing out of Washington that states that about five thousand pounds of the plastic explosive Semtex has mysteriously disappeared from a storage facility at Fort Benning in Georgia. The report states that the alleged theft was not discovered until an audit was recently being conducted. A spokesperson stated that if the audit had shown a small quantity of the explosive missing, then they would usually credit that loss to bad record keeping, but due to the amount missing, a full-scale investigation has been started. That amount of explosives, in not just the wrong hands, but in any hands, could mean trouble. As we learn more, we will pass it along. This is Vanessa Cole reporting live from Fort Benning, Georgia for WASH-TV Washington. Lenny, now back to you in the studio."

"Thank you, Vanessa."

*****

Yuri was relocated to Pakistan so that he could have the ability, the privacy, and the unlimited resources to do what he had to do in order to fulfil his obligation. He was working some days up to twenty hours a day in the attempt to get everything complete by the time restriction that was imposed on him. There were times when he would fall asleep standing up. Some days, all he wanted to do was to lay down and go to sleep. But the ones that oversaw him would not allow him to rest very much. All that they wanted from him was for him to do what was required and nothing else. He was allowed to speak to Svetlana on one occasion that was all. The transmission was severed when his daughter started to ask

28

too many questions and when she started to cry. Yuri is continually assured that his daughter is safe and healthy and that they would be together after he completes his task.

As time progressed, Yuri attached his drone device to a few different aircraft, but each time, the tests failed. The craft either went down prematurely or the controls malfunctioned. So, as a safety measure, after about the fourth loss, he did request that a pilot to be in the craft so that they would not continue to lose aircraft until he finally had the system perfected. He did not have a problem with attaching his system to smaller crafts, but the larger the craft were, the more complex they were and that was what worried him. He kept telling them that he is a software designer, not an aircraft manufacturer. Although he did have a few aircraft technicians working with him, he did not understand the full-scale mechanics of such a vehicle. Designing remote controls for small drones with a half dozen moving parts is a world apart from designing remote controls for a forty-five-ton aircraft. But Yuri continued to trudge on, he had an objective, and he really had no other choice.

*****

Many others with the special skills that were needed were occasionally checked on to make sure that they too were keeping sharp with their skills. From what the organization could observe, their mission was right on schedule. There were a few road bumps in the beginning, but that was all smoothed out within a few months. The many years of planning were finally about to pay off. All that they needed was to have the aircraft fitted with the remote control and then they could finally set an exact date.

*****

"Good evening, I am Lenny Woods, and this is the six o'clock edition of WNEW-TV Action News. We begin tonight with a report out of Russia at an area known as Novy Port. It has been reported that there have been two operational *TK Class* nuclear submarines with long range missiles that are unaccounted for. The CIA has released a previous classified report that states that these two submarines do in fact carry two nuclear tipped missiles each. Ever since the breakup of the former Soviet Union, the submarines have been stored at the former naval base awaiting cleansing and scrapping. When the submarines were recently sold at an unseen auction, the new owners decided to offer the scrapping contract to private contractors. The identity of the private contractors and the location of the submarines can't be confirmed. As we get more information, we will pass it along. For WNEW, this is Lenny Woods."

*****

A meeting was called at the house in Chantilly. All seventeen men arrived at different intervals and each one was greeted at the door by the resident. The resident hugged each one as if they were a long-lost brother that had just found his way home.

Each man was directed to a room off the foyer. As each waited for the rest of the group to arrive, they shared stories of how their lives had changed over the past many years since they all sat in that same room. Some said that if it was not for their mission, then they would prefer to remain in the field that they were chosen to learn. They all knew that their placement here was not to live the *American dream*. They were here to fulfill a dream of their own. A dream that would be a living and long nightmare for many Americans.

As the last one arrived, the resident closed and locked the door, then he directed the last man to the parlor. As all the men sat there, the resident remained standing at the end of the table. He reached for and raised his glass. "Brothers, I would like to welcome you all back here and I would like to propose a toast. Please, stand and raise your glass in honor." They all stood and raised their glasses.

"It has been a long and prosperous road these past years. You all have learned your lessons well and those lessons will take us all into bigger and better days in the name of Allah. We will be able to show America what we are made of, we will bring them to their knees forever." The man raised his glass as high as he could. "Let this red wine represent the blood of America. We will consume this blood as a token. So, in the name of Allah, I thank you all." The men followed suit and raised their glasses in reverence before consuming the wine.

The man in charge called for the servers to bring the meal. They all ate and talked openly during their feast. When they were all satisfied that they could not consume any more, the servers were called once again to clear the area and they were all invited back along with the cooks. The man in charge invited them all to stand by the huge fireplace and he handed them all a glass of wine. He raised his own glass and offered them all a private toast. "Ladies and Gentlemen, I thank you for your time here today. You will never know how big of a part that you all played here today in helping us to celebrate our mission. You all will never know the outcome of our mission, but I thank you all for your time and service." He raised his glass. "Cheers to you all." They all repeated his words and drank. The man stepped back, and all his comrades removed handguns and executed every one of them. He raised his glass again. "Allahu Akbar."

The men raised their own glasses and in unison called out. "Allahu Akbar."

The leader called all the men to another room, and he handed each of them a set of papers. On those papers were instructions on when and where each of their personal charges were to be placed so that they could have the most effect. Everything was coming along as planned, the mission would be a success.

The head man spoke up. "Before we part here today and start down the road of no turning back, does anyone have any questions or concerns?" He scanned over each man and not a flinch from any of them. "Outstanding, now, let's finish our drinks and then we depart. Mustafa, is everything ready for our departure?"

"Yes Deval, charges are placed, we are ready."

Deval raised his glass once more. "Brothers, finish this glass of American blood and we will go." They all quickly drank their glass of wine, and they all tossed the glasses against the fireplace breaking them. Deval was the last to toss his glass. "The wine was their blood; the glass was their spirit. Let us all leave."

The men all vacated the house and went to their respective vehicles. As the last vehicle was rolling down the long driveway, a series of small explosions could be faintly heard emitting from inside the house and the barn. No turning back now.

*****

Two days later, at 8 a.m., a Maryland Energy Commission van with two occupants slowly rolled along the Susquehanna River on Shures Landing Road headed towards the Conowingo Dam Hydro Station. The driver did not say a word, but the passenger did speak. Looking around, he stated. "It is very pretty here, I really do hate to see it go, but we have a mission, and the mission will carry on. Pull up over there and park. We need to go sign in at the security desk."

The two men went to the front door and the man pressed the button. A few seconds later, the door latch clicked and there was a buzzing sound. The man pulled the door open, held it and gestured for Larry to enter. "Lieutenant, you first, please."

The duo walked in, and a lonely guard came out from behind the desk. He stood there for a moment before speaking. "Gentlemen, if you would like, I will assist you in bringing your equipment in. But first, I need you both to sign in." Larry was a little surprised that the guard did not ask for any identification or the nature of their business.

Without thinking, Larry spoke up. "You aren't going to ask us why we are here before you offer to help us bring our equipment in?"

The guard showed no emotion and he just sort of bit his lip before he answered. "Lieutenant Rollins, I know full well why the two of you are here. Like you, I too am not too thrilled to help with this situation, but unlike my co-worker that was approached before me, I would like my daughter back with me alive and huggable, not in multiple pieces." The guard looked at the other man, and the man just grinned.

The man spoke up. "Gentlemen, we have lots of work to do, so, if this chitchat is over, then I suggest that we get our equipment, and we get started." The three men went to the van and retrieved the equipment.

Once they were back inside, the security guard stayed at the desk while Larry and the man went on their way. The man had a GPS device that would guide them to the exact spot that they needed to be to plant the Semtex. It took almost four hours for the two of them to go down deep under the dam. There were a few times that Larry reminded the man that if it was not for the life of his daughter, then there was no way that he would ever consider doing anything like this. He told him that for the record, "You know, when this is all over and I get my daughter back, I am going to send her away."

The man looked at Larry. "Why would you do that, Lieutenant?"

"Well, sadly, I do not even know your name, but that is irrelevant. But what I do know, is your face. That is all that I am going to need to track you down."

The man looked at Larry and laughed. "Lieutenant, why would you do that?"

"Well, since I do not know your name, I will call you George. So, George, I promise you that when this is all over, I will track you down and I will show you exactly how I feel about you and your crew. I promise you that when I do find you and capture you, I will under *no* circumstances hand you over to the law. Why? Well, since you did not ask, I will tell you." For the first time, the man looked a little nervous.

"George, I will find you and I will serve justice on you and record it for all the world to see. I will hang you up from the ceiling and I will slowly remove your skin as a symbol of not allowing you to hide anywhere. I will not kill you nor dissect you as you threatened to do to my child. As a matter of fact, I may even do this in front of a full-length mirror, just so you can see the glory that I would be having." Larry had the upper hand for the moment and the man was looking even more nervous.

Finally, he spoke. "No more talking, just keep moving, we have a lot of work to do!" The man pushed Larry by the shoulder to keep him moving. "We have one more charge to place before we leave. Go, go!" It was Larry's turn to smile.

When they were done at the Hydro station, the man looked at his watch and directed Larry where to drive. The man looked at his GPS. "At the top of the hill at the stop sign, make a left. That will be Shuresville Road. Stay straight on that road until you come to Stafford Road. At Stafford Road, make a left and stay on that road until we come to Lapidum Boat Ramp. There is a boat waiting for us there that will take us to where we need to be. We are on a time schedule and so far, we are doing fine."

It only took about twenty minutes for the two of them to reach the boat ramp. Once they arrived, they saw a man standing by the boat ramp and he started to approach them as they were parking. The two of them got out of the van and George opened the sliding rear door. He directed the man as to which cases that he was to grab. "We need all the gray and tan cases. There should be six of each." George looked at his watch, we have about seven hours of day light left to complete our task, so I suggest that we get on our way."

The three men carried their cases to a State Highway Administration boat and loaded them on board. Larry stood there a moment and shook his head. Under his breath, he spoke. "Just how far does this go?"

George looked at Larry. "Lieutenant, if you would be so kind, please climb aboard, we have work to do." Larry and George climbed aboard, and the boat captain handed them both a life jacket. "Gentlemen, if you would not mind, please put these on."

They both donned their vest, and the captain removed the lines and slowly backed the boat out. Once clear of the dock, he punched the accelerator, and they were on the move. When they were nearing the I-95 Bridge, George removed his GPS device, and he directed the captain to a certain pillar on the southbound span. George and Larry climbed onto the pillar base and the boat captain passed both a gray and tan case that George asked for.

The captain looked up. "For the record Lieutenant, I really would not do this if I were not forced to. I just hope that the authorities have some type of mercy on me when they catch us. I am just grateful that I will be one that will not be in this area when all of this goes off."

Larry looked down at the captain. "I too apologize that you have to be a part of this."

George opened the cases and removed the devices and handed one to Larry. He pointed up the service ladder, "Lieutenant, if you would be so kind to go first, then please, be my guest." The two of them climbed the service ladder until they came to a platform. George once again removed his GPS and looked at it. He turned until he had a reading. "Lieutenant, if you would be so kind, please place your charge on that joint that is marked 'R-T-one-two-one-seven'."

Larry looked at George. "Not to sound impressed, but it appears that you boys must have really done your homework."

George smiled and looked Larry straight in the eye. "Lieutenant, do you think that we just got up today and decided to execute this mission? We spent years working out all the details. We went to school, we learned, and we did what we had to do to gather as much information and resources that we could before we ever even came for you. So yes, Lieutenant, we really did our homework." Larry just stared at George.

George again looked at his GPS and made a few adjustments. "Now, Lieutenant, I need you to climb the ladder to the next landing and place that charge onto the joint marked 'R-T-two-three-five-seven'. That joint is located over there on the other side." Larry looked up and then he made his way to the next landing. He placed the charge and went back down to George.

The three men made the same trip to the northbound lanes and performed the same actions. They then moved onto the freight train bridge between I-95 and Route 40 and placed the charges on the pillars as directed by George. The two men went back to the boat and proceeded to the Route 40 lanes and did the same routine. When Larry placed the last charge on the bridge and returned to the boat, George thanked him. "Thank you, Lieutenant, that was excellent."

Larry looked at the boat operator and then at George. "Can we go home now?"

George smiled. "Lieutenant, we have but one more bridge, the train bridge."

Larry looked at George. "You really are fuckin' insane, aren't you?"

"Now, now Lieutenant, like you, I have a job to do." George nodded his head and made a motion towards the train bridge. The boat captain turned the wheel and headed off in the direction that he was directed to travel.

When they arrived, Larry just sat there for a moment. George leaned over and picked up the last set of charges and stuck them out for Larry. "Lieutenant, if you would not mind." Larry sat there just staring down at the charges. "Lieutenant, it's a little late to start to have a conscience, would you not agree? This is the last one. Just think, by you placing this charge, you are one step closer to getting Bella back. Now, Lieutenant, if you would be so kind." Larry was reaching for the charge when a siren blared, and a command came over a loudspeaker.

"You three individuals in the boat. Stop what you are doing and prepare to be boarded."

George froze for a second, then regained composure. George slowly placed the charge under the tarp, then he smiled. "Gentlemen, I will handle this. Remember, one word of alerting them of anything wrong and you will get your children back real soon. Just stay calm."

The boat approaching them was the Department of Natural Resources Police. There were two men aboard and they were not heavily armed. All that Larry could see were side arms. As they were but a few feet away, the boat captain stood up and started the conversation. "Good afternoon officers, my name is John Meyers, I am with the State Highway inspection Team, how may we be of assistance?" George just gave the captain a dirty look, then continued to smile. The officer not driving asked for their bow line. Larry tossed the line and the officer secured it in the grapple.

"Gentlemen, may we see some identification and inspection paperwork?"

"Certainly", came the response from John. He retrieved his work folder and passed that and his ID over. Larry and George soon followed. The officer looked at Larry and John's ID's. Then he looked at George's ID and then at George.

"Bloom? Leonard Bloom?" George nodded his head in acknowledgement. "Sir, Mr. Bloom, if you do not mind me asking, what is the nature of your business out here with a bridge inspector? If Homeland is involved, is there something that we should be aware of?"

All eyes were now on George. "No, no officer, we are just being cautious. Any large objects of infrastructure have fallen under our watchful eye ever since nine-eleven. When an inspection is performed, whether it be any type of bridge or tunnel that is linked to a major artery, we attend the inspections."

The officer looked at George for a few seconds and then he handed the ID's back. He removed the bow line and shoved his boat away. As they started to drift, he called out. "Thank you, gentlemen. Sorry to hold you up in your work. Have a nice day." With that, the DNR police were gone.

George sat there quiet for a second, then he turned to John. "You know Mr. Meyers, if things had gone any other way than what it did, then it would have been you, that would have been responsible for six unnecessary deaths today. Just for the fun of it, if you ever had the chance to disobey a command from me again, then I will personally see to the dispatch of your son. Do we understand each other?" John just sat there with a fire in his eyes, and he said not a word.

George reached under the tarp and retrieved the charge. "Now Lieutenant, let's try this again." Larry took the charge and climbed out of the boat. As he neared the ladder, George removed his phone and opened an app. "Lieutenant, Pier two-seven-B-R-one-six. Got it?"

Larry looked at George. "Oh yeah, got it."

After all the charges were placed, the three men made their way back to the boat ramp. George was the first one out of the boat. "Gentlemen, you are both free to go wherever you desire to go. For now, your services are complete. I thank you both and I must admit, you both did rather well." George looked back and forth between the two men. "When we have completed our mission, we will gladly return your children to you unharmed, and they will each have a backpack with them with one million dollars in unmarked cash. As I stated before, you are free to do whatever you desire with the money. When either the authorities catch up to you or you take it upon yourselves to go to them, you may hand it over or you may say nothing about it at all. That is entirely up to you. But for now, good day gentlemen."

Larry and John sat there a few minutes after George left. Larry turned to John. "I really do apologize to you for you having to go through this ordeal, but for me, this is only the beginning."

John looked at Larry. "What exactly do you mean?"

Larry smiled. "As I promised him, I will track down him and his family and I will do what I told him that I will do. So, you and I can either part company now, or if you like, you may join me. The way that I feel is this, nobody fucks with my family and gets away with it. After I get my little girl back, she will be sent away safe, and I am going hunting. So, in or out?" John just sat there thinking.

CHAPTER FOUR

It was Monday, May 28, 2012, Memorial Day. That day was one of the busiest and most traveled days of the year. Millions upon millions of people got from point *A* to point *B* in personal vehicles, airplanes, buses, trains and if need be, some even walked. It was a mass exodus in any direction if you would care to look. Everyone was going about their own business to either get to the beaches or to get home in time to get things ready for going back to work the next day. The roads themselves were packed and bursting at the seams.

At around one o'clock in the afternoon, two D.C. Police vehicles and a Park Police SUV pulled into the Anacostia Park just southeast and across the Anacostia River from Washington, D.C. The Park Police vehicle was towing a trailer with a tarp covering the load. As the vehicle neared Poplar Point, it stopped, and the passenger got out. He reached into the back of the vehicle and removed four traffic cones. He placed them across both lanes of the road and then he got back in the vehicle. The vehicle continued until they came upon the old guard building near the edge of the Anacostia River.

At that point, the two D.C. Police Officers and the driver of the SUV exited their vehicles and approached anyone that was there. They informed them that they needed to vacate the area due to an emergency. There were a few that wanted to protest, and the police officers threatened them with arrest if they so desired. After they was sure that no one else was in the area, the passenger of the SUV removed four more traffic cones and walked up the road a little way before setting them up. After doing so, he headed back to the vehicle. Once he arrived back, he looked at his watch and then at the officers. "We have about one hour until we perform our mission. If you desire Mr. Curran, please make yourself comfortable for the time being."

The driver of the SUV is Bruce Curran. Bruce is a veteran of both the Afghanistan and Iraq wars. He is highly decorated, and his specialty is the mortar. He was squad leader in both wars, and he knew more about the M252 Mortar than anyone else. With his knowledge and personal experience, he was usually able to drop a round within fifteen meters from as far out as five-thousand meters. There was probably nothing new that you could show him about his weapon. Before he was about to commit treason and a terroristic act, Bruce took the advantage of a few minutes to reflect on what was about to happen. For the safety of his child, he could not do anything. He felt as though he had no other choice but to help these people commit a heinous crime.

The two officers got back into their cars, and each went a different direction on the road so that they could set up a roadblock well ahead of the cones that were placed out.

Bruce went down by the river's edge and found a nice quiet place to think. It was about eighty-two degrees and there was slight breeze coming off the water. Bruce sat there with his eyes closed and head tilted back just a bit so that he could feel the sunshine on his face. The one thought that kept going through his mind was, *just how big is this situation*. A few minutes of solitude was broken when the man came down to where Bruce was. "Mr. Curran, if you would not mind, it is about time to get set up. So please, come join me." Bruce sat there for a moment just looking up at him. The man could sense what was going through his mind. "Mr. Curran, I can assure you, this operation is way bigger than any operation that you have even been involved in. You could not begin to fathom just how deep and how well planned this has gone. We, when I say we, I mean the organization that I am a part of. We have been practicing this operation over and over for about twenty years. We have come here to the United States with the intentions of being integrated into society and learning different trades to the best of our abilities in order to fulfill our obligations for this mission. We have become doctors, lawyers, policemen, as you have just learned and many other professions. We are deep in the government and deep in the military. So, Mr. Curran, as you will soon learn, we will succeed in our mission. Now, if you would not mind, we need to set up."

Bruce was very reluctant to stand, but he knew that if he did not, that his daughter Chelsea would never feel his embrace again. He somehow gathered the strength to stand and walk over to the trailer. As the man removed the tarp, "Mr. Curran, if you would be so kind as to give me a hand to get this in place, then you can make your final adjustments." Bruce lent a hand to get the M252 mortar pedestal off the trailer and set up near the building by the water.

"Do not worry Mr. Curran, although we have the coordinates that we need, we also have a spotter on the roof of the hotel on Seventeenth and E Streets. You know, just in case you are off a bit. Our spotter has clear view of where the round is to land, and he will relay whatever adjustments that you will need."

Bruce sort of chuckled. "You really got this all figured out, don't you?"

The man in turn chuckled. "Mr. Curran, as I stated a few minutes ago, this is a failsafe operation that has been run over and over and over for years. So yes, *we* have it all figured out." The man looked at his watch. "Mr. Curran, it is now six minutes past two. If our timing is right, we will begin our part in about twenty minutes. So please, get your charges timed and ready.

*****

Traffic was as heavy as anticipated on the I-95 corridor. Thousands upon thousands of vehicles crossed the I-95 Millard E. Tidings Memorial Bridge over the Susquehanna River each hour. People were going both north and south in an attempt to get back to their lives before the next morning was to call them back to work. The route 40 Thomas J. Hatem Bridge was heavily laden with the hustle and bustle of end of holiday travelers also.

At exactly 2:17 p.m., the train bridge over the Susquehanna came alive with the southbound Dixie Belle and the northbound Boston Light. Three hundred yards before they were to pass, the charges that Larry placed on the pillars went off leaving a gaping expanse of two-hundred feet of where the track used to be. With these trains moving over ninety miles an hour, there was no time to attempt to bring them to a halt. The engineers did not even have time to reach for their radio before the lead engine began to pull the attached cars into nothingness until they hit either what was left of the bridge or the river itself. Everything, the sounds of the bridge crashing and the sounds of the cars hitting the river was over in a matter of seconds. Stillness.

Exactly fifteen seconds after the train bridge was destroyed, the charges on the route 40 bridge began to detonate. About four-hundred feet of roadway along with hundreds of cars just disappeared one after the other into the space where the roadway was. Vehicles that did not initially go over the edge were

45

pushed over the edge by additional vehicles that could not stop in time. Fifteen seconds later, the charges on the freight rail detonated. Then, as like clockwork, fifteen seconds later, the charges on the Tidings Bridge began to go off. As with the route 40 bridge, the 95 bridge received an opening in the roadway that was well over three hundred feet long. As with the route 40 bridge, hundreds of vehicles were not able to stop when the roadway disappeared. With the sudden loss of the four bridges and the accidents that occurred after the explosions, a few thousand people died in the matter of a little over one minute. As the motorists that were able to do so, began to emerge from their vehicles to get off what was left of the bridge, fifteen seconds later, a sudden violent rumble off to the west got their attention. The bridges shook, and the people stood there staring at something that was to make them freeze in their tracks.

As they looked to the west in horror, they saw something that only movies are made of. They saw a wall of water almost a hundred feet high coming straight for them. People began to scream and with all the wrecks covering the road, their attempts to run for safety were non-existent. Many tried to climb over the wrecks, but that was a slow process that would turn out to be futile. After removing the town of Port Deposit from the map, the wall of water hit the Hatem Bridge first. Whatever the initial explosion did not remove, the approaching water did. Anything that was in the rushing water's path was taken with it.

The added debris in the fast-moving water then slammed into the freight bridge, then continued on to the crippled route 40 bridge removing what was left and the carnage continued to carry on until it finished removing what was left of the passenger train bridge.

Along the path of total destruction, towns along the waterway that included private residences, shops and a hospital were swept away, Havre De Grace was severely hit. Thousands more were killed as the wall of water and debris came slamming into the holiday tourists enjoying a beautiful day in the sun.

When the first explosion occurred, many flocked from inside the restaurants to get to the water's edge to see what had happened. Unbeknownst to many, the firsthand sightings that became horror in their minds, would only be there for a matter of seconds until they too would be part of history. When all was said and done, over thirty thousand people perished that day in the matter of minutes. To date, this was to be the worst terrorist attack that the United States had sustained. This attack would bring the East Coast infrastructure to a crippling halt.

*****

Washington, D.C.

2:18 p.m.

Vice President John Beard literally went racing through the hallway on the way to the private quarters of President C.J. Wolford, he was frantic. He was yelling along the way, "MOVE! Move, get the fuck out of the way! MOVE!" When he was down the hall from the entrance door to the private living area, he yelled to the agent stationed there. "Quick, open the fuckin door! We're under attack!"

The agent took a second to let that soak in, then he opened the door and yelled. "Mr. President, CODE RED! CODE RED!"

VP Beard went racing into the private residence. "C.J., C.J., the

U.S. was just attacked a minute ago! We don't know by who or why, but up in Northern Maryland, on the Susquehanna, someone just destroyed all infrastructure connecting north and south. I-95, Route 40 and both train bridges along with the Conowingo Dam were just blown. Unspecified reports say that many thousands initially dead. We need to get you out of here and to Camp David right now! Let's move!"

When VP Beard was rushing down the hallway, the Secret Service was also informed, and they were now in the private suite with the president and the first family. One of the agents took charge. "Mr. President, you and your family have to go right now. Let's move!" He grabbed the upper arm of President Wolford and started to whisk him away. Two other agents each took ahold of an arm of the first lady and all but carried her out and down the hallway.

Before they exited the building, there were about two dozen agents already outside making sure that the pathway to Marine One was safe and secure. When they were sure that it was safe to move, one of the agents opened the door, "MOVE! MOVE NOW!"

The president and the first lady were pulled along on the way to the helicopter when one of the agents yelled, "INCOMING! HIT THE DECK!" The agents involved pushed the president and the first lady to the ground and they used their own bodies to help shield them.

The mortar round landed about halfway between the residence and Marine One. The spotter on the roof immediately called out on the phone, "Left, one-seven. Left, one-seven!"

Although Bruce heard the man on the phone loud and clear, the man with Bruce still called out the adjustment. "LEFT ONE SEVEN!

LEFT ONE SEVEN!" Bruce made the adjustment and dropped a round down the tube.

A few seconds after the first-round hit, the agents were up and pulling the president and first lady to their feet. "LET'S MOVE! LET'S MOVE! GET ONBOARD MARINE ONE!"

They did not make it but a few steps when an agent yelled again. "INCOMING! HIT THE DECK!" As they all hit the ground, the next round came in. The round hit its mark, Marine One was no more. Between the round being a High Explosive and the Marine One having a full tank of fuel, the explosion lifted and threw most of the group off the ground many yards away. As they were attempting to recover, the lead agent called out to see if everyone was okay.

Beside cuts, bruises, hearing loss and a few concussions, they were all able to stand. The bloodied lead agent called out for them to get back inside. "QUICKLY! WE NEED TO GET OUT OF THE OPEN!"

The spotter yelled in his phone, "DIRECT HIT! DIRECT HIT!" The man turned to Bruce and thanked him for his service, and he also apologized to Bruce because he would not get to see his daughter again.

Bruce was furious. "What? But we had a deal!"

The man smiled and told Bruce, "Sorry, Mr. Curran, but in about five seconds, we will all perish." Bruce turned to lunge at the man, but he did not make it. As the man stated, their time of existence was up.

*****

Dulles International Airport

2:17 p.m.

Three minutes before landing for routine maintenance, Taiwan Flight 193 was being talked through the landing procedure. The air traffic controller was looking at his screen and making adjustments to keep everyone safe in the chaos of landings and take-offs that are a daily practice here. "Taiwan Air One-Niner-Tree, you are clear to land on runway Hotel-Romeo-Tree-Niner-Niner." The controller continued to watch his screen when he noticed a blip on the screen. As he focused on Flight 193, the call signal was flashing and changed from TA-193 to TA-262. "What the hell? What the hell is this?" The controller called out to his supervisor. "Jimmy, hurry on over here and have a look at this. The call sign for Taiwan Air One-Ninety-Three started to blink and then it changed to Taiwan Air Two-Six-Two! What the hell?"

As the supervisor was headed over to the controller, his phone rang. When he answered, he was informed of the attack in Maryland and the attack that just happened seconds ago on the South Lawn of the White House. With phone still in hand, he stopped at the controller. "What? What did you just say?!"

The controller repeated himself. "The call sign for Taiwan Air just changed itself on the screen to TA-Two-Six-Two."

The supervisor turned ashen white. "Impossible! That flight disappeared over the Indian Ocean seven years ago!" As they looked at the screen, they noticed that the plane had started to change directions. The supervisor called out, "Get me on the line to Air Defense!" At the sound of those words hanging in the air, all power went out in the tower. Lights and screens were dark.

*****

As the battered president and the first lady were being ushered back into the safety of the Whitehouse, he was still able to hear fairly well out of one ear. What he heard was not good. As he turned to see what the sound was, it was too late to say or do much. Taiwan Air Flight 262 was a spilt second from making contact with the White House. All President Wolford could get out was, "OH SHIT!" The impact from the aircraft, plus the thermal nuclear warhead from one of the stolen Soviet submarines incinerated the Whitehouse and everything within five miles around it. Anything within twelve to fifteen miles of the initial blast was also killed or destroyed. The devastation would spread well beyond the anticipated fifteen-mile kill zone. Hundreds of thousands died in the matter of seconds without ever knowing that it was happening. The mushroom cloud from the detonation could be seen for a hundred miles out. What the initial explosion did not kill, the impending radiation fallout would take care of.

With all communications and power grids in the U.S. totally shutdown, the mass chaos that followed the destruction in D.C. could not be relayed. As the physical destruction was going on outside, Premium Server outside of Langley was busy sending out viruses to each web site known to man. The server farm also sent messages to satellites instructing them to alter their orbits and begin to fall back to earth. There were a few thousand satellites that were now fiery projectiles that were cascading down to the earth with nothing to stop them. Airliners that were in the air lost all power and they too were mega-missiles destroying anything that was in their path as they hit the ground. Thousands of aircraft fell from the sky all at once.

The server farm also hijacked and altered the supposedly impenetrable electronics of the military. Everything that had some sort of electronic device was now unusable. Everything from small craft to aircraft carriers to fighter jets were now useless. What was once in the skies was now coming down.

Vice President Beard, along with many cabinet members that were in the Whitehouse that day, did make it to the safety of the bunker that was well below ground and beyond the reach of the nuclear explosion. The shock wave from the explosion did rattle the bunker and knock a few things off the shelves, but no one was injured. Although there was no communication, just from the extent of the shockwave, everyone in the bunker knew that the president did not make it.

CHAPTER FIVE

There was a lot of discussions going on at the same time concerning the possible demise of President Wolford. The Speaker of the House, Nicholas Mitchell, was the first to attempt to get order back in the great hall of the bunker. He made his way to the podium and with all that he had and as loud as he possibly could, he placed his fingers in his mouth and let out an ear-piercing whistle that finally brought some silence to the room. "Thank you!" He looked around, "I admit, that I, along with everyone else in this room has not a clue as to what we are facing up above us. What we need to do is to follow protocol and move forward."

Rumbling started again, and he raised his voice. "Please! Please, let's try to keep some order here." The rumbling subsided for the moment. "I may not be the smartest man in this room, but I am pretty sure that the president..." He hesitated for a second, "And his family did not survive. So, by protocol, the vice president is to be sworn in as acting president." He looked around. "Chief Justice, are you here with us?"

A hand from way in the back of the crowd goes up. "Great! Would you and Vice President Beard please step forward?" The two made their way forward. Speaker Mitchell looked under the podium and located the Bible. Before they got started, "As you all are aware, since we are not certain that the current president is alive and well, Vice President Beard will become acting president until we receive any confirmation whether good or bad."

Speaker Mitchell looked around. "So, with that in mind, each and every one of you in this room will move up one step to the position that was above yours before we all came down here. Not that I desired the position and/or the responsibilities that come with it, but I too, will move up from Speaker of the House to the position of Vice President." He looked over the room. "Okay, shall we move forward? Chief Justice, if you would not mind." Speaker Mitchell stepped off to the side.

*****

In Northern Baltimore County, Larry was busy doing searches on the web when everything went dark. A few seconds later, it felt like an earthquake just hit. "What the hell?" Not rightfully sure as to why, but he ran outside to see whatever it was that he hoped to see. What he did see was something that would stick to his memory forever.

As he gazed towards the sky, he initially saw what he thought was an aircraft hurdling towards the ground as if no one were in control. It took a few seconds for him to wrap his mind around what he thought that he saw. Then as he looked up again, he saw the beginning of the many satellites that would tumble back to the ground. All that came out was, "WHAT THE HELL!! They did it today!"

As he watched the skies, a young woman came staggering up the long driveway to Larry's house. "Help me, please help me." The woman, all bloodied and traumatized, collapsed in the middle of the driveway.

Larry ran over to her and got down to the ground. He pulled out his cell phone and punched in '911'. Nothing! He looked at the screen and it was blank. There was no indication of power. He pressed the power button and waited...nothing. "SHIT!" was all that he said. He turned to the woman and checked for a pulse, "Ma'am, can you hear me? Ma'am!"

She opened her eyes and began to speak. "I...I think they are all dead."

Larry looked puzzled. "Who?! Who is all dead?"

She looked at Larry. "Everyone in the cars. The cars just stopped running and we had no control, we just hit each other. They are down the hill on Mountain Road. I tried to help them, but no one answered."

Larry told her to stay there and that he would be right back. He ran into the house and got a few blankets. He ran back to the woman, and he tried to make her as comfortable as possible. "Stay here and try to stay calm. I am going to try to get some help. I will be back as soon as I can."

Larry made his way down the quarter mile driveway and came out onto the roadway. All he saw was wreckage as far as he was able to see. Vehicles were all about and he did not hear anyone calling for help. As he stood there a moment, he realized that he actually heard nothing at all, no birds, no nothing. There was an eerie silence as if he had gone deaf.

Slowly, he made his way along the road in the direction of the local fire department. A quarter mile or so up the road, he came upon a few motorists that were suffering from only minor scrapes and bruises. The one thing that Larry did notice about all the wrecked vehicles was that there was not a single airbag deployed. It took a few seconds to sink in, but then it came to him. "Shit! An electromagnetic pulse. No wonder things are not working."

Larry did come across a few firefighters that were helping people that were injured in the accidents. The biggest problem that they would face would be how they were to get people to the hospitals without any transportation. Larry had a solution. His neighbors owned a horse farm, and he was pretty sure that they would have a few carriages and that they would be willing to help. He told the station chief that he would be back shortly with some help.

*****

Chief Justice Joseph Pine made his way to the podium, and he asked for silence in the room. "Please everyone, please refrain from speaking for a few minutes." The room was silent. He picked up the Bible and he held it in the palm of his left hand. "Vice President Beard. Please place your left hand on the Bible." He did as he was asked and slowly placed his hand on the Bible. "Please raise your right hand and repeat after me." He did as he was asked, and the swearing-in took only but a minute. The Chief Justice looked to Nicolas. "House Speaker, are you ready?"

Nicholas took a deep breath and exhaled sharply before moving. He was ready and then again, he never really foresaw the day nor did he ever in his wildest dreams ever believe that this day would come. He stepped up to the podium. The Chief Justice smiled and asked him, "You ready for this Nick?"

Nicholas smiled back, and gently replied. "No...but do I have a choice?" There was a quiet chuckle from a few close enough to hear. Nicholas did as he was directed, and he took the oath of office for vice president.

The Chief Justice motioned for John to join him and Nicholas at the podium. "Ladies and Gentlemen, may I have your attention." The room went quiet again. "I would like to present to you the acting President and Vice President of the United States, President John Beard and Vice President Nicholas Leonard

Mitchell." When they were done, there was a round of applause and a few cheers that were tossed around.

After the cheering resided, President Beard stepped to the microphone. "Okay folks, we need to get moving forward. Even though we are down here, we can only fantasize as to what is going on up above us. So, my first act as President is to retrieve the radios from the Faraday cage and just hope that someone on the upper side has done the same. Because honestly, I believe that a nuclear strike has occurred above us and if that is the case, then there are no communications as we knew it." He pointed towards the Secretary of the Army. "General, if you would not mind, please retrieve the radios, we need to see what is going on up there."

*****

Larry made his way to his neighbor's farm and knocked on the door. When the resident answered, he told Larry that he was totally unaware of what had happened. Larry filled him in on as much as he knew, and the neighbor was more than willing to lend a hand and his horses. The man called for his son and nephew to help them out.

It took them about fifteen minutes to get four teams hooked up to carts. As they were headed out of the driveway, a few people were making their way up the driveway to get help. Considering what happened, Larry assured them that this was the most help that they were probably going to receive. The ones that were not that badly injured volunteered to lend whatever help that they could.

The people that were the most injured were loaded onto the carts first. There was a 24-hour medical center not too far from where they were. But the only problem was, no one could get any information as to whether they could accept any injured or not. They had no other choice, all that they could do was to go there and see for themselves.

*****

President Beard and his newly appointed cabinet made their way to the underground Oval Office. "Gentlemen, I am truly sorry that things are as they are, but we have to make the best of what we have here. So...with that in mind, we need to see if that radio has been located." Just as he was about to leave, the door opened, and the general came in pushing a cart. President Beard looked at him and the cart with the old metal boxes on it. "Wow, are they dinosaurs or what?"

"Well, Mr. President, whether they are dinosaurs or not, we can only hope and pray that they work and if they do, we can also hope and pray that someone up top has one that works also. So, let's get these things out of the box and see if they fire up."

They cleared the table and popped the latch on the old metal canister. When they opened the lid, the general was taken back to a time many, many years ago when he was a young officer serving in Viet Nam. "Wow! I have not seen one of those since I was a kid starting out in this service to my country."

The general removed the hand radio and the backpack radio with the curled cord attached to the handset. "Well before we could attempt to use this hand-set, we are going to need to charge the batteries. But, as for this one..." He turned the pack around and pulled the crank out and began cranking. The looks on their faces was priceless. "What? Haven't any of you ever seen a field radio like this?" They all shook their heads.

President Beard was the only one to speak. "No General, I cannot say that any of us have ever did."

"Well, Mr. President, this is probably the only thing that will survive forever. There is never a battery to charge. When you crank, there is a tiny generator inside that gives you enough power to last for quite some time. Let's see what we have here."

The general cranked the radio a few more times and picked up the receiver. "Well, here goes nothing. Hope someone is listening." The general pressed the button on the side of the receiver. "Mayday, mayday. Is anyone listening?" He released the button and all that could be heard was white noise. He pressed the button again. "Mayday, mayday, anyone listening." He released the button...nothing. "We're fucked! One of a few things is happening here, either that thing doesn't work, there is no one up above that is alive or no one else up there has a radio. That is something that we may never know." He tossed the receiver on the table and walked away.

They all stood there in silence for a moment when suddenly, there was a noise that came through. "Hello, hello, are you still there?" There was a sudden outburst of cheers. President Beard spoke up. "Quiet, quiet! General, this is your show. See who it is."

The general picked up the receiver. "This is General Seltzer, Secretary of the Army. Whom may I be speaking to?"

Silence, nothing but silence. They all just looked at each other. President Beard looked to the general, "What happened? Do you need to crank that thing some more or what?"

"No...it should be fine. We should have enough power to last us for..."

There was a reply that came across the radio. "I apologize for the delay, General, my name is Lieutenant Rollins, Lieutenant Larry Rollins, United States Army." Once again, there was a round of cheers.

"Shh, shh, quiet." The general handed the receiver to the president. "Here, Sir, press this to talk and release it to hear."

President Beard took the receiver. "Lieutenant Rollins, this is President John Beard. What unit are you with?" There was silence for a moment.

The radio crackled again. "President Beard? Does that mean…"

The president began. "Lieutenant, currently, we really do not know. We are currently inside the bunker below the White House. We are cut from all communications except this one here. We have no idea as to what is going on up there."

"Mr. President, as far as I can tell, all communication has been severed. Apparently, there was some sort of nuclear blast that has caused massive outages. It also appears that an EMP has been released that has disrupted all that has electronics. Aircraft, satellites, and anything else that had been in the air is now falling to the ground. Automobiles have crashed and piled among each other." The gasps went around the table, and they all just looked at each other.

"As for Washington, Sir, I, along with many, do not have any information on that subject. It just so happened that the person that owns this radio is a collector and he had it stored in what he called a…" Silence for a few seconds, "A Faraday Cage. Whatever the hell that is, I am not sure, but it worked." A little long needed laughter went around the room.

"Lieutenant, if you don't mind me asking again, what unit are you with and how many are with you?"

Again, silence for a moment. "Ah, Sir, I am an ordnance specialist with the Six-hundred-eighth out of Fort Benning, Sir."

"So, you have the battalion there with you?"

"Sir, yes and no. Currently, I am on leave, and I am home in Baltimore County, Maryland. So, to answer your question...Sir, I am alone." Now, once again, there was silence on Larry's end, only this time, he knew why.

After a few minutes, a reply came back. "Ah...Lieutenant, could you give us a few minutes to discuss things here and let's say that we talk again at..." President Beard looked at his watch. "Lieutenant, the time now is fourteen-forty-five, how about we talk again at sixteen-hundred, okay?"

Larry looked at the radio owner. "You got any way to track time?"

The man smiled. "Well, believe it or not, I do have a sun dial in the side yard."

Some odd reason, looking around at the collectables surrounding him, Larry did not doubt for one minute that there would be such an item available. "Mr. President, at sixteen-hundred, I will be back. Hopefully, I can have some more information for you."

"Great, Lieutenant, we can use this channel again when we talk again at sixteen hundred." Larry looked at the dials, the frequency was set at *5960*.

*****

As the new presidential cabinet was busy trying to figure a way out of the bunker, little did they know that a search and rescue team was currently gearing up and about to slowly make their way by foot towards D.C. Once they arrived in Hagerstown, the unit was taken into the old high school so that they could go over the game plan.

The team was led by Colonel Bradley Corde, a well-seasoned Army Ranger and Scout. Colonel Corde was to lead a platoon of thirty-two soldiers that were highly skilled in this type of mission. Once they were all present and settled, he began his spiel.

"Ladies and Gentlemen, listen up. My name is Colonel Bradley Corde. Since we are all going to be attached at the hip for only God knows how long, you may drop the formalities and call me either Colonel, Brad or Corde. I am pretty sure that along the line, a few more names may spill out of your lips."

He looked around the room hoping for a response. "Okay. I should not have to tell you this, but I will anyway. It is not going to be easy. Once we step out that door tomorrow morning, it will be at least a twenty-four-hour adventure by foot just to get to the White House location. Depending on what we may encounter along the way, we may be on foot for, once again, only God knows how long."

He scanned over the troops before him. "I would like to emphasize that this is strictly a volunteer mission, so, with that thought in mind, if any of you desire to stay back here, then, by all means, stay. If you do decide to stay, there will be no hard feelings towards you. I must also point out that there may be a good chance that a part of this unit will not make it through the entire mission. Anything can happen during this search and rescue. So, once again, if anyone wants to stay, then please step out so that the rest of us can get down to business." He scanned the room, and no one moved. "Outstanding, then I suggest that we proceed."

*****

Larry was at the radio at precisely 1600 when the radio crackled to life. "Lieutenant Rollins, Lieutenant Rollins, do you copy?"

Larry grabbed the handset. "Yes, Sir, I copy."

"Lieutenant, have you attempted to reach out to see if anyone else has a radio out there?"

Larry looked at the radio owner and the man shook his head. "Ah…negative, Sir. The radio owner says no." The man shrugged. "But Mr. President, I will be having to leave shortly, but the radio owner will be here if you need anything. Well, Sir, then again, there is only a limited amount that he can offer other than encouragement."

"I realize that Lieutenant but thanks any way. I am sure that somewhere out there, there is a unit on the way attempting to reach us."

Larry just thought to himself, 'Not that anyone would even know that they were there'.

Larry asked the man to please try to reach out to see if anyone else may have had a radio in a *Faraday Cage* as he did. He also left him with instructions of whom to contact in case he failed to arrive back here at a designated time. Larry told him that he had to make good on a promise that he offered to his friend, George. He stated that he had to go back to his house and retrieve some information that he was working on before everything went dark. He thanked the man for all he did, and he assured him that one day that he would compensate him for his time and effort.

The man stopped Larry before he got to the door. "Lieutenant, if you would like, I have something that you can take along." The man disappeared to the basement and came back a few minutes later with a Viet Nam era radio. "Here, Lieutenant, you may take this with you."

Larry looked at it and chuckled. "Wow, talk about a dinosaur."

The man looked at Larry. "Well, if you don't want it…"

Larry was quick to cut him off. "NO, NO…I'll take it."

The man smiled. "Thought you would." He went on to explain that he kept that relic tucked away in a Faraday bag in a Faraday cage, he was not taking any chances with his *baby*.

Since Larry was not familiar with that style of radio, the man covered all that Larry would need to know. Larry held it up and joked that he felt like *G.I. Joe*. The man went on. "It may not be modern, but Lieutenant, it is one-hundred percent American made. It has been and will continue to go through more shit than you could ever begin to imagine. Tell you what else I will do for you." The man went into a drawer and retrieved a strap for the radio. "Here, this will make travel easier." Larry thanked the man for his continued patronage, and he assured him that he would return his *baby* to him when all this was over.

Larry made his way back home and retrieved some papers that he was working on before all went black. He realized that he did not have all the information that he desired to take on his journey, but he knew that he had to do with what he had available. He was bound and determined to find what he was after.

He went to the garage and scrounged through the drawer in search of his bike pump that mounted to the bike. After a few minutes, he was able to locate it. Along the way of the search, he came across a few things that he would need to secure his yard cart to his bike, and he also came across two spare inner tubes. After securing the cart, he loaded his gear, the whole time hoping that he did not forget anything. He stood there in thought for a moment looking at his yard cart. Then to himself, he spoke aloud. "Damn Larry, you should have bought that *BIKESHAW* when Ray had the availability to build them."

He did one final look over. Last, but not least, Larry went to his gun safe and removed the firearms that he believed that he would need. He slipped his dual shoulder holster on and checked his Glocks to make sure that they were loaded. Once satisfied, he slipped them into their holsters and put a light leather vest on. He gathered up enough rounds to his satisfaction and took them out to the cart. He went back into the house and made sure that everything was secured before dropping a note on the kitchen counter. He left instructions for *just in case*.

CHAPTER SIX

President Beard brought together his new cabinet to make a major announcement. "Gentlemen, I am pretty sure that I speak for everyone here, because I am president." A few chuckles went around. "To continue on, I, along with many here, if not all of you, do not have a clue as to how many may actually be left out there and if they are, we have not a clue if and or when they are coming, nor do we even know that they know that we are down here. Agreed?" He looked around to see everyone's head bobbing in agreement. "Great, I have a plan. Let's clear this table."

The president went to the cabinet and removed a couple tubes. He went back to the table and popped the ends off and slid out what appeared to be maps. He unrolled them, and he asked to have the corners secured. "Now gentlemen, what we have here was only to be seen in times of emergencies. And you know what? This is a time of emergency. We need to get out of here just in case there is no one coming in to get us out."

The maps were the original maps that were drawn of the secret tunnels that run under D.C. President Beard handed things over to General Seltzer. "General, if you would not mind, since you are more familiar than I am, I would like you to take over from here."

"Thanks John." He looked up. "Ahh..., I mean, Mr. President."

"Quite all right, it will take me a bit to get used to it also. Continue on."

The general took the floor. "Gentlemen, as you can see on the maps, there really are secret tunnels that our founding fathers, well, mainly George Washington himself, built as a *just in case* escape route. But... those tunnels were built long before nuclear weapons were ever thought of, so the chances of them actually surviving are slim to none. So, during the cold war, President Kennedy was the first to authorize the construction of deep, blast proof tunnels. It took many years and a lot of secrecy to pull the construction of those off, but we have them."

The general pointed out a few tunnels that were still viable to his knowledge. "I personally know for a fact that these four tunnels are intact and useable. Well, that is until a few hours ago. Right now, I can only speculate that they are still passable. Due to possibly having to use them someday, deep piling construction was limited in these areas."

The general looked around. "There is only one sure fire way to see if they are still any good and if I had to pick which one would be the best, then I would pick this one." He pointed to one that would take them the furthest away from D.C. before it came out to a secluded area. "So, if it is all right with everyone here, I for one would like to volunteer to suit up and forage out and see firsthand if this here tunnel is still usable. Anyone have any objections?" No one objected.

President Beard jumped in. "Okay, with that thought in mind, is there anyone that would like to venture with him? I would go, but as you are all aware, if I go, then there has to be twelve secret service with me."

They all had a little laugh on that until one man raised his hand. "I'll go with you Leon that is the least that I can do, considering what we are facing here. Besides, not much that the newly appointed Secretary of Defense can do down here right at this moment."

*****

Larry made his way slowly, but surely. Along the way, he passed many people out and about trying to make some sense of what they were witnessing. A man stopped him and asked if he had any idea as to what is going on. Deep inside, there was a burning of hatred that Larry wanted to spill out and tell the man what he knew. But, at that moment, he felt as though that he should just keep his secret inside where it is currently safe. Inside his head, the voices were screaming, but how was he to tell anyone that he was a big part of what had happened. Larry trudged on.

Since the Conowingo Dam was gone, Larry was just hoping that the bridge over the Susquehanna on route 372, Holtwood Road, was still available. He was also hoping that the rush of the escaping water did not undermine the pilings. If it did, then his next chance of getting into Lancaster would be the long way with the same hope that the route 30 bridge is still intact also. He figured, what the hell, if need be, he would ford the river, and drag everything with him.

When he made his way down route 74 and he was about to turn right on 372, he stopped for a moment to say a prayer. First, he bowed his head, then as he went on, he tilted his head up, opened his eyes and looked towards the Heavens. "Lord, I know that I have been a big part in this mess, but I felt as though I had no choice. But please Lord, please do not punish me as I try to do what I have to do. Please let the bridge be there when I get there, Amen." He sat there for a moment with head tilted back, tears streaming down his cheeks and eyes closed. He tried to fight back the tears before he opened his eyes so that he could see straight.

Before he started down the hill, he did a final check on his gear. He mounted his bike and turned right onto 372. There were a few vehicles scattered in different fashion along the way, but the road was clear enough that nothing impeded his advance. At about a quarter of a mile before the bridge, the road took a small dogleg to the right. When he made his way around the bend, Larry was able to see that the bridge was intact and that there were people crossing the bridge. Larry let out a sigh of relief. He looked up. "Thank you, thank you for hearing my plea."

Larry made it over the bridge with no complications. While doing so, there were a few people that attempted to stop him and ask what was going on. He just called out that he had no clue and he kept moving. Lancaster is only about thirty-five miles from his house, so he figured that after crossing the bridge, that he only had about thirty miles to go. He held a pretty steady pace, and barring any obstacles, he should be there in way less than three hours. He was not sure if *George* would be where he hoped, but he knew that if he was not, then whomever was there would tell him where to find him.

*****

General Seltzer was able to enlist the help of five other men. They went to what is called *The Bunker* and found NBC (Nuclear Biological Chemical) suits that fit them perfectly. There was a small group that went with them in order to help them suit up, but once they were about ready to go into the escape chamber, the group left *the bunker*.

Once inside the chamber, General Seltzer asked them all to please have a seat on the bench. "Gentlemen, I thank you all for what you are about to do here. But, if there is anyone that may be having second thoughts, then please speak now and go back into *the bunker*. If you do decide to go back, then please know that no ill will would be held against you. This is purely volunteer, no

69

heroics here. Understood?" No one said a word. "Sad thing to think of, but there is that chance that we may be the only ones that are alive on this planet, well, only ones besides Lieutenant Rollins and the ham radio guy. We may get out there and travel for days without ever being able to remove our helmets. So, once again, anyone want to stay?" Still, no one said a word. "Well, let's go."

They helped each other to get their helmets on and locked. They all faced each other and each one gave a *thumbs up* signal. "Okay men, let's move out." The general went over to the panel and pressed the airlock button. Nothing! "What? What the hell?" He pressed it again, still nothing. He looked at the others. "Well, guys, looks like we are going to have to fight this journey all the way." The general opened the panel and pulled out the hand crank. "Anyone care to join in?"

One man stepped over and placed his hands on the crank with the general. "Ready, Sir?"

"Any time you are, Sir." They turned the crank and slowly, the large door slid open revealing a long, semi-lit hallway. Once they had it opened enough to fit through, one by one, they entered the hallway. Once all were in the hall, two other men volunteered to crank the large door back into place so that the airlock would remain sealed in case any of the others decided to use it.

They made their way to a small alcove and the general introduced the men to a collection of *Two-man pedal cars*. The men looked a little surprised. "What? Did you think we were going to walk the fifteen miles in these suits carrying our gear?" They all got a little chuckle out of that.

One man spoke up. "You know General, if some of the others had known about these cars, they may have joined us."

The general smiled. "I know."

When they got in the cars, the general removed a small Geiger counter and switched it on. He removed the calibration block and checked the accuracy, the counter showed point seventy-two. "Okay men, counter is calibrated. He replaced the calibration block and then he raised the counter in the air. There were a few clicks, but nothing to show that they would be in any danger if they removed their helmets.

The general was the first to remove his. "Gentlemen, it appears to be safe for the time being, you may remove your helmets." They did as they were directed. "If you all would like, I will take the lead car and I will leave the detector on. If I notice any change for the worse before we get to the next safety chamber, then I will let you know. Understood?" They all nodded and grunted in agreement.

It took about an hour and forty-five minutes to reach the next chamber which would connect them to the outside world. Before they went inside the chamber, they all once again donned their helmets. The general looked at the group. "Okay, need two more volunteers for the crank." They looked at each other, the general smiled. "Okay, how about this. Whomever did not crank the last time, then they can crank this time." Four of the group looked at the last two men and they all sort of nodded their heads towards the door.

"Okay, okay, I'll do it", came a gruff response from one of them. "Come on Briggs, you grab the handle too."

The two of them started to crank the handle when the general decided to press the button. The door opened and the men stopped cranking. "Wow, Sir. Think maybe you could have tried that before we started cranking?"

"Didn't know. But what I do know is this, by that door opening by the push of a button, then chances are, the outside world still exist. But, until we are sure that it is safe, let's keep our helmets on, okay?"

When they entered the chamber, the general took out the Geiger counter once again and switched it on. Nothing. "Well, so far, so good. But still, keep your helmets on until we break the seal over there. But first, we close this back up. Hit that button please Jim."

At the exit door, the general spoke up. "Gentlemen, hopefully, once we cross over unto the other side, we will be able to drop this gear. If everything pans out, then I will request a volunteer to go back and start to get everyone out. So, with that in mind, here we go." The general pressed the button, and all kinds of wheels and gears could be heard moving about. After about fifteen seconds, a loud *Clank* was heard and a rushing of air.

The general leaned in. "Here goes nothing." He pushed the door and slowly, it swung open. He opened it enough to step through. Once again, he took a reading, nothing. "Okay gentlemen, we are good. If one would like to volunteer to go back, then fine, otherwise, Mike, if you would be so kind."

Jim spoke up. "Sir, if you would not mind, I will go."

The general smiled and focused his glare at Mike. "Thanks Jim, I knew that you would."

Once the remaining part of the group was outside the chamber, the general pressed a button and the door closed and secured itself. He pressed a few buttons on the keypad and then he addressed his crew. "Okay everyone, there are lockers in a room off to the side here. You will also find a cache of assorted weapons that will suit our needs. Please feel free to choose the weapon of your choice."

CHAPTER SEVEN

Larry was making his way at a reasonable pace. There were a few obstacles along the way, but not what he had imagined. As he was only a few minutes out of Lancaster, he began to notice that there were a few vehicles that were still running, not all, but a few. Due to Conowingo being out, there were still major dead spots where there was no electricity. The amount of draw that it would take to cover the down grids would have been too much for any switching station to contend with. Now, he was happy with what he could get.

When Larry was getting his research done before everything went down, he was thinking ahead enough to print out a map. He did not know for sure if his GPS would work or not in the future, so something in the back of his mind told him to print the map. Besides, he knew that it was not like the old days as to where you could go into any gas station and pick up a free map or as far as that goes, any map at all. Sad, but there is a generation out here that has lost all sense of direction, time and all common sense altogether. The young generation these days could not find their way home without a device if they were only five miles away from home. Larry was outfitted to continue to move forward.

He stopped in town to get a little rest while he went over what he had before him. He sat down at a bench in the town's park and removed his backpack and then some of the contents from within. From what he researched; he was only about five minutes from the residence that he connected to *George*. When he got done getting his bearings, he stood up. "Oh, damn!" Although he was still in top physical shape, it had been years since he had ridden his bike and even longer since he had ridden this distance all at one time. The lapse in time sure was showing today, of all days.

"Never knew that not biking for so long could play such a major part in pain." He walked around a moment to try to shake it off.

He placed everything back into the backpack and got back on his bike. He slowly made his way out of town and made a right onto New Holland Road and headed towards Zooks Corner. As he went along, he commented to himself occasionally. "Who in the hell came up with these names? Where did *Zooks Corner* come from?" Shaking his head, he continued. "Not really sure, but George, Leonard Bloom or whatever your name really is, I am coming. Get ready for company."

It would be dark in about forty-five minutes, so when Larry reached Zooks Lane, he just hung out for a bit acting like he had bike trouble and he was doing repairs. He wanted to make sure that he had the cover of darkness when he went in.

Once it was dark, Larry slowly walked his bike with the cart down the lane working his way to Waterford Drive. When he reached his destination, he rolled his bike into the cover of the trees. He opened a strongbox on the cart and removed two silencers, which are commonly called *Coughers,* due to them sounding like a cough when the weapon is fired, and a night scope. He removed each of his Glocks and checked to make sure that they were loaded and ready. He twisted a cougher onto each one and placed them back into their holders. He grabbed another backpack that he had on the cart, and he slung it over one shoulder.

After throwing a camouflaged poncho liner over his gear to conceal it, he started off. He stopped at the road and removed his night scope. He scanned the area and he noticed that the house had cameras. Hitting a switch on the scope, he was able to see that there was no heat signature coming from the cameras which told him that they may be down due to the widespread power failure. Larry looked around to make sure that there was no one outside. "So far, so good. I really didn't desire any company."

He placed his scope inside of his vest and he removed his night goggles and placed them on. Slowly, he made his way across the road and slouched down. He looked back over his tracks just to be safe that no one was behind him. He remained in a crouched position as he made his way up the short tree lined driveway. He saw a small shed off to the side and he made his way over to it.

Larry went around the back side and had a seat against the shed wall. He lifted his goggles and took out his scope. It was still on heat signature, and he scanned the house. He saw five signatures and from experience, he knew they were all adult. He was scanning the rest of the house when he heard a child squeal from laughter. The sound did not come from the house, it came from a barn style building behind him. He swung around and his heart stopped. Larry started shaking from what he was seeing. There was at least a dozen or so heat signatures of children and at least three from adults. "My God! Bella Marie", was what came through his lips! He turned back around and leaned against the shed wall again.

He sat there a few minutes with heart and mind racing. "What? What do I do? Think Larry, think! You need more than you, but do you have the time?" When he pulled himself together, he knew that he had to get to a safer place to go over his notes. He placed his scope back in his vest and donned his visor. He retraced his steps back to his gear. When he reached his cart, he pulled the poncho liner up and got under.

With penlight between his teeth, he scoured through his papers until he came to the list of names that he could find that were also dragged into this chaos. The only one that he would be able to reach inside the dead zone would be John Meyers. Larry looked his address up on the map and he saw that it was only a few miles away in Pennsylvania. "Kirkwood, I can be there in less than half an hour." Larry looked up. "Please God, please guide me to John's house and please, let him be there and receptive to me. Thank you." Larry left his trailer behind; he could make better time without dragging that along. He made sure that the poncho liner was secure, and he quickly made his way toward John.

As he made his way starting down route 30, he saw a small crowd and red and blue flashing lights, he really wanted no parts of that. He lowered his goggles and scanned the area. He saw what he thought was a way around this. He was one street over when he skirted the commotion. Apparently, there is a curfew in effect and the police are stopping people and sending them back home when they see them out. Larry did not need to be stopped and there was no way that he could possibly clue any of the authorities in on what was going on. When he got to a corner, he was very careful to avoid people. When he thought it was clear, he hurried across the street to the next set of buildings. He kept this up until he was sure that he was in the clear.

It did only take about thirty minutes to reach John's residence. Larry was not sure how he was going to confront John, neither was he sure if he would even be welcomed. But what choice did he have? Larry left his bike laying on the grass beside the porch steps and he removed his scope. He looked for heat signatures in the house before he went to the door. He did see two signatures of what appeared to be adults. He placed his scope back in his vest and started towards the porch. Under his breath came, "Here goes nothing." Larry knocked on the door and stepped back. A few seconds went by and nothing. He knocked again...nothing. He was about to knock a third time when he heard an all too familiar sound of the breach of a shotgun open and close.

The one with the weapon spoke up. "PUT YOUR HANDS UP! UP HIGH!" Larry did as he was told.

Without turning around, Larry kept his hands high, and he now spoke. "Mr. Meyers, I am not sure if you remember me or not, but my name is Larry Rollins. I was the one that *George,* dragged into this mess and he had me plant the explosives on the bridges. May I please turn around?"

John kept the shotgun high. "What the hell do you want? You got my little boy killed. I should blast your head all over my front door."

Larry was not too sure what to do. One thing not to do was anything stupid. He kept his hands high, and he remained looking away. "Mr. Meyers, please, before you do something that will get your son killed, please Sir, hear me out. I do believe that your son is fine."

John poked Larry in the back with the barrel. "What do you mean? My son was probably killed when all of this went down."

Once again, Larry asked him to hear him out. "Mr. Meyers, if you would allow me to, I can prove what I say. Please, at least allow me to have a seat and I can show you. I promise that I will not do anything stupid. Just to show you that I want to help and not hurt you, I will let you know that I have two Glocks un..." Larry was cut off by the poking of the barrel.

Larry continued with a little gruffness. "Mr. Meyers, I have two loaded Glocks with silencers inside each side of my vest. If you would like to have your wife remove them, then maybe we can talk."

John poked him again. "How do you know that I am not alone?"

"Mr. Meyers, I am a Military man, I have a scope, which is also inside of my vest, and it allows me to see heat signatures. I looked before I knocked. Now please Mr. Meyers, we are wasting precious time here. *Please listen to what I say!*"

John thought for a moment. "Okay, okay Mr....what did you say that your name was?"

"Larry Rollins."

"Okay Larry Rollins, I will have my wife remove your weapons and then we talk." John called for his wife, and she removed the weapons.

Larry sat on the porch, and he handed his backpack to John's wife. "Mrs. Meyers, inside my backpack, you will find a stack of papers, please remove them and hand them to me." She did as she was asked, and Larry removed a list of names and a map.

"Not thirty minutes ago, I was in Zooks Corner at a residence that I believe *George* is in. Even if he is not there, I do believe that the children are there."

That statement really got the interests of John. "Why do you think the children are there?"

"Well, I was checking out the house and I was about to go in when I heard a child squeal from a barn looking building. I turned to see the signatures of at least a dozen children and a few adults with

79

them. I cannot guarantee that your son nor my daughter is among the ones in that building, but I cannot do it alone. That is why I am here now. I need some assistance in going in. I just wish that I had more time and more people to help me."

John finally laid his shotgun down and spoke man to man to Larry. "Sir, I can see the sincerity in your face, and I hear it in your voice. How many more people do you need?"

Larry almost burst into tears. "You serious? You can muster up people just like that?"

"Mr. Rollins, while you were doing your homework, you should have looked up my family tree. Then you would have seen that most of the homes around here are owned by my family. Within ten minutes, we can have at least a dozen men, all armed and ready. What do you say?" What could he say? Larry stood up and went over to John, shook his hand and gave him a big manly hug. John just stood there as his wife smiled.

When they were done, she handed Larry his weapons butt first. "Here you go, you may need these Lieutenant."

As John stated, within ten minutes, there were fourteen men armed to the teeth sitting on bikes ready to move out. Larry looked around, "Wow! John, you are amazing."

John smiled. "Lieutenant Rollins, trust me, you are not the only one that wants to hunt down *George* and make him pay." He waved his hand. "We are all hunters, so...we have our own scopes and night goggles. So, Sir, if you would be so kind, please lead the way."

Larry was so overcome with bliss that he almost fell when he attempted to mount his bike. With the wave of an arm, "Gentlemen, let's roll."

CHAPTER EIGHT

They were all loaded up and about to start out the door when a soldier came rushing through the door. "Colonel! Colonel Corde! I have a message for you that I believe will assist you."

The corporal handed him the paper and the colonel opened it. He got a big smile on his face. He handed the paper back to the corporal and patted him on the shoulder. "Thanks Corporal, please take care of this." The colonel looked out over his troops getting themselves ready and he attempted to speak above them all. "Folks, may I have your attention please. I think that you may want to hear this."

The group went silent. "Some good news that I would like to share with you all." All eyes were upon him. "It appears that the local citizens around here have come to our aid. Someone went as far as to contact the local bike shop and inform them that we are setting off on a mission and they decided to donate bicycles and trailers to assist us in getting to D.C. in a much better time and fashion." A loud cheer went up and the colonel waved for them to quiet down. "I just sent the Corporal out to inform the shop owner that we would accept the bikes and the trailers, he should be back in a few minutes. So, with that in mind, let's say that we go outside, get our gear together and be ready when they call for us to come get the bikes."

*****

General Seltzer and his group made it to the door that was sealed and separating them from the outside world. He stopped and faced them. "Men, here it is, the farthest reaches of the underground tunnels. Once we open this door and we blow the outside hatch, well...we will know by our surroundings if we are alone. Everyone ready?" All heads nodded up and down in unison. "Alright guys, get your helmets on and let's check each other before we proceed."

When the general was satisfied, he gave a thumbs up signal and pressed a series of buttons. The large door made some clanking sounds, blew some pressure relief valves, squeaked and finally clicked. The general looked back at the men. "Here goes nothing." He pressed another series of numbers, and they all heard a faint boom and felt the ground move a little. They all looked at each other. The general looked at them and laughed. "What, did you think that we would leave the entrance exposed for someone to come along and decide to see what was down there? No, no, no. the entrance has been covered and concealed for many, many years. I was just amazed that the charges were still good. So...shall we pull this one open and see what is in color on the outside, Dorothy?"

One by one, they emerged outside of the tunnel. To their surprise and prayers, it was a beautiful sunny, late spring day. The general removed his Geiger counter and took a reading, all looked good. He removed his calibration block and checked it. "Point seven-two." He removed his head cover. "Gentlemen, we are good. The calibration reading is higher than the actual. Feel free to come out and take a deep breath."

When they all removed their head cover, they stood there in awe. The air was fresh, the birds were happily singing, and butterflies were all about. Bees were busy going about pollinating the spring blossoms. The general laid his head back and just took in the surroundings. The smell of the honeysuckles in the late morning was something to cherish forever. He took a deep breath, then exhaled sharply. "Gentlemen, if you all will think back to your academy days, then you will remember that if you hear birds after a nuclear blast, and you see butterflies, then chances are, the nuclear blast was not strong enough to make it this far. Then again, we are fifteen miles out of D.C."

One of the men spoke up. "General, just where in the hell may we be?"

The general chuckled. "Michael, we are in Piscataway Park, just outside of Accokeek."

Michael nodded, "Ah, okay." He looked a little lost. "Ah, General."

"Yes Michael, what is it?"

"Ah, General, where is Accokeek?" Laughter went out.

"Michael, Accokeek is on the east side of the Potomac, just west of Waldorf."

Michael looked confused. "You telling me that we went under the Potomac? Wow! That's cool." Another round of laughter.

The general got serious. "Alright guys, first and foremost, we need to contact the authorities. Frank, if you would be so kind as to get the radio fired up. Then maybe, just maybe, we can get someone here to get us out of here."

"Sure, thing General."

"Mr. Briggs, as for you, if you would be so kind as to leave a message and then secure the door, then I would be highly satisfied."

"Yes Sir, General, right on it."

*****

Larry stopped everyone just as they all mounted their bikes. "Before we get into town, I need to let you know that there is a curfew going on and the police are stopping all that they encounter. One thing that we do not need is to be held up in any way. So, when we get to town, we will dismount and take it slow. Any questions?" One man put his hand up. "Yes, what is it?"

"Sir, some of us are already aware of that, and we sent our distraction team ahead of us." A few got a little laugh out of that, Larry did not.

"I'm sorry, what do you mean?"

"Sir, a few of us have daughters that are of age. We do believe that they can be quite the distraction."

Larry smiled. "So be it. Then I suggest that we get underway."

Larry led the way. Once they reached the town, they went slowly along making sure that no one spotted them. Once the last rider was clear of the last street, word went up to Larry that all was clear and for him to step on it.

They made their way along Willow Road at a pretty good pace. Once they reached New Holland Pike, they all grouped together. Larry led off. "Gentlemen, we are only a few minutes out. When we get closer, we will dismount, and I will lead you to where we can conceal the bikes. Everyone ready?" All heads nodded in agreement. "Let's do it."

When they came upon Waterford Drive, Larry stopped and got off his bike. In a whisper. "Gentlemen, follow me." They made their way down the road until they came to the place that Larry stashed his gear earlier. "One at a time, carry your bike back here." They all did as Larry said. When they had all secured and covered their bikes, Larry motioned for them to get down. "For those that have night visors, please put them on." When they were done, he gave directions. "I will lead and one by one, come across the road when I give you the okay and join me at the back of that shed." Larry pointed across the road. "Once we group up there, we can decide who is going where. If there are no questions, then let's begin."

Larry went to the edge of the road and removed his cope. He set it on heat sensor. He scanned the road and what all was before him. When he was satisfied, he made his way across the road to the shed. He scanned around and then motioned for the first one to come over. One by one, Larry got them over safely. Larry scanned the barn and just as it was before, he saw children and at least three adults. When the first six were with him, Larry decided to send them to surround and secure the barn. "Guys, I see three adults and about a dozen children inside. I have not seen any clue that any weapons are involved, but, just in case, be on your toes. I may send two more men over in a few minutes so that they can enter the barn while the rest of you hold the perimeter. No one moves until I give the signal. Got it? Now get going."

One by one, Larry waved the next group over. When six more were with him, he ran everything down to them. Slowly, one by one, they disappeared into the dark and around the house. Larry turned and waved the last three over. John was the last to arrive.

"Mr. Meyers, you can..."

John cut him off. "Lieutenant, I do believe that by now, you can call me John."

John stuck his hand out and Larry accepted. "Okay, John it is. Call me Larry."

John shook his hand and smiled. "So be it Lieutenant."

Larry felt as though he and John should take separate buildings, just in case. John agreed. John asked if he would mind if he chose the barn and that Larry took the house. "Lieutenant, just do me one favor."

"What's that Mr. Meyers?"

John smiled. "If *George* is in there, please keep him alive long enough for me to get my piece."

Larry stuck out his hand and John accepted. "Agreed."

John took a deep breath and tapped one of the men on the shoulder. "Let's go save the day, shall we?" One at a time, the two of them made their way to the barn's front door. And they waited there for Larry to get to the house and give them a signal.

Larry made his way onto the front porch along with one of John's cousins. One was on one side of the door, and one was on the other. Once again, Larry switched his scope to heat signature and he scanned the house. In a whisper. "Two rooms in, two bodies sitting down watching television. Two on second floor and it appears that one is in the shower." Larry removed a picture of *George* and held it up for the other man to see. "If this is one of them in there, please only shoot to wound, not kill." The man nodded. Larry checked the doorknob, it turned. He pushed on the door. A little above his breath, "Damn, deadbolt." Larry removed a set of lock pins.

The man spoke up. "Here, let me do that. You keep an eye on the idiots inside."

Larry looked at him. "You know how to do this?"

The man smiled and reached into his pocket. He whispered back. "I just love *Show and Tell*, don't you?"

Larry looked at what the man was holding, and he read it out in a hushed manner. *"Lancaster Lock and Key*. You serious?"

The man smiled. "I'm fuckin' this kitty, you just hold the tail out of the way."

*****

Between having to pedal the car by himself and the rest breaks in between, it took Jim over two hours to get back to the bunker. When he did arrive, there was an anxious welcome party just hoping that all was well. They cheered as Jim made his way out of the chamber and into the bunker. Some shook his hand and others clapped him on the back. President Beard made his way to the front. "Well Jim, please tell me some good news."

Jim looked him in the eye then lowered his head and shook it. "Not good Sir, sorry." The tension was thick enough to cut with a knife. After a few seconds, Jim raised his head, took a deep breath and got a big grin. "IT'S GREAT NEWS! We made it to the outside and all is still there as far as we know." The crowd roared and applauded.

The president raised his hand and motioned in a hush manner. "So, you made it outside, did you see anyone?"

"No, no Sir, as soon as we discovered that the radiation or the nuke hadn't destroyed the planet, the general sent me back to retrieve everyone."

"Well Jim, I for one am ready to get out of here. How about everyone else?" The roar was deafening.

The acting security agent approached the president and leaned into him. "Sir, as much as you desire to get out of here, I cannot allow it." Although the agent said it in a low key, most of the room heard it.

Vice President Mitchell stepped up. "He's right John. Sad, but true. Now, you and I are one of the last that would be able to leave here until we know for sure that we have an acting government facility up above. It may be hours and then again, it may be months or years until we can leave here. Until everyone is certain to the extent of damage that D.C. took, we cannot go." President Beard never took that thought into mind. All he wanted was to get out and do what he was supposed to do, run the country.

*****

Colonel Corde and his posse made good time by having the bikes as transportation. They made their way along route 355 skirting I-270. Every so often, he would stop and take a reading. By the time that they got to Gaithersburg, they were getting readings that were beginning to get a little too uncomfortable for the general. He turned to face the group. He waved for them to gather. "Folks, we are starting to pick up some readings that will only get worse. So, as much as I hate to do it, we are going to have to suit up. Yes, it is going to suck having to wear the suits and pedal the bikes. Just keep an eye on your suit's A.C. and adjust it accordingly as we move along. The worse thing that you can do is create a puddle around your feet that you would not be able to safely remove. Then again, at the same time, we can't afford to have a foggy visor either. So, like I said, work with it."

It was not until they reached Rockville that they started to see the carnage of the radiation. There were bodies strewn about, many were laying on their back with appendages curled and head cocked back with mouth open. The scene sent an image through the colonel's mind of a dying cockroach. Even the animals, from birds to dogs to horses with the policemen still in the saddle pinned under the weight of the animal, were laying all about. It looked like something out of a horror movie. The colonel raised his arm to signal a stop.

Colonel Corde dismounted and hit his intercom button. "Alright everyone, I believe that from here on out, it may be best if we walked. I realize that we still have a few miles to go, but from what we have seen already, I really do not believe that we will be doing any rescue." They all just stood there and looked at him with disbelief.

One spoke up., "Sir…" She hesitated for a second. "Sir, do we just keep going or do we do something here with the bodies?"

Colonel Corde looked at her for a few seconds. "Captain Sheer, there is nothing that we can do for these people. If we stop to remove or bury them along the way, then we may be lucky if we reach the White House by retirement age. So, I say let's keep going and complete our mission. Any more questions, Captain?"

He could see her head shake inside the overlarge bubble helmet. "None, Sir."

"Okay, let's move out. Remember, with these ratings getting higher as we approach D.C., use the buddy system and keep an eye on each other's generator. One thing we do not need is a suit going bad." Everyone did a quick buddy check and when all was good, they began to move again.

Although they have all trained for this time and time again, reality never seems to kick in until it hits close to home. They all tried to stay focused on what was directly in front of them, but at times, it was too much just not to look. There were bodies in every direction and in every conceivable position. There was one man that was on a bike, and he must have been sitting still leaning against a pole with his drink bottle. His fried body was now attached to the pole, and you could see where his water bottle melted and dripped through his hand to the ground. His hand was still in the gripping, drinking position. He along with many others never had a chance.

When Captain Sheer came across the woman in the park that was apparently playing with her baby, that is the part where she lost it. Colonel Corde ran over to her and turned her away from the scene. "Captain! Don't you fuckin' lose it out here! Not now, not ever! Look at me! Better yet..." He swung her back around to see the charred remains of the woman sitting on the bench with her outstretched arms holding her toddler up in the air. They were to be forever frozen in that position. "Look at them! Do you want to be like them? If you do, I will pull your fuckin' lifeline now. We, when I say we, I mean this team, we need you and your head on straight. You are not here for a stroll in the park. You are on a mission and that mission must be completed. Do I make myself perfectly clear?"

Captain Sheer just stood there with her gaze affixed on the charred woman and child. "Captain! Do I make myself clear?" No response. Colonel Corde grabbed her airline and gave it a tug.

That snapped captain Sheer back to reality. "What the hell Colonel?"

"Now that you are back, do I make myself perfectly clear?"

She looked him dead in the eye and took a deep breath. "Perfectly clear. I am okay now Colonel. I apologize. I lost it for a moment. It won't happen again."

He stared her right back. "It better not. Next time, I will pull hard enough to break your air seal. Now, MOVE OUT!"

Walking the bikes was the easy part, the hard part was seeing the remains of all that had not a clue that their time was up. Sure, they had to veer around vehicles and bodies, but all was good. Once they came up to what he took to be Massachusetts Avenue, they rested in what once was Bryce Park. The trees were all gone or smashed down to splinters. There was not a whole bunch left to see. What had been standing was now laying over and burnt to a crisp. Since the satellites were no longer where they should have been, Colonel Corde relied on the old-fashioned map to get him where he should be.

The Colonel pulled everyone together. He pressed the button on intercom and began his speech. "Alright, folks, listen up. We are just a short distance from the White House. We have two options of travel here. Of the two, I prefer Massachusetts to Connecticut and work our way in. If anyone else has a different approach, please speak up now." Nothing. "Alright, we rest up here for about a half hour, then we move out."

CHAPTER NINE

The man took but a few seconds to unlock the deadbolt. He turned the doorknob ever so gently. Larry grabbed the man's hand and called out. "Hold on! I see heat above the door! Don't open, its rigged!"

"Shit! Thanks, I almost blew this, no pun intended. Can you see what it is?"

"From my experience, it is a trip wire, but it would be nice if I could see it from the other side." Larry looked around. "Give me a minute. I want to see if I can get an eye from a window off to the side."

Larry slowly made his way off the porch and found a window about ten feet off the corner. Before raising up, he did a heat scan to see if that too was wired, nothing. He scanned all the rooms. All were still in the same places. He slowly raised up to the window and much to his surprise, the window was actually open a few inches. Under his breath, "Son-of-a-bitch!" He dropped down and went back to the front. "Pssttt. Psssttt." The man turned to see Larry. Larry signaled to give him two minutes, he was going in. Larry turned back. "Pssttt, psssttt."

The man looked his way and whispered. "What?"

Larry whispered. "Rather than pssstt, what is your name?"

The man smiled. "Fred, but psssttt is fine." Larry gave him a thumbs up.

Larry went back to the window and scanned it for heat. Nothing! He slowly pushed the window up. When he was sure that he could fit in, he stopped pushing. He flipped his goggles to night vision and looked around. He saw an old bike laying off to the side and retrieved it to use it as a step. Once he got one leg inside, he flipped back to heat. Under his breath, "Still settled." He continued to climb inside. He quietly made his way to the door and disarmed the tripwire before slowly turning the knob. The whole time, in his mind, he is saying, 'Please don't shoot me'.

Larry cracked the door. "It's me, don't shoot!"

Fred whispered back. "I did think about it."

Larry leaned in close. "Do you want up or down?" The man chose up. "Okay, I will give you to the count of thirty, then I get the assholes down here. Clear?"

"Clear. See you in a few." Larry placed his hand on the man. "Hold on." He hit his mic button. "We are in, on my mark, we count to thirty and then we hit at once. If you got this, each of you just hit the button twice, don't speak. From the back of the barn, got it?" Larry and Fred listened for the mic response, and he continued to ask from the front of the barn and then the back of the house. "Great, on my mark, start counting now, thirty..."

Fred slowly and quietly made his way to the second floor. He had his heat signature on, and he saw that the one that just stepped out of the shower was a woman. Either way, he had a job to do. When he got to twenty-five, he switched on the night vision. When he reached *thirty*, he stepped inside of the bedroom, flipped off the light and confronted the individual in the room. The subject startled and reached for a weapon. Fred called out. "Don't do it".

The subject smiled and called out, "Allahu Akbar."

He looked at the subject and responded. "Yes, he is." Fred pulled the trigger and put a well-placed round right between the subject's eyes. He dropped.

He quietly made his way to the bathroom; the woman was just finishing drying off with the hair drier. He raised his visor and placed the red laser on her forehead. "Care to be next?" The woman just froze for a second, then she glanced over to the counter where a small Glock lay. He gave a little laugh. "Go ahead you piece of shit! Think I won't shoot a woman?"

The woman glared back over to the counter and laughed. "Go ahead, your child dies anyway."

"Wrong...not today." He placed a round in her forehead also. He called on the radio. "Second floor neutral and clear. Coming down."

The men downstairs heard the thump upstairs, but they just laughed and thought that the two of them were having wild sex. Larry made his way back to the second room and confronted the men. When they saw him, they jumped up to get a weapon. Larry put a round into the knee of one man and stopped him there. The other man made it to his weapon and grabbed it. In a diving move, he turned and pointed it at Larry, but Larry was quicker. Larry placed two rounds into the man's chest and the man never got a shot off.

Larry was soon joined by Fred along with another man that came in from the back. They all gathered around the wounded man. Larry spoke to Fred and the other man. "Think you guys can handle this from here? I need to get to the barn."

Fred slapped Larry on the back. "Go, they probably need you there more than here anyway."

"Thanks." Larry made his way out the back and ran to the barn.

*****

President Beard was not too thrilled about having to stay put, but it is what it is. The new House Speaker confronted the new President. "John, in many aspects, life as we knew it is gone. I am sure that you are as surprised about all of this as all the rest of us are. Honestly, never had I ever thought that I would one day be *House Speaker*. Honestly John, just the thought scares the hell out of me! I was more than thrilled when I was appointed *President Pro Tempore of the Senate*. That spot was big enough for me. At least in that position, I could still go out and dine with my..." His speech stopped and fell off in midair, when he suddenly realized that now, his wife and most assuredly his whole family, was now, one of the thousands of casualties up on the surface. His knees buckled, and he fell into a chair.

The president ran over to console him "Damn Bill, I apologize. Never had I taken a second to realize that all of our families are now gone!" President Beard himself fell into a chair next to Bill. Both men sat there and cried. No one dared to come close to either one of them due to reality setting in on everyone that was left there in the room. Most everyone had family that they were planning to return to at the end of the day. Now, even if they got out, there was no home nor any family to return to. Besides the sobs that were all about, everything else was quiet for quite a while.

When the president was able to pull himself together, he wiped his eyes, blew his nose, took a deep breath and stood erect.

"Alright everyone, I apologize for the little breakdown." Mumbling and head shakes were all about the room. "I would like my newly appointed direct cabinet to meet me in the conference room in ten. Feel free to crack open a case of those stored snacks and bring them with you." He hesitated and looked around, "I am sure that we will all be getting used to them very shortly."

*****

Mr. Briggs called out. "General Seltzer, Frank was able to raise someone, but I think we may have a problem."

"Why is that Mr. Briggs?"

"Well, Sir, I am having a little trouble getting him to believe me. He thinks that because I am on an old non-used airwave that I may have bought this at a flea market and now, I want to take advantage of the current situation to play a hoax."

The general looked at him. "Give me that damned mic. What the hell is going on an old non-used airwave have to do with anything? Maybe he is a hoax." The general grabbed the mic, "This here is General Leon Seltzer, Army Chief of Staff for the White House. Whom do I have the pleasure of speaking with?"

He released the button and all he could hear was laughter. He was beginning to get a little riled. When the laughter stopped, the man spoke. "Okay, okay, I will play along. Where are you?"

The general looked at Mr. Briggs with a puzzled stare before answering. "Sir, I along with a few volunteers are currently in Piscataway Park attempting to contact the authorities." The general let go of the mic button and waited for the long silence to end. After a moment, he pressed the button, "Sir, do you hear me?"

Response came back. "Yes, yes, I hear you. I was just doing a little checking. Piscataway Park would put you at about fifteen miles outside the heart of D.C. I just have one question for you General. That is, if you do not mind."

The general looked a little confused and looked to Mr. Briggs. "What the fuck question would he have for me?"

Mr. Briggs shook his hand towards the mic. "Well General, I am sure that if you press that little button and ask him, he will be sure to tell you."

The general looked at him. "Alright smartass, I figured that much."

The general raised the mic. "Okay Sir, I agree, but to whom am I speaking with so that I may be so kind as to address you properly?" He looked at Mr. Briggs, winked and nodded. "How was that?" Mr. Briggs gave a thumbs up.

"My name is House, Michael House."

"Okay Mr. House, whenever you are ready, fire away." He looked at Mr. Briggs. "This ought to be good."

"Now General, if you are whom you say that you are, there are three little words that are inscribed above the doorway leading out of the office of the Army Chief of Staff. If you repeat them to me, then I will know that you are who you say that you are."

The general looked at Mr. Briggs. "Really? How in the hell would he know anything about that?"

Mr. Briggs shook his head and shrugged his shoulders. "Not a clue. But, like before, press that little button and ask him, not me." General Seltzer gave him the death stare.

The general picked the mic up and hesitated for a few seconds before answering. "Listen up, Mr...."

He looked to Mr. Briggs for the gentleman's name. "House, Michael House."

The general winked. "Okay, listen up, Mr. House, I am not sure where you are getting your information from, but I will play along. There are no words."

The response was quick to come back. "Wrong answer. I will be signing off now."

"NO, WAIT! There are three words, but how would you know that?"

There was a little chuckle heard on the other end. "General, my great granddad was in the position that you claim to be in. I remember being in that office when I could barely read and seeing those words. I asked him what they meant. He picked me up to be closer to them and after a long story, he told me. So, if you read Latin, I am waiting."

Mr. Briggs still looked lost. "Is he for real?"

"Apparently." The general lifted the mic. "Mr. House, the immortal words that I used to look at every time that I would exit that room are, 'Veni, Vidi, Vici', in English, I came, I saw, I conquered. Now, can we continue?" There was a small round of applause that came across the airwaves.

"Congratulations General, I do believe that you are who you say that you are. Now, we may continue. How may I be of service to you, General?" The general got a big smile on his face.

Looking at Mr. Briggs, he snickered. "See, I told you that we would prevail."

Mr. Briggs just nodded. "Uh huh!"

"Mr. House, are you able to contact the authorities?"

There was a little chuckle that could be heard over the airwaves. "Well General, this is your lucky day, you just happened to get the right person. I am actually the Police Chief of Accokeek. Now, Sir, how may I be of assistance?"

The general felt a world of weight being lifted off his shoulders. "Mr. House, is there any way that you may have any vehicles that are running so that we can get out of here?"

"Well General, first off, please address me as Mike. Second, at this present time, we do not have any motor vehicles available, but we do have horses and wagons. General, you got any cowboys with your posse? If so, then they are more than welcome to have a ride."

The general gave a little chuckle. "Not sure Mike, but if you would still like to be so kind, we will take the lift anyway. Where do we meet you?"

"Hold on..." Mike grabs a map. "Where are you now? Any clue?"

"Mike, we are currently on Mockley Point. Can you find that?"

There was a deep laugh that came across the air. "Mockley Point? Are you shittin' me General? I used to play in those bunkers when I was a child. Tell you what, if you start off on a southwest course, you will come to Mockley Point Road. Continue on that road until you come to a tee. At the tee, go left, that will be Bryan Point

Road. We will meet you somewhere on that road in about an hour or so. Sound good?"

The general was more than ecstatic. "That sounds more than good, we will see you then."

"Oh, General, how many did you say was in your party and what kind of gear are you hauling?"

"Currently, there is five of us here and we came as light as possible. We were not aware of what we would be facing"

"Okay, General, give us a bit and we will be there."

*****

When Larry got to the barn, he saw that there were three adults, two female and one teen male that was already subdued and lying face down on the floor. Larry looked around. "BELLA! BELLA MARIE!" Nothing! He looked to one of the men that came in before him. "Is this all? I mean, is there any more children?"

The man shrugged. "Not sure, this is all that we found here." Larry asked the men to do him a favor and get the children out of the barn.

Larry went over to one of the women and kicked her hard enough in the side to roll her over. He stuck the barrel of his Glock in her mouth hard enough that it broke some teeth. His cocked the hammer back. "Where the fuck is my daughter?!" The woman sort of smiled and laughed. Larry was beyond pissed, he pulled the trigger and that put a silence to her laughter really quick. He jumped up and kicked the male hard enough to roll him too. He also slammed the barrel in his mouth resulting in knocking out teeth. He cocked the hammer. "You want the same as she got?"

101

The boy looked petrified. Larry pulled the gun out of his mouth and swung it around to the boy's knee and pulled the trigger. The boy screamed in pain and Larry silenced him with the barrel in the mouth again. "Well, you gonna tell me or do you want more?"

The boy attempted to smile and that pissed Larry off more. He removed the barrel and placed it between the boy's legs. "Think that's funny, huh? Want to try laughing with no balls?!"

The boy stopped laughing. He turned his head to the side and spit out blood and teeth. Through garble, he tried to communicate. "Wha ya want?"

Larry pressed the barrel tighter to the boy's crotch. "I want to know where my daughter is. Who has her?" The boy was about to speak when the other woman started to sound off. Larry swung the gun around and placed one clean shot into her forehead. "SHUT THE FUCK UP!!" The boy started to shake, and he peed himself. Larry placed the barrel between his legs again. "Now, you were about to tell me where my daughter is or the next thing that you will be aware of is the taste of your balls in your throat. I will pull this fuckin' trigger and take you apart piece by piece, do you understand me?" The boy nodded yes.

Larry removed the Glock, wiped it off on the boy's shirt and placed it back in the holster. "Start talking." At first, the boy hesitated. Larry reached to the Glock.

"Wait. I will tell you, but you need to promise me that you will not kill me and that you will get me to a hospital." Larry agreed. "Bella is your daughter?"

Larry looked at him. "Yeah, why? What does that matter?"

The boy shook his head. "Nothing, it is just that she would always say that her daddy was coming and when he did, that he would kill everyone here." The boy hesitated a second. "The one that took her, his real name is Deval."

"Is that his first or last name?"

The boy shook his head. "Not sure, but I do know that he also goes by Leonard Bloom."

"Anything else?"

The boy hesitated. "He also took a boy named Johnny."

John Meyers jumped up. "My Johnny!"

Larry felt a surge of ice go down his spine. He grabbed the boy by the throat. "Where did he take them?"

The boy fought to breathe. "Not sure, we were just assigned to keep them here and to keep them alive. But somehow, Deval had a feeling that you were coming, and he took them."

"When?"

"About three hours ago."

Larry stood up and looked all around. He looked down to the boy. "How were they traveling?" The boy hesitated, and Larry removed his Glock.

"They were on foot."

"Which direction?"

Before the boy could answer, Larry pulled the hammer back. The boy winced. "They were on foot. I heard him say something about

Lancaster Airport. I do know that after this was all over, we were all to meet in Montreal."

"Anything else?"

Larry pointed the Glock at the boy's head. "NO! NO, THAT IS ALL!"

Larry shook his head. "Okay, that is all."

Larry lowered the weapon to within a few inches of the boy's head. "What!? I told you everything! Besides, you promised not to kill me and to get me to a hospital."

"That I did. But Leonard Bloom, Deval or whatever the hell his name is, he promised me that I would get my daughter back after this was all over. He lied, and so did I. See you in hell." Larry placed one round into the boy's forehead.

CHAPTER TEN

After a much-needed rest, Colonel Corde aroused the squad. He hit the button on his transmitter. "Okay folks, listen up." The group all rose to their feet and gathered around. "During normal times, we would have about three miles and one hour to travel. But, as you have all come to see, our travel has been anything but normal. So, with that thought in mind, I suggest that we get started. We can continue to walk the bikes. You never know, we may have a use for them at some point. Or if we encounter a slight hill and clear roadway, maybe we can use that to our advantage to drift down the hill. But, yes, another *but*. If we have to, we ditch whatever we do not immediately need, and we continue on. Agreed?"

Before they rolled out, they each did a once over to make sure that each other was secure and in no danger of getting a radiation leak. They grabbed their gear and headed down Massachusetts Avenue. The farther they proceed, the worse the situation became. They did not make it but about a quarter mile when the colonel came on the intercom and told everyone to ditch the bikes and anything that pertains to emergency medicine that would take care of more than their immediate group. "Folks, I shouldn't have to say it, you can see for yourself. But...I do not feel as though this mission will result in any type of rescue nor recovery."

Looking around, deep inside, the colonel wanted to turn around and go back to Hagerstown. The closer they got to their destination, the more destruction that was about. As far as anyone could see, there was no form of buildings standing that could even be recognized as a building, just massive amounts of debris that appears to have been blown all in one direction. If there were ever any trees, there is now no visible sign that they ever existed here. There were plenty of huge bubbles of asphalt in what the colonel took to be a road that were the size of medicine balls and hard as a rock. At times, they struggled and had to help each other over the bubbles. It was almost like they were trying to get through a concrete jungle that had been leveled.

At about a half mile into their trek, the colonel went around a massive bubble and suddenly stopped. He stood there for a second, then he fell to his knees. Captain Sheer was the next to go around the bubble, she too stopped in her tracks and knelt next to the colonel. One by one, each soldier came around the bubble, stopped and joined the colonel.

The colonel hit the intercom switch. Choking back tears, he began. "If any of you, and I am to blame as well, but if any of you had any doubt if there was hope, here it is." Before them, there was a cross standing between them and their destination. There appeared to be no damage on the object, it looked as though someone erected it for them. Everything around them was unrecognizable as to what it formerly was, but this cross, it was pristine.

The colonel continued on. "I know this cross. It was way up on top of the Woodrow Wilson House on the corner of Massachusetts and Twenty-Fourth Street." He raised his eyes to the sky. "My God, what has man done." The colonel bowed his head and said a prayer. "Folks, I do not know if we are at that corner of the house or if we are blocks away, but anyway, let's keep moving."

*****

President Beard brought everyone together in the meeting room. "Alright Gentlemen, we need a game plan. We cannot sit here with our thumbs up our asses as we wait for someone to decide to come get us. Hell, the outside world has not a clue as to who, what or whatever survived the attack. From here, we know nothing either. Although we had that short conversation with..."

He looks over the group and one calls out. "Rollins, Lieutenant Rollins."

"Right, thank you Bill, Rollins, Lieutenant Rollins. Besides, we have not heard from him in what, one day, two days? Being in here, I have no track of time. Personally, I need some fresh air. I know that my security would be against me going out, but I am the president, I can do that!"

The group just sat there and looked at him like he had lost his mind. "What? You all don't agree? Anyone else have a better idea?"

One man rose his hand. "Sir, Mr. President..."

He hesitated. "Yes, Daniel, speak your mind."

Daniel cleared his throat. "Sir, I..."

The president cut him off. "Please Gentlemen, we are all just men stuck down here together, so please, let's say we skip the formalities. Okay?" They all nodded, "Good, now Daniel, what did you have to offer?"

Daniel stood up, puffed out his chest and began. "Wellll, John..." They all burst out in laughter at his forwardness. "No seriously Sir, I mean John. You are now acting president and we need to keep you in that position as long as we can. And honestly, this is about the safest place on this planet right now. Hell, even a nuclear blast could not get in here."

President Beard nodded his head in agreement. "As much as I want out, you are one hundred percent correct Daniel. So, with that in mind, we need to see if we can somehow reach Lieutenant Rollins again. Hopefully, he is still alive."

Daniel raised his hand. "Yes Daniel. You got more?"

"Ah…yes. Sir…" He hesitated a second. "John, it has only been hours, not days."

President Beard gave him a stern look. "Why thank you Daniel. Thanks for breaking my hope!" All eyes in the room started to wander from one person to the other.

*****

Considering the situation, it was a pretty good hike from Mockley Point until they were greeted a good way down Bryan Point Road by the *Cavalry* of six men on horseback. The lead rider stopped his horse and then spun in a few circles. The general was in the point position. He walked up to the rider. "Chief House?"

The man smiled. "Yes, Sir, that I am. That must make you General Seltzer."

The general smiled and extended a hand. "That it does Chief. Nice to make your acquaintance."

About a minute later, there were two buckboards that came into view from around the dogleg in the road. The chief called out. "Gentlemen, if you would be so kind, please climb aboard and make yourselves as comfortable as possible and we can get you out of here."

The chief called out to one of his men. "Zeke, would you be so kind as to give your ride to the general here? Well, that is if the general knows how to ride a horse."

He looked toward the general. "General?"

The general smiled. "Chief, I hate to admit it, but I've ridden more horses than women."

They all laughed. "General, either you are a lonely man, or you don't get out of the barn much. But either way, I like that. Can I use that line sometime?"

"If you get us through this, you can use it all you like."

It was not that long of a ride until they were at the Police Station. As they rode along, the chief and the general drifted to the rear so that they could talk. "Alright Mike, what can you tell me? The last that I knew, besides a radio conversation that we had with an Army Lieutenant, there was some sort of terrorist attack in Northeast Maryland."

"Well General..."

The general cut him off. "Mike, please call me Leon."

Mike reached his hand out. "Nice to meet you, Leon." Mike smiled and exhaled sharply, "Wow! Never in my wildest dreams would I have ever thought that I would actually meet and then shake the hand of *The Army Chief of Staff* based at the White House. Although my great granddad held that position years ago, it was a different world back then, not as political as it is today." He looked at the general and grinned. "Now, Leon, you do realize that I will take advantage of this relationship, right?"

The general laughed. "I would not expect any less."

"Talk about friends in high places."

"As I was about to say before I went rogue on you, it does appear that a terrorist attack has in fact occurred. From what I have received from some small amateur ham operators that had radios stashed in *Faraday Cages*, the East Coast infrastructure has been destroyed in the form of bridges and the Conowingo Dam."

"What? Sorry, please continue."

"From what my department has learned, as of yet, no one has taken responsibility for the attack. Then again, with all communications down, besides the old radios, anyone that would claim responsibility would have a hard time getting the word out. Currently, no one knows exactly how far out this has reached. We do know that there was an EMP, well at least there was one above our area for at least twenty or thirty miles. Any and all electrical devices are basically fried."

The general stopped his horse. "Are you for real? An EMP?"

"Apparently Leon. It also appears that it was designed to wreak havoc on the ground as well as the air. It was raining aircraft and satellites for about forty-five minutes after the first sign of the attack. What was up, was soon to be down. There is no way to determine how many lost their lives. Like I said, we have no clue as to how far out it reached. And to top it off, we also have not a clue as to when we may have any confirmation from other states. The big questions are: are we only effected in the surrounding area, or is this a worldwide thing? They are the million-dollar questions waiting for a five-cent answer."

General Seltzer just sat there a moment taking it all in before he spoke again. "Mike, I am sure of one thing."

"What's that?"

"We do have an acting president that is alive and well."

"You shittin' me? Who?"

"John Beard. He along with his immediate cabinet is safe, deep in a bunker under what was once the White House."

Mike stopped his horse and got a big smile. "You are serious, aren't you? Man, that is cool. Well, yea and nay. Sorry. So...that must mean that President Wolford is in fact gone?"

"It appears so Mike. When we all headed to the bunker, he and his family were headed out to Marine one in an attempt to get to Andrews. But, if what we believe happened actually happened, then there is no way that any of them made it out. So, with that potential hanging in the air, we, when I say we, I mean the White House Staff and cabinet thought that we should keep it on the safe side and shuffle the cabinet. I did not have to abandon my post, but everyone else in the presidential line moved up one notch."

Now, it was Mike's turn to sit there and take it all in. "Wow! I'm sorry that I can't offer much for information. I, along with my department has tried reaching out and we have gotten little to nothing in the way of response. Hell, you just told me more than I already knew. To be totally honest, I really did expect to see the military bustling through town or at least making contact. But...nothing."

He fell silent for a moment. "Wow Leon, President Wolford gone. I...I just can't wrap my head around that. He was the best one that we had in a long, long time. No offense or disrespect, but it is gonna take a lot of doing for Beard to try to fill those shoes."

111

"Well, Mike, if you would not mind, when we get to your station, would you mind if one of my men got on the horn? He may have a trick or two up his sleeve. We actually have access to frequencies that you may not be aware of."

Mike looked at him and smiled. "Somehow Leon, I am sure that you do."

Much to their surprise, when the group arrived back at the station, there was a few military personnel there. It turned out that the local Guard Unit had come together, and they offered the assistance of their MP's and UP's to help keep things in order. There was not any trouble that was expected, but one can never be too cautious.

CHAPTER ELEVEN

Larry and John made their way back to the house to confront the man that took the leg shot. On the porch, they were informed that the man had nothing to offer concerning any of this. John was furious. "What do we do now Larry? How in the hell will we find them?"

Larry placed a hand on John's shoulder. "I know where they are going, and I know how. I just need a little more information. Give me a few minutes, then we will start out, okay?" John agreed, but he also wanted to be the one to extract information. Larry smiled, "tell you what, you can start, and I will finish up. Okay? That way, none of this is on your conscience."

They made their way back in to where the man was lying there holding his leg and screaming that he would kill them all. John walked over to him and kicked him as hard as he could in his shot knee. The man screamed in immense pain. John bent over. "You piece of shit, care to threaten me again!" John kicked him again and then he grabbed him by his collar and sat him up. John got down to eye level. "You know, you will tell me what I want to know, and you will do it either with a lot of pain or an enormous amount of pain. Either way, I guarantee that you will tell me."

John began to rise until he noticed that the man sat there attempting to get a snicker on his face. John pushed the man down against the floor and removed the man's belt. He sat him back up and fastened the belt tight around the man's legs just above the knee. The man just looked at John. It was John's turn to be the one to snicker. "Sorry Pal, but I need you alive, I cannot have you bleed to death before I get my answers."

The man looked at Joh. "Thank you." John laughed and removed his large Bowie knife. "Don't thank me yet!" John placed the blade under the backside of the man's knee and quickly sliced upward. The man's leg fell off and landed next to him. For a split second, the man did not realize what had happened. When the pain kicked in, he screamed louder than John had ever heard a man scream. John sliced a piece of the severed leg off and shoved it in the man's mouth. "SHUT THE FUCK UP!" The man could not scream, and he started to gag. "Don't you fuckin' choke to death!" John took his knife and slit the sides of the man's mouth and used the point to flip the meat out. John looked him square in the eye. "You ready to tell me what I want, or do you desire to snicker and have another body part shoved into your mouth!" The man nodded yes.

 Larry patted John on the shoulder. "I got it from here John."

John rose and gestured to Larry. "All yours Lieutenant."

Larry got down to eye level. "What is your name?" The man sat there and did not grunt a word. Larry reached his hand up. "Knife please John." John handed him the knife. Larry looked at the man again. "You know, it is only polite to answer someone when they ask you a question. So, either you are ignoring me, or your ears are clogged, let's see." Larry quickly places the blade on the man's left ear, and sliced it clean off. The man screamed and Larry picked up the ear and shoved it in the man's mouth. "Like my partner told you a moment ago. "SHUT THE FUCK UP!"

Larry continued. "Can you hear me now? You can nod if you like." The man sat there a second until Larry moved, then he nodded his head up and down furiously. "Good! Now, either I can cut your ear out of your mouth, or you may remove it yourself." The man slowly reached up and took his ear out of his mouth. Larry shook his head, "Uh-uh, don't put that down, hold on to it, I may need it in a few minutes."

The man looked at Larry and through a blood-filled mouth, "You are fucking insane."

Larry smiled. "Thank you. You people made me this way. Shall we continue?"

The man just sat there looking at Larry. "Care to know what really, really pisses me off? When I ask someone a question and they force me to force it out of them. So, last time before I really get pissed. Name!" Larry raised the knife to the man's other ear.

"Okay, okay. My name is Salim." Larry lowered himself to eye level.

"Salim what? Smith? Jones? One chance to answer!"

The man took a deep breath, "Salim Abdella."

Larry stood back up. "Now, that wasn't that hard, was it?" The man just glared and did not speak. "So now, you will tell me everything that I need to know for the moment, okay Salim?" The man nodded. "How is Deval getting to the airport? Is someone picking him up?"

The man just smiled. "You will never understand the power that my people will have over America. It will not be long until America comes to their knees, and they worship us."

Larry stood there a second, then he dropped to his knees. He held his head low for a moment. "You know Salim, you are correct. Now, I am here on my knees at your level. I will continue to lower myself to your level." Salim smiled. Larry reached and removed a

Glock and placed it against the good ear of Salim. "Now. Now I lower myself to your level. You will soon hear me worship you." Larry pulled the trigger and sent Salim to the other side.

Larry stood up. "Ready to go get Deval?"

John smiled. "By all means, Lieutenant. Lead the way." John got on the radio. "Listen up, remove the children, take them to safety at my house and burn everything here that is standing. I don't want to come back and find even so much as an uncharred timber." The two men in the house with them acknowledged and they proceeded upstairs. They ignited the bedding and the curtains to get the fire started. The men in the barn hustled the children out and they too ignited whatever was available that would start quickly.

Larry and John recovered their bikes. Larry turned to John, "If we stick to the roads, we can probably make better time than if we went through the trees and forded the river. A little way up, we can cross using Mill Covered Bridge. Since Deval is on foot and dragging two children along with him, we should be able to overtake him in a short amount of time before he reaches the airport. You know John, you don't have to be a part of this. So, last call, care to stay?"

John looked at him and chuckled. "You gotta be fuckin' kiddin' me. He has my child also. I would not miss this for the world."

Larry stuck his hand out and John accepted. "Okay, mount up and get your night vision on." Right as they started, Larry yelled out, "Deval, Leonard Bloom or whatever you want to die by, I promised you that I would come for you. So, here I come!"

*****

116

When Colonel Corde reached the area that he believed used to sustain the White House, he paused and said a prayer. He looked around and there was nothing in view but a large hole in the ground and a mound off in the distance. He pressed his mic button. He sharply exhaled. "Well folks, we may have traveled in vain. Before us, is where I believe the White House once stood." They all just stood on the brim and looked down. The colonel pointed off into the distance. "See that mound?" They all turned to see where he was pointing. "That my friends, was where Capitol Hill used to be. It was so named that, due to the fact of that mound was the highest point in this area. Now..." The colonel spun around with his arms outstretched. "One day, surely not Monday, but one day, man gets to start all over again."

For his records, the colonel removed his Geiger counter and took a reading. "Huh, that's strange."

Captain Sheer approached him. "How so, Colonel?"

"The reading on the counter is one hell of a lot lower than what I expected. Actually, it is lower than it was five miles ago." They stood there a second. "So, that must mean that all of the nuke material did not release here. Some of it must have been blown out before the canisters were ruptured."

The colonel called them all to attention. "We may have some live canisters or warheads in this area. Well, as far as that goes, we may locate some on the return trip. Just be visual and cautious at the same time. You spot anything, call out." The colonel switched off his mic and switched on his recorder and made notes. The last recorded word was a short one. "Sad".

*****

117

General Seltzer and Chief House were the last to ride in. They just took their time and had quite a conversation along the way. When they reached the police station, they went around back and dismounted. One of the deputies came running out. "Chief! Chief!"

Mike looked at him like he was a child running to greet daddy. "Wow Rickey, happy to see me?" The deputy just glared at him. "Well...sort of. Anyway, a little while ago, we picked up some chatter from someone that claims to be a Lieutenant that is hunting down the terrorist."

"Did you get a name?"

The deputy pulled out a folded piece of paper. "Yes Sir, Rollins, Lieutenant Rollins."

The general looked at him, reached and grabbed the paper. "Give me that."

The deputy was shocked. "What the hell?"

The chief took the stump. "Rickey, this is General Seltzer, the *general* that I spoke with on the radio."

The deputy felt like he was two inches tall. "Sorry Chief, sorry General."

General Seltzer read the message. "Son of a bitch. Apparently, Lieutenant Rollins located where the supposed mastermind was holed up and he and a group were headed to get them. Chief, I need to get on your radio!"

The sheriff led the general to the radio room. The general looked around. "Wow, this takes me back a few years. How in the hell did you get this to survive the blast?"

The sheriff went back to the doorway and slid a pocket door closed. "General, being this close to D.C. and with the knowledge of never having knowledge, my great grandpappy had this room built many years ago. General, welcome to the largest Faraday cage in the world. Well, the largest as I know of."

The general looked around. "Damn! Gotta be the biggest damned microwave oven that I have ever seen." He spun around in circles. "You say your granddaddy built this? The one that held the position that I now have. Well...I guess I still have it."

They all chuckled. "The one and only General. He always said, *Boy, you never know when the big one will hit*. And damned if he wasn't right."

The general continued to look around. "How or where or better yet, let's go back to how did he get all of the Faraday screening? Or better yet, do I really want to know how?"

"General, my great granddaddy was a man of many resources and friends. I am just thankful that he was where and who he was. Otherwise..." His words fell silent.

The general took control. "Okay, get this fired up and lead me in the right direction."

One of the deputies took over. "Right this way, Sir. I am still on the frequency that the L T was on. He was chattering with someone going by the call sign of *Eagle One*, that is if that makes any sense."

The general laughed. "Son, have you any clue as to who Eagle One is?" The deputy shook his head. "Eagle One is the call sign for the president of the United States when he is unable to either be in the airplane proudly called *Air Force One* or the chopper named

Marine One. Eagle One is when he is immobile and in the nest. Just as he is now."

The deputy looked at him. "Sir, are you associated with the president?"

The general smiled. "Son, I have known President Beard for many years, we are good friends."

The deputy continued to stare at the general. "President Beard? You mean Pres..." He never finished his words before the general gave him a sad look.

"Okay Deputy, enough chit chat, fire it up."

"Yes, Sir!" The deputy threw a few switches and the board lit up.

"Thanks." The general leaned in and pressed the button. "Groundhog to Eagle One, Eagle One, do you copy?" The general released the button. There was some snickering behind him, he turned around.

Mike was smiling. "Really Leon? Groundhog?" Another round of laughter.

The general tried a fake smile. "Hey, I am the Army Chief of Staff. We move on the ground, so, I am known as Groundhog." This time, the general laughed with them. "You know, I never thought about it, but that is pretty funny." More laughter until the radio crackled to life. "Shh, shh, quiet down."

"Groundhog, this is Eagle One, copy." A round of applause went out.

Once again, the general called out. "Shhh, quiet!" He cleared his throat. "Eagle One, Groundhog here. Out of the hole and the sun is shining in a new field."

This time, the applause came out of the speaker, and they all heard, "Shh, quiet down please. Leon, John here, how you doin' Buddy?"

The general looked at Mike and smiled. "Chief, me and the president are tight. I call him John and he calls me Leon."

The chief leaned in. "Personally, I may start calling you *Suck Ass*." All in the room laughed.

The general hit the button. "John, I am great. Sorry, but we need to keep you safe in the nest for a bit until we can come up with a game plan."

"I know Leon, I'm not going anywhere." When he said that, the president looked around him and a few of his secret service agents gave him a thumbs up sign.

"So where are you now, Leon? Have you made any contact?"

"Actually John, I have. At this moment, I am in the office of Police Chief Mike House. He is Chief of Accokeek Police Department. He sent the cavalry out to get me and my men. I mean that in the literal sense. They came out on horseback and wagons." The president had the mic button pushed in and the whole room heard them all laughing.

The President asked to speak to the general alone for a moment and everyone left the room. When they were alone, the general told the president so. "Leon, I need you to go to Three Mike Tango Oscar Seven. Think you can do that on your end?"

The general looked around the board. "Ahh, I believe so John. If not there within thirty seconds, come back here, okay?"

"Gotcha Leon. Thirty seconds from *mark*."

The general turned a few knobs and adjusted the tuner. "Here goes nothing. Groundhog to Eagle One, you read?" The general waited the thirty seconds and was just about to switch back when he heard some chatter over the radio.

"Hold on. Wait a minute, let me see. Just leave it there." The sound of someone clearing their throat. "Ahem, Eagle One to Groundhog, do you copy?"

The general pressed the button and chuckled. "Yeah, Eagle One, I copy. I was about to switch back until I heard you hens clucking over the buttons."

President Beard asked everyone to leave the room so that he may have a private chat with the general. When the last was out and the door was closed, "Leon, we are on a secure airwave. If anyone else was to attempt to access this channel, they would just receive a scrambled signal."

"Okay John, what's up?"

"Leon, remember that we had contact with a Lieutenant Rollins?"

"Yeah, he was somewhere up in Northern Maryland. Why? What's up?"

"Well Leon, from what we have received here, it appears that he is trying to be the knight in shining armor. He apparently is going after someone that he believes is the mastermind behind all of this. Not rightfully sure how he came up with that idea or the supposed identity of that individual, but he is on the chase. This is where you come in."

"Okay John, where am I to fit in?"

"Leon, with everything that has happened, there are a lot of vigilantes out there just itchin' to put the blame on someone. We cannot afford to have a war going on while we attempt to bring the government back to life. So, this is what I need you to do. I need you to get a posse together and go get the lieutenant and stop him before someone innocent gets hurt. Think you can do that?"

The general sat there for a moment thinking that over. "Well John, not rightfully sure where to start looking for him. Also, in case you have not heard, transportation is very limited right now. They only things that will work around here are bikes and horses."

"Okay Leon, so where is the problem?"

"There is a few, John. One, without proper communication, it is quite rough to figure out where to start. Two, even if we knew where to start, we don't know where to head to catch him."

There was silence for a moment. "You know Leon, I hate to pull rank, but I am afraid that I am going to have to give you a direct order to carry out this mission."

"What? Really John?"

"General, my title is President. You will address me as such. And you will carry out this order or when I get out of here, I will take it upon myself to have you court martialed and executed for treason. Do you understand that?"

This time, there was silence on the other end. "Okay, okay, Mr. President. I will carry out my order. Out." The general hit the power button so that he would not have to listen to another response. He scrambled the nobs so that no one could get the frequency to their conversation. The general just sat there a minute just trying to put two and two together. A knock on the door brought him out of his trance. He looked up to see Mike standing there. The general waved him in.

"What's wrong Leon? You look like you just broke your favorite toy."

The general sat there quiet for a few seconds. "Mike, it appears that I am going to have to leave, and I may need your horses."

"Ah, okay and no. My horses are our only means of transportation for the time being."

"I know that, but I was just given an order to get to Northern Maryland to try to stop someone from doing something that they may regret later. So, I am taking your horses."

"Now General, I can't give you my horses, but I may know where you can acquire some good horses for a long trip. Tell you what, give me about fifteen minutes and I will have an answer for you."

"Now Chief, I'll tell you what. You have those horses for me in fifteen minutes or I will take yours." The chief and the general had a stare down for a moment.

"Fifteen minutes General, fifteen minutes."

"Oh Chief, if you would not mind, I will also be in need of another radio. That is if you can spare one. In case our group would have to separate, I would feel a lot better if I had contact with my people every once in a while. Thanks."

CHAPTER TWELVE

It only took a few minutes for Larry and John to reach the covered bridge. Once they were inside, they dismounted their bikes and had a seat on one of the long, arched support beams that ran along each side of the bridge. Larry took out his flashlight and map. He held the flashlight between his teeth and studied the map for a moment. Sucking up slobber, he tried to talk, but it came out garbled. He removed his flashlight, wiped it off and then tried it again. "John, if need be, on our bikes, we can be at the airport in less than two hours. That is if we have to hump it. But with Deval and the children being on foot, it would take them about ten hours to reach their destination. That is barring any assistance that they may receive along the way. We should be able to overtake them on Hunsicker Road somewhere around here." Larry takes his finger and draws an imaginary circle around a stretch of road.

John sat there stretching his neck and looking over Larry's shoulder. He sat back for a second. "I only have one question. Think that I may already know the answer, but I want to hear it from you."

Larry lowered his map and turned toward John. "Okay, fire away."

John sort of lowered his gaze towards the flooring. "If and when we do catch Deval. What are your plans for him?"

Larry stood up and turned directly to John. "If? There is no *if*. We will encounter him, and we will get our children back. As for what I am going to do, I will do what I promised him that I would do. I will cause him as much pain and agony as he caused a lot of people. He will beg me for death. But that is the last option. He will tell me everything that I want to know. He will even tell me where to find his family so that I can get them and dissect them also. That, I will guarantee you."

John just looked at Larry. "You really are serious, aren't you?"

Larry stared right back. "They started the war and they set the rules. I am just carrying on from where they failed, and I am applying their rules." John just stared and remained quiet. "John, I was raised, and I was trained to abide by the Geneva Convention. But, when these fuckers decide to cut the heads off people, use children as human bombs and have no respect for human life, then John, the Geneva Convention goes right out the window. They want to kill innocents and have no conscience, then I am able to lower myself to their standards. I will not have a problem skinning Deval while he is alive. I am actually hoping to have his family first, that way, he can enjoy my technique before I kill him." Larry folded his map back up and placed it in his vest pocket. "Okay, time to roll. We have a bad guy to catch."

The duo was just a quarter mile from route 272, Oregon Pike, when John noted some movement. He softly called to Larry. "Larry! I see someone." They stopped their bikes and Larry removed his night vision glasses. He scanned until he saw what John saw.

Larry's heart skipped a beat. "Oh my God, it's them." Larry zoomed in and he saw Deval towing each child, with one in each hand. At that moment, the thought going through Larry's head was that he wished that he had his sniper rifle. He would shoot Deval in the leg to keep him from being able to run.

They pulled off to the side and started to come up with another game plan. Larry pulled out his map and had another look. "Hunsicker changes to Valley after the bridge. About a thousand feet down Valley, we will know better as to where we can get out in front of them. Look here." Larry pointed to the map. "If they take the road on the left, then that will enable us to go straight and come out ahead of them. Then again, at the same time, if they go straight, we go left, and we come out in front of them. So, let's keep our distance and stay with them." They mounted back up and started down the road.

* * * * *

Colonel Corde stood there just looking around at all the destruction. Once again, he called out. "My God, what have you allowed man to do?" He stood there attempting to hold back the tears when Captain Sheer came upon him. "Colonel, anything that I can do?" The colonel kept his gaze away from the captain. "No. No Captain, I am fine. Just have a lot weighing on my mind."

He turned to face the captain and she could see the tears welling in the corner of his eyes. Being in the suit, the colonel had no way to wipe his eyes. So, he just let them flow down his cheek. "You know Captain, although I have seen a lot and been through even more, there are just somethings that really get to me. At times, I am not sure if I am getting soft in my older age or if I have just seen enough and my soul just can't retain anything more." He shook his head and paused between each word. "I …just…don't…know."

They stood there silently facing each other for a few minutes when another soldier approached. "Sir, Ma'am, sorry for the intrusion, but can you fill me in on what we are to do now?"

The colonel stood there for a moment before speaking. "Sergeant, gather your team together and inform them that we are to move out in five minutes. Remind them to keep a sharp eye out for any ordinance that may not have exploded."

"Yes Sir, but can you tell me where we are headed to?"

"Sergeant, we are headed back to Hagerstown. There is nothing more that we can do here."

President Beard was starting to get a little antsy being holed up underground. There was quite a bit of space in the bunker, there was just not that much to do. The bunker was designed and built to sustain life, not to be a lifestyle. The storeroom was stocked with just about any type of canned food or bottled drink that one could desire. The provisions were supposed to be able to last at least eighteen months for a party of thirty. Currently, there were forty-two that were down below.

The president called a few of his cabinet together for a meeting. Once the six were there that he called for, President Beard closed the door. "Gentlemen, you are probably wondering what I called you in here for. There is a reason why only the six of you were called." He stood there leaning on the table just looking back and forth at each one.

Finally, one of them spoke up. "And, why is that John?"

The president stood erect and reached into his back pocket. He removed a deck of cards and tossed them on the table as he cheerfully announced, "It's poker time!" The smiles were priceless. The president went to the refrigerator and opened the door. "Gentlemen, name your poison." They glared upon a very well stocked, stuffed refrigerator full of assorted beers.

"I figured that as long as we are stuck down here, well hell, we may as well make the best of it. Unless someone has a better idea as to how to pass the time, then I suggest we get started and enjoy ourselves." The cheers were many but were kept to a minimum roar so as not to alert the others. President beard slid open a cabinet panel and removed a box. He opened it and removed a humidor. He flipped it open, "Gentlemen, may as well make this meeting official, cigar anyone?"

* * * * *

General Seltzer called his men together in a private meeting. He explained what all he was told by the president, and he let them all know that they would be riding cowboy style to Pennsylvania. Mr. Briggs raised his hand. "Ah...Sir, I ah....well I never been on a horse."

The general laughed. "Mr. Briggs, nothing to it. Besides, I really do not believe that we will be running full force like you see in the movies when they are chased by the Indians. We will be trotting, that is all. The problem is not getting on or riding, you will mainly just feel some discomfort when you dismount. Okay Mr. Briggs?"

"Well, do I have much choice?"

The general smiled. "No, not at this time." The rest of the crew got a good laugh at that statement.

The general had a good idea as to where they were to be able to get started, he just did not know where Larry was headed. He told his men that since there is the chance of running into radiation from the blast that they would have to take a longer route and almost must skirt along the bay before they headed north. At the present time, they needed to keep as much distance between them and Washington, D.C.

Once they came upon route 231, they headed east so that they could take the bridge over the Patuxent River. Once they made it on the bridge, someone called out that there was a watering hole over the bridge on the right. The general stopped his horse and told them that if times were different, then he would stop and buy the rounds. But, right now, they had a lot of traveling to do before they could celebrate.

They were a little more than halfway over the bridge, when a group of armed individuals appeared and entered the roadway. The general called for his group to stop. They sat there a few minutes watching the other group just stand there watching them. Someone heard something to their rear, and they looked back. There was now a group of armed men standing on the bridge where they first entered.

In true horseman style, the general spun his horse around in circles to keep an eye on both groups. "Gentlemen, without moving too quickly, slowly and carefully reach down and unlatch your holders." After a few more circles, the general brought his horse to a halt. In a low tone, he called to Mr. Briggs. "Mr. Briggs, I need you to hold the fort down while I go see if I can speak to whomever is in charge." Mr. Briggs acknowledged, and he added, "That may be a good idea. Because right now, my ass already hurts too bad to get off this horse. Good luck General."

The general slowly rode toward the end of the bridge. From the group, there was one individual that emerged, and he was carrying a shotgun laying over his shoulder. The man slowly made his way towards the general. When they were about ten feet apart, they both stopped. Neither one said a word for a moment until the general decided to break the silence.

He readjusted himself in the saddle. "Good afternoon, Sir. I am General Seltzer, I am the Army Chief of Staff for the White House, whom may you be?"

The man just looked at him studying him for a moment before he spoke. "Okay, General. Seltzer, was it?"

The general looked at him. "Yes, Sir, that is right, Seltzer."

"Okay General Seltzer, if you are from the White House, then how in the hell did you survive?"

He sat there in the saddle wondering how to handle this.

"Mister...sorry, you never did answer when I asked your name."

The man hesitated a moment. "Bridge, call me Mr. Bridge."

The general took a deep breath. "Okay Mr. Bridge, I will answer your question. I, along with a small group of the cabinet made it safely into an underground bunker before all hell broke loose." Mr. Bridge just stared at the general.

"Okay general, how did you get out of the bunker when no one else seemed to be able to get out?"

He chose his words carefully before he spoke. "We..." He spun a little in the saddle and waved his hand towards his group. "We are just a small group that was sent out by President Beard to see if we could actually get out and if it was safe in order to get him out."

The man looked at him like he had two heads. "President Beard?" The man hesitated. "Vice President Beard is now President? What happened to President Wolford? Didn't he make it? What..." The words just fell silent.

The general took a deep breath and then he exhaled. "Mr. Bridge, sadly, President Wolford apparently perished before he could get to safety. I personally do not know what D.C. looks like. I just know what the gauges told me. And what they did tell me really makes me believe that there was no way that he made it. I'm sorry."

The man stood there a moment with his head hung down. He raised his head and took a few steps to the side. He removed the shotgun from his shoulder and waved it in the air. The men that were on the far end of the bridge dissipated. The man walked over to the general and extended a hand. "General, I would like to apologize. My real name is Ridgely, Thomas Ridgely. Sorry for the cold start." The general accepted his hand and told him that he understands. Thomas explained that they are the first ones that they have encountered that were not highly sick from radiation. He told the general that they were just trying to protect the community from exposure.

"Mr. Ridgely, I would probably try to do the same as you if I was in your shoes. No offense, but we are on a mission, and we really need to get moving. We have a long way to travel."

The general sort of threw his thumb over his shoulder in the direction of his men. "See that one sitting there in front?"

Thomas peered around the general's shoulder. "Yeah, General, I do."

The general smiled. "That poor guy has never been in a saddle and right now, if he gets off that horse, he will never get back on." They both laugh and the general extends his hand. Thomas takes it and thanks him for his service and his determination.

Thomas tells the general that they will not be able get any powered transportation for about another twenty miles. He informed the general that he has heard from family members miles away that told him that the only vehicles that will still run are the older vehicles from the early 70's before all of the electronics kicked in. Thomas told the general that he would send a letter with him that would make it easier to acquire transportation. The general thanked him and waved for his group to join him. He informed Mr. Briggs that they may be able to get off the horse and in a vehicle in a couple of hours. The look on his face was of both relief and pain.

*****

Larry and John were not too far behind when they passed under the bridge. Larry saw the trio turn left and he told John that they would give them a minute before they hurry past them going straight down Valley Road. "What do you think Larry, should we split with one going with them and one going the other or should we stick together and head them off together?"

Larry thought about that for a moment. "You may have something there. Maybe we should split. Let's check our radios before we start."

They were ready to start when Larry asked John which way he wanted. "Well, considering how you feel about Deval or whatever his name is, I think I will stick with him, and you stop him ahead of us."

Larry just sort of smirked. "Okay John, I see your point. Tell you what, I will promise you that I will not dissect him for the time being. Okay?"

John agreed. "Good, let's get started."

John dropped his night vision goggles over his eyes and turned to Larry. "We will see you in about twenty minutes."

Larry dropped his. "Twenty minutes it is. See you soon." Larry headed off at full speed and John started off slowly. He knew that the last thing that he would want to do would be to catch up to them too soon and spoof them.

Larry made it to the rendezvous point and waited. He looked at his watch and figured that they should be coming in about five minutes. He sat off to the side in the tree line to stay concealed. A few minutes later, he looked at his watch. To no one in particular, "Okay, where are you, George. Come to poppa."

A few minutes later, Larry saw movement up the road. Slowly, he removed one of his Glocks and he ever so slowly pulled the slide back to make sure that there was a round in the chamber. He watched the movement for a moment until he realized that it was John on the bike, not Deval and the children.

Larry slowly stepped out so that he would not startle John. As John neared Larry, Larry stuck his arms out in surprise. "What the fuck? Where are they?"

John stopped. "They were right in front of me before they went around the turn."

"Well, they just didn't disappear! What the fuck happened?" Larry pulled his map out and points at it. "We are here. And where did you last see them?"

John pointed. "Right here. I saw them last right when they went around the turn."

Larry studied the map. "Shit, he must have dragged them through the woods to the highway. We can go back down this road and we should be able to catch them if they did make it to the highway. If we don't catch them, then we need to hightail it to the airport. One way or another. Ready?"

John inhaled and then exhaled sharply. "Let's do it"

They headed off to Landis Valley Road and made a left headed towards route 272, also known as Oregon Pike. Once they arrived at Oregon Pike, they left their bikes off to the side of the road and they scanned the area. After about ten minutes, John saw something. He tapped Larry on the shoulder. "Larry, look!"

Larry turned his head and the sight that came upon him was what they came for. "Deval!"

CHAPTER THIRTEEN

President Beard was starting to fidget quite a bit. At times, he would be out in the great hall pacing back and forth. Other times, he would be in a boardroom throwing things about. It was not until his security adviser was informed by an agent that he believed that the president was having a meltdown.

Mort Brady was now in the same boat and the same mind set as most of the rest of the cabinet. He was casts into a position that he never really saw or thought that he would ever be in. But, on his way to confront the president, he allowed his mind to drift back to when he was a child and his mother punished him. "Well now Mortimer, just remember, it is what it is." Mort thought, *it may be, it is what it is, but I don't have to like it.*

Mort knocked on the door just to get a reply of something being thrown against the door. He knocked again and announced himself. "Hey John, it's me, Mort, can I safely come in?" No answer. "John, I'm coming in." He attempted to turn the knob, but the door was locked. He continued to knock, but a bit louder. Nothing. He put his ear up to the door and listened. Not a sound.

Mort called for the agents milling about and told them that he feared that the president may be down. One of them in turn knocked and called out for the president. Nothing. The other fumbled for the correct key as the first continued to knock and call out. When the correct key was found, the agent unlocked the door and slowly pushed it open while continually calling out to the president to announce himself and his entry.

Once the door was open far enough that they could see into the room, one agent quickly made an entrance and swung around to get a view behind the door. "Clear!" At the sound of that, Mort and the other agent made their way into the room. No sign of the president. With most of the furnishings strewn about, it took a few seconds to scan the room to make sure that the president was not laying on the floor. The two agents, with weapons drawn, went over to the closet and pulled the door open. Nothing!

To no one in particular, one agent let out with, "What the hell?" They all three kneeled and looked under the table. Nothing. They jumped up and one ran to the door and announced that the president was gone. In the matter of a seconds, there was an additional six agents in the room. One of the first on the scene took charge. "Spread out! Search every nook and cranny. He just didn't vanish into thin air!"

One of the agents caught the light just right as it reflected off the table and he saw a smudged shoe print. He looked up. "Air vent. The president has gone through the air vent!" The lead agent yelled out the door for someone to locate the drawing for the ventilation system. Three or four people in the great room scrambled to find the right drawing.

When it was located, he made a mad dash to the board room. "Mort, Mort, I got it."

They cleared the table and spread the drawing out. Mort ran his finger along the many tees and elbows. On one path, he came to a stop. "Shit! Shit! Shit! The airlock! Check the air lock! He may be trying to get out!" Every agent in the room scrambled out the door and down the hall to the airlock. When they reached the door, they peered inside and saw nothing. One tried the door, and it would not open. "Damn it! He jammed the door. Get the ax."

Mort caught up to them. "No! You can't break that seal. Without us knowing what the reading is on the other side, we would face the danger of exposing and possibly killing everyone here in the bunker. There has to be emergency suits somewhere around here. Find one, at least one."

A suit was located, but it was a size *small*. Mort looked at it and then he looked up and down at a nearby agent. "You sure as shit won't fit into this. Call everyone into the room. We need to quickly find someone that can fit into this suit." When everyone was assembled, Mort took to the podium. "Folks, like right now, we need a volunteer to go through the vent system to get to the escape chamber." Mort looked around, not a hand went up. "Really?! No one? Well now." He looked over to the one agent. "Agent, as you were a few minutes ago. Go get the ax and chop open that door and expose us all."

The agent looked at Mort. "Are you serious, Sir?"

Without as much as a blink, "Dead serious!"

As the agent turned to leave, an aide spoke up. "Wait, I'll do it. But, for the record, this crap is way above my paygrade! Give me the damned suit." Mort told the agents to help the man into the suit and to help him get up into the duct system.

As he was being suited up, Mort gave the man the rundown. "No heroics, got it? All we need you to do is to get inside of the escape chamber and take a reading. If it all looks good, then and only then do you remove whatever it is that has the door jammed. Have I made myself clear?"

The man nodded in agreement. "Oh, before I go through with this, there has to be an agreement. For me doing this, I want a half million dollars upon our departure from here."

The group around him looked at him with puzzlement and amazement. Mort smiled and placed a hand on the man's shoulder. "Tell you what…" Mort looked lost. "Sorry, I don't even know your name."

"My name is Cashius, Cashius Spector."

Mort smiled again. "Thank you. Now Cashius, here is my counteroffer. Ready?"

Cashius nodded and smiled. "Ready."

Mort gave a little squeeze to his shoulder. "Cashius, if you don't fuckin' get your little bitch ass in that fuckin' vent and do what I just explained to you, I will cut your throat right here and now. That's my counteroffer. So, what will it be? You have five seconds."

Cashius looked quite nervous. "I will do it. I was just trying to make a buck."

"Good, get your ass up on that table." Cashius was given a flashlight and a paper with the instructions where to turn in the duct system so that he can make his way to the chamber. He was also given the code to open the pressure lock that separates the chamber vent from the main vent. Without that code, Cashius would not be able to get through to the chamber. "Here, this will get you through. I just hope that Beard didn't somehow fuck this up."

It was a slow process to get through the duct. Cashius may have been small, but he was also nervous as can be. He was sweating profusely and that was causing his face shield to fog up. He tried to wipe it, but common sense did not function at that particular moment. He did not think that the fog was on the inside. When he could not clear it, he became more nervous. He was one step from a panic attack.

Everyone in the board room could hear Cashius and see his vitals as he was having a meltdown. Very slowly and softly, Mort spoke up. "Cashius, listen to what I am saying to you. Okay?"

Cashius was breathing heavy and quickly, but he did manage a word. "Yes."

"Now Cashius, I want you to stop for a moment. Just lay back and listen to the sound of my voice." Another acknowledgement came though. "Cashius, I know we are pressed for time, but if we rush at this point, then time would run out real fast. Take three deep breaths and exhale slowly, okay? You don't need to answer, just do it."

They listened as the instructions were followed. "Now Cashius, if you would lift your left arm, you will see a control box on your wrist area. Let me know when you got it."

"Got it."

"Okay, good. Now, release the latch and flip it open." "Okay. Opened."

"Doing good Cashius, doing good. Now, enter these numbers into the keypad and then press the enter button. Don't worry if you enter the wrong number, the system is set to accept only certain numbers. Cashius, press one-five-eight-two, then press enter. You will appreciate this." Cashius did as he was directed. He could see again, the face shield instantly cleared up.

Cashius felt a sudden calm come upon him. "Okay guys, I'm good now. Sorry."

"No problem, whenever you are ready, you may continue." Cashius took a few more deep breaths, exhaling slowly and then he started moving again. They all listened as he moved and grunted along. It took about five minutes for him to reach the vent. Once again, they saw his heart rate rise.

"Cashius, what is it, Cashius? What's wrong?"

"I can't get the vent open. I entered the code, but the latch won't turn!"

"Okay, okay, keep calm. We will figure this out together." There was a pause of about thirty seconds.

"Got it! I got it! I kept wiggling it until something fell out that had it jammed."

There was a short round of gasps in the room. "Great, now Cashius, I need you to go through the vent and drop down to the floor."

Cashius looked down and the floor seemed to be a great way down. "I, ahh...I am not sure if I can do this, it is quite a drop."

Mort pressed the mute button. "If he stops now, I will climb in there and drag his sorry ass out here, suit or no suit." Mort pressed the call button. "Cashius, listen to me again. There are a lot of people counting on you, not just here, but possibly all over the remaining country. We really need to get you to the floor."

Mort looked at the prints. "Cashius, I see from the prints that it is only about nine feet from floor to ceiling, so..." He paused and looked at the ones in the room, "If you get through the vent feet first and hang on to the edge for a few seconds to stop your momentum that should leave you only about three feet to drop.

When you do drop, roll as you hit the floor. Doing that will allow you to dissipate the force. Got it?"

There was no immediate reply. "Cashius, you still with me?" No reply. Mort hit the mute button. "What the fuck? Looking at the monitors, it is showing that he is still conscious and moving. Why won't that little bastard answer me?" Just then, they heard him drop and hit the floor.

Cashius screamed out. "Son of a bitch! I made it, I fuckin' made it." There was a cheer going through the room. Mort told everyone to hush, and he hit the mute button to open the channel again.

"Congratulations Cashius. We are on our way to the chamber. Don't open the door until I get there and tell you to. Got it?"

"Got it Mortimer."

When everyone arrived at the chamber door, Mort pressed the intercom button and told Cashius to go to the far wall and open the cabinet. Cashius went over and opened the cabinet.

"Okay, now what?"

"Take out one of the meters and turn it on so that you can get a reading." Cashius looked up and down the cabinet shelves.

"Ah...Mortimer, what exactly am I looking for?"

"Cashius, there should be some Geiger meters in there. They are small square black boxes."

"Sorry Mortimer, none here."

Mort turned the intercom off and turned to face everyone. "Well, ain't this just fuckin' peachy. What the hell do we do now? That bastard Beard knew that we would come after him and he also knew that anything that he did would slow us down." Mort thought for a moment. Cashius came over to the door and knocked. Mort turned the intercom back on.

"Sorry Cashius, we were just trying to figure things out. It looks like you are going to have to go into the next chamber and see if maybe there is a meter there."

Cashius looked behind him. "Okay, as long as I am here. Give me a few minutes." He went over to the door. "What is the code?" Mort thought for a moment and then he blurted out the code. "No good. The light stays red."

"Well Cashius, it looks like you will have to do this the hard way. If you open that panel, you will see a crank. Pull it out and I think that you will catch on really quick." Cashius did as directed. He started cranking and slowly, but surely, the door moved. He just kept cranking.

"Damn Mortimer, think they could have geared it any lower? I will be sweating like a pig in a few minutes."

"You are doing great Cashius, just keep moving forward. Now, all you need is enough gap to squeeze through." Cashius cranked a few more minutes until he was sure that he could squeeze through. He let the crank handle fall and he squeezed through the door. There was no sign of him for a minute. Then, through the opening popped a hand holding a black box.

"Is this what you desired Mortimer?"

The guys all answered at one time. 'Yes!'

144

"Now Cashius, if you would, come on over here to the door and take a reading." He held the meter up to where they could see it through the window. Mort was smiling, "Point seven two. Great Cashius. Now, if you would, please go over to the other door and take a reading."

Cashius did as told and he called back. "Same level Mortimer."

More cheers. "Okay, great Cashius. Now, if you would, come on over and open this door. I will apologize in advance, but you may have to do some more cranking."

Cashius looked doomed. "Okay, but can I take this hood off?" Mort informed him that he could.

It took a few minutes to get the door opened. These really were not designed to open manually. Before Cashius had the door opened, he was stripped out of his protective suit and most of his other clothes. When they were all able to get into the chamber, Mort looked at Cashius and chuckled. "Well now, didn't know that there was a strip show in here." Cashius was not as amused as everyone else was.

Mort directed two agents to get the other door opened. When that door was opened enough to get an arm through, Cashius stuck his arm through with the meter and took a reading. He pulled the meter back in. "Same as the other readings, point seven two."

"Great, let's get this opened and get Beard."

Once the largest could squeeze through, they all made their way to the pedal cars. This group was in a lot better shape than the first group that went down this tunnel. It only took a few minutes for the group to make it to the other end. Just as they were about at the end, they saw movement. One of the agents jumped off the car, drew his weapon and called out for the person to stop. When that person turned around, they saw that it was President Beard. He looked at the group. "It appears that there was only one charge to open this door and it also appears that they sealed it up and destroyed the access panel once they all got out. Otherwise, I would have been long gone."

The lead agent stepped up. "Sir, we need to get you back into the bunker where it is safe."

"Safe? Are we not as safe here as we would be there? I am not sure if I can take any more of this. I'm going nuts being down here. I need to get outside."

"Mr. President, we can all agree on that statement, but right now, I need you to agree to come with us back to our quarters. Maybe the doctor can give you something to take the edge off."

President Beard stood there for a moment. "Okay. I'll go, but you get that doctor into me as soon as you can. Agreed?"

"Agreed Sir."

CHAPTER FOURTEEN

Colonel Corde and his platoon took their time heading back to Hagerstown. A good part of the way, they walked their bikes when they could have ridden. It was not until they were a short way from Urbana District Park that the colonel came out of his stupor and came back to reality. The sound of children laughing and playing brought him back. When he realized that they still had their contaminated suits on, he ordered everyone to stop and called to have the decon tent set up. The colonel was the last one to get cleaned up.

As they sat around drying themselves off, the colonel pulled them all together. With his head hung low and in a low tone voice, he began. "Folks...I really do not know where to begin." He looked around at everyone staring back at him. "I failed. I have never felt defeat as I do today. I not only failed the president, but I included you all and I have failed all of you." No one said a word. "I have been doing a lot of thinking these past many miles. I have decided that once we return to Hagerstown, I will resign my commission."

One spoke up. "But Sir, You..."

The colonel held up his hand to stop any more rebuttal. "Sergeant, I have made my decision."

The group just sat there quiet while they continued to towel off. The colonel rose. "Captain, when everyone is done, please make sure that the decon tent and the area around it is secure." The captain acknowledged and she put a few soldiers in charge of making sure that the order was carried out.

The colonel started walking towards the park when he confronts a man. Although he was not in uniform, the man approached and saluted. "Colonel, I am Lieutenant McMasters, I am currently on leave status from Fort Lewis Washington, but I can suit up and join you in about ten minutes if you could use me."

The colonel just sort of looked at him blankly. "Sorry Lieutenant, but we are headed back from a mission and now is not a good time to recruit someone else."

"Sir, with all due respect, I am not asking to be recruited, I am desiring to serve as I took an oath to do. You are the first platoon that I have encountered or as far as that goes, you are the first of any military personnel that I have seen. Sir, I am just ready to kick the ass of whomever may be responsible for this mess. So, Sir, I am ready and able to join you."

The colonel stood there for a few seconds while the words of a determined soldier sunk in. Finally, he spoke. "Lieutenant, you have got five minutes. As soon as my group is done wrapping up, we roll out. Whether you are here or not, we roll. Understood?"

 The lieutenant smiled. "Sir, understood quite well." He looked around, "Ah Sir, may I ask you a question?"

"By all means Lieutenant, you have four minutes left."

"Sir, I don't see any of yours around, so will I be taking my own vehicle, or do you have transportation coming?"

That statement got the colonel's mind clear. "Lieutenant, you have a vehicle that can run?"

He smiled. "Yes Sir, we have been working on them for the last few days and we have gotten about twenty vehicles revamped and on the road. We have established a boundary for traveling south, but around here and headed north, we are good to go."

The colonel smiled. "Well now Lieutenant, I do believe that you have earned a place in the lead vehicle. I can't wait to tell my platoon."

The two of them made their way over to the group. "Okay, listen up everyone, I have some good news to share. First off, this is Lieutenant…" He paused and whispered to him. "What is your last name again?"

He leaned into the colonel and in a low tone. "McMasters, Sir."

The colonel smiled. "Thanks." He cleared his throat. "This is Lieutenant McMasters; he will be joining our platoon. He is on leave from Fort Lewis, and he wants in. But there is even better news." They all sort of perked up. "Lieutenant McMasters has offered to allow us the use of transportation." All ears were now tuned in. "He has been diligently working the last few days to get some vehicles up and running, so…no more bikes and or walking back to Hagerstown." There was a loud cheer and a few whelps that sounded out. "So, as soon as everything is squared away, we pack up our gear and we get to ride."

*****

Larry and John made their way off the road, and they lay down in the grass to await the arrival of their guest. John rolled to look at Larry. "Now Lieutenant, please tell me that you will confront first and kill later."

Larry looked at John. "I would not want to lie to you John, so I will not make any promises. I will do what I have to do, no more, no less. Now get down and stay quiet, they are almost in ear shot."

A few hundred feet from Larry and John, the man stopped. He strained to see what was ahead of him. Larry whispered to John.

"He may have made us. If he turns to run, I will have no choice but to put a bullet in his head." The man stood there for a few more seconds and then started moving again. He tugged at the children to follow him. Slowly and cautiously, he made his way towards Larry and John. Larry tapped John on the shoulder and John looked to him. Larry signed, *wait my signal.*

The man was slowly approaching the duo. Every so many steps, he would stop, look and listen. Larry was getting quite antsy. In his mind, he was screaming, *a few more steps. Just a few more steps.* The trio made their way to within twenty feet of Larry and John. Larry reached over and tapped John. They both jumped up and they sprinted to the man and the children. Larry started first. "Deval, halt!" The man was so startled, he stumbled.

The man raised his hands. "Please, please don't hurt us. We have no money. It is just me and my two children."

Larry dropped his night vision and looked at the man and the children. "What? What the fuck?" Larry flipped the hat off the man's head so that he could get a better view. "Who the fuck are you?"

Larry spun the other way and took a few steps. He turned back to the man. "What are you doing out here in the dark with the children?"

The man was quite nervous. "Sir, I am just trying to make it home. We were on our way home a few days ago when our automobile died. We witnessed a lot of people being robbed during the day light so I figured that it may be safer to travel at night. Please Sir, I beg of you, please let us pass. We have nothing to give to you. The children have not even eaten in two days."

Larry stood there a moment, then he replaced his Glock back into its holster. He removed his backpack and opened it. He reached inside and removed a few MRE's and handed them to the man. "Here Sir, here is a couple meals for you and the children. We are not out to rob you. We are actually looking for a man with two children in tow. One of those children is my daughter and the other is this man's son."

The man stood there a second. "Not sure if this is the one that you may be looking for, but about fifteen minutes ago, a car pulled up to me and the man in the passenger seat screamed out the same word that you screamed to me."

Larry looked puzzled. "The same word? You mean Deval?"

"Yes, that's it. I did not understand, and I asked him what he said. He said never mind and they drove off. Not but a few hundred feet in front of me, I saw the headlights come upon what appeared to be an adult and two children. They got into the vehicle, and they drove off."

Larry grabbed his head, spun in a circle and screamed. Looking up, "What the hell! Why me? What did I do to deserve this?"

The man whispered to John. "Is your friend okay? I mean, he seems to be quite stressed." John assured the man that Larry was fine. He gave him a quick rundown of the current events. The man told John that he has sympathy for Larry and that he hopes that he can find the one that he is looking for.

*****

It was only a few more hours of horseback until General Seltzer held up his hand to stop. He turned in his seat. "Anyone else hear that?" They all listened; it was Mr. Briggs that spoke first.

151

"Besides the sound of my ass screaming, I hear an automobile!" He broke it down into syllables and with a little more excitement. "I hear an au-to-mo-bile!" Looking up, he placed his hands together. "Thank you, Lord. Thank you, thank you, thank you!" He moved a little in the saddle. "Lord, one more thing, please help me out of this saddle." They all got a little chuckle out of that.

The general chimed in. "Well, Mr. Briggs. I will tell you what I will do for you. If we can acquire an automobile, I will see if they will throw in a pillow for good measure. How does that sound?" Mr. Briggs was grinning ear to ear. Well, that is until he would move in the saddle that was when he would wince in pain.

"Alright men, let's keep moving forward and see what we can find." It was only a few more minutes until they were in the town of Barstow. The general followed his ears to an auto repair shop that sat along route 231. When they were coming up the front drive, a greasy looking man dressed in dirty overalls with one strap hanging emerged with a shotgun teetering down under his left arm. He stopped a few feet out in front of his business and waited for the group to ride up to him. The general called a halt. "Gentlemen, wait here a moment, let me see if we can negotiate any."

The general rode up to the man and he asked permission to dismount. The man looked at him, turned his head without losing eye contact and spit out a mouthful of tobacco juice. He turned his head back to the general and did not say a word for what seemed like five minutes. The general again asked permission to dismount. The man looked at him and gave a slight motion with his head.

Slowly, the general eased off the horse, but this time, it was the general that never broke eye contact. He remained beside the horse. "Sir, my name is General Seltzer, I am the Army Chief of Staff. Whom may you be?" The man just stood there staring, never saying a word. The general was beginning to feel like they were in a standoff.

The general was about to advance a bit toward the man when a woman emerged from what appeared to be the office. "George, what the hell is wrong with you? Invite those military men in here." The man just continued to stand there. The woman came charging out and headed straight for the general. She looked directly at the man as she directed her speech towards the general. "Sir, please excuse my ignorant ass husband. As a baby, he was dropped on his head. George, give me that damned thing before you get us both shot."

She told the general to bring his men in and sit a spell. General Seltzer turned and called as he waved his men in. Slowly, Mr. Briggs made his way up to the rest. The woman extended a hand to the general. "Hi, my name is Beatrice, but everyone calls me Bea."

The general accepted her hand. "As I attempted to tell your husband, my name is Seltzer, General Seltzer."

The woman kept a grip on his hand. "General Seltzer as in Leon Seltzer, Army Chief of Staff?"

For the first time in his life, the general felt a little embarrassed and he blushed. "Yes Ma'am, that would be me."

"Well kiss my ass, George, this man is a hero, show him some respect." George just stood there. She helped him along with a slap to the back of the head. "Damn it George, get off your high horse and act like your mother raised you properly." George finally shyly extended his hand.

Bea looked at the rest of the crew as they arrived up to them. She waved. You boys come on down from there and come on in. I will round up some drinks for everyone." They all slipped out of the saddle but for Mr. Briggs. She looked up at him. "Well Sir, do you need a special invitation?" Mr. Briggs just sat there.

The general smiled. "Well Bea, I, along with Mr. Briggs there am not too sure if he can get down without a lot of assistance." They all got a good laugh out of that, well, all but Mr. Briggs.

Bea looked at George. "George, get a ladder for this man to use." George disappeared into the garage and emerged with an old rickety wooden ladder. The general and Bea held the ladder as Mr. Briggs painfully made his way out of the saddle. When his feet were on the ground, he could barely manage to walk. Bea grabbed him. "Come on with me, I have just the thing that you need to cool down that backside."

They all made their way to the house and along the way, the general explained that they were on a mission, and he needed to acquire an automobile. Bea told him that George could get them fixed up with transportation after they all had a good meal and some time to rest. To all in earshot, a good home cooked meal sounded really good. "Well Bea, I cannot argue with a good home cooked meal. Now that I think about it, none of us have eaten in two days."

She slapped him on the shoulder. "Then it is settled, come on in."

"But I need to point out that we cannot stay for too long, we are on a mission with a strict timeline."

"Well then General, I suggest we get inside and get the dinner rolling." She focused on George. "George, these men are going to need transportation, how about you gittin' that ol' four wheeled swamp van of yours up and runnin'? That way, they can take some extra fuel, all their gear and some grub for later on." She looked at the general, leaned in and whispered. "Sir, sometimes, I just wonder about him. I really do believe that he really was dropped as a child." They both smiled and went into the house.

CHAPTER FIFTEEN

Larry and John just stood there for a moment while Larry tried to figure things out. Larry went back to the man. "By any chance, do you know what make and color the vehicle was that they all got in?"

The man lowered his head. "I am sorry Sir, but I do not. I just know that it was an older vehicle that was dark in color. With no lights out here, it is really rough tryin' to see anything. If I had seen the two of you, I would have skirted around you."

Larry removed his map and put on his night vision. "If we had a vehicle, we could be at the airport in just a few minutes. We are only about two or three miles away from the airport. At a good, steady clip, we will still be about fifteen minutes until we get there. So, we need to hoof it real fast if we are to get Deval and the children before they get in the air." Larry thanked the man and assured him that in the end, that everything would be just fine. Larry checked his straps on his pack. "Ready partner?"

John finished checking his and looked up. "Ready partner." They retrieved the bikes and headed off at a pretty good pace.

It was a little under fifteen minutes until they got to the airport. They arrived at an outer fence of the airport and Larry removed his binoculars. He scanned the runways, but he saw nothing. "Shit, John, I have not a clue which way to go. I don't see any lights of any sort. Here, you have a peak while I try to see if there are any heat signatures."

Larry passed the binoculars to John, and he in turn slowly scanned the field from one end to the other. "Sorry Lieutenant, I don't see anything. Tell you what, let me punch a hole in this fence and we can at least get that out of the way."

Larry was slowly scanning for heat signatures when he quickly turned back. "John! Look again. Out there to the left of that hanger at ten o'clock."

John looked and he saw nothing. "Sorry Lieutenant, nothing."

Larry passed the glasses. "Here, you look. That way I know that I am not going crazy."

John took the glasses and scanned where Larry told him to look. "Son of a bitch! I think that you are right. I see something th…" His words dropped off as he passed the glasses back to Larry. "Shit! Here Lieutenant! That is someone."

As Larry was looking again, John made good time punching a hole in the fence. "Let's roll Lieutenant." John shoved the bolt cutters back into his backpack and he made his way through the fence. Larry was quick to join him. They sprinted across the field as fast as they could.

Once they reached the edge of the runway, they got down low and pulled out the glasses and scanned again. Larry saw three adult signatures and two children. "John, that has to be them, here, have a look."

John took the glasses and he too saw the five signatures. "Lieutenant, I think that is them. What is the plan?"

Larry rolled over on his back and looked up. "First, we need to make sure that there are no other bodies in the area." Larry looked up at the overcast sky. "Best thing that we have going for us at this moment is the overcast, moonless night. When we charge over this runway, we should be pretty invisible to anyone that may not have heat glasses."

John rolled onto his back. "So, what is the plan. You want north or south side Lieutenant?"

Larry rolled back onto his elbows and scanned the area good. Using the heat signature glasses, he slowly scanned one end of the field to the other. "As far as I can see, they are the only ones here besides us. So, you choose, north or south Mr. Meyers."

John smiled and rolled back over onto his elbows. "I'll take north Lieutenant." Although it was a dark, starless night, John and Larry stayed hunched down as they quickly made their way across the runway. Larry said that once John went around the corner of the building, that he would give John to the count of sixty before he entered the hanger. Before entering the hanger, Larry cracked the door open a bit just to make sure that there was no light inside that would blind him when he went in with his night googles. All he saw was one man holding a flashlight as a second man was working on an older model Piper Cherokee.

When he got to what he believed was sixty seconds, Larry slowly slipped inside the door and held it until it came closed. Of all things, he did not want to alarm anyone in the hanger. Larry made his way as far as he could while still maintaining cover. Larry saw John enter the far-right back corner. John saw Larry looking, and he gave him a *thumbs up*. Larry motioned for John to use the night vision binoculars. When he saw that John was ready, Larry signed instructions to him. John gave another thumbs up, and he put the binoculars away. Bella and John Jr. were seated on the floor about twenty feet from the men. Larry and John knew that they were at a safe distance from danger.

Ten seconds later, both Larry and John emerged from behind their cover. Larry called aloud. "Deval!" The man with the flashlight attempted to draw his weapon. Both John and Larry placed one round into the man, and he fell backwards and to his right. Deval was about to reach in his jacket. "Don't do it asshole. Stay where you are!"

Bella heard his voice and she screamed out. "Daddy!"

Larry kept his weapon on Deval. Just so that Deval knew that Larry was serious, he used the laser and he kept it on Deval's head. "Bella, I need you and John Jr. to come over here. Just arch yourselves around those men and do as I say."

John Jr. was a little hesitant. John called out. "Johnny, it's Dad, do as the man said. You and Bella follow his directions."

The whole time, the mechanic stayed buried inside the motor housing. Larry called out. "Man inside engine compartment, one chance to live. I need you to emerge out here with both hands in plain sight." The man moved a little but remained as he was.

John was now about ten feet behind the man. "Asshole, you have five seconds to do as told or I will be the one to put a bullet in the back of your head." The man stood there a few seconds and then he tried to be a hero. He quickly pulled out of the compartment, turned and was about to lunge at John when John ended it for him. John looked down at him. "I hate fuckin' Iranians."

Larry kept his weapon trained on Deval. Deval glanced at the now dead mechanic and his bodyguard laying on the ground. Larry saw his eyes shift to the dead bodyguard's weapon laying just a few feet away. Larry let out a little chuckle. "Go ahead Deval, but your ending will not be here today. I will take you apart piece by piece." Deval continued to eye the weapon. "Really asshole? Did you really want to test me? Look at your comrades, how good did they score on their tests?"

Larry and John had about enough. John shoved Deval. "Get on the ground. Now!" Deval did not say a word, he just gave John an evil look. John placed the barrel of his rifle against Deval's calf. "Either you do it like I said, or I will cripple you for your few remaining days." Deval continued to look at John, but he did slowly work his way to the floor. John kicked open Deval's legs. "Spread 'em. Arms out to the side, do it!"

Larry holstered his weapon and he patted Deval down. He recovered one handgun from a back holster. He was about done until he saw a small bulge up at his collar. Larry reached inside Deval's collar and tried to pull out whatever it was. He could not get it to move. "What the hell is this?" No response. Larry pulled out his knife and cut the back of Deval's collar. Larry froze for a second and then he jumped up. "John, get the children out of here! Fast!" John did not hesitate.

A moment later, John returned to Larry. "What's up?" Deval moved to where he could sit up. John drew his weapon on him. "Get back down asshole!" Deval laughed. John kept his gaze on Deval, but he focused his attention to Larry. "What did I miss?"

Larry turned to John. "Not rightfully sure at this moment. Some sort of device mounted on his upper back."

Deval moved so that he could stand. John jumped and drew his rifle up to his shoulder. "Stay down!"

Larry interceded and took his hand to lower the barrel. "Let him stand. I need answers." Larry walked behind Deval, and he carefully spread the back of his jacket so that he could get a better view. He raised his flashlight up and scanned the device. He stepped back and then he went around to face Deval straight on. "Okay Deval, I'll play along for a few minutes, what the hell is that?"

Deval let out a big belly laugh. "Lieutenant, you say play?" He laughed again and then had the most serious look on his face. "This ain't no fuckin' game Lieutenant! This is real life."

Deval started to pace, then John began to raise his weapon, "Please. Let him walk John. I need answers." John lowered his weapon and he backed up a few steps.

"Okay Deval, you got my attention, let's hear it."

Deval walked up to Larry. "Lieutenant, I mean you no harm. You can relax."

"If it is all the same to you, I will stay on alert. So, let's hear it."

Deval took a deep breath. "Wow, where to begin." Once again, he let out a chuckle.

"Okay, tell you what Lieutenant, why don't you get the children back in here. I need you to see something."

This time, Larry chuckled. "Not a chance. Continue on."

Deval got serious. "Get the fuckin' children back in here before they literally lose their heads!"

This time, it was Larry that was serious. "What the fuck did you do Deval?" Larry turned towards John. "John, go get the children." He focused on Deval. "For your sake, I hope that you did not do what I think that you did."

John returned with the children. Larry turned a slight bit. "Bella, come here sweetheart." Bella hesitated. "It's ok, sweetie come to me for a moment."

Slowly, Bella made her way. "Daddy, I'm scared, what's going on?"

"Sweetheart just come to me. Everything will be okay."

Bella made it to Larry's side. He put his arm around her shoulders, and she wrapped her arms around his waist. He gave her a slight squeeze. He slowly moved his hand up and towards the middle of her shoulder blades. His hand stopped when he felt the same thing that he did on Deval's back. His eyes locked on Deval's.

Deval smiled. "Care to hug the other one too Lieutenant?" The fire in Larry's eyes was burning.

Larry cocked his head. "John, please take the children over there for a few minutes. I need to have a one on one with Deval."

Deval looked at Larry. "Well now Lieutenant, looks like I still control the situation here." Larry wanted to shoot him right there.

Larry stared Deval down for a few minutes. Finally, he turned towards John. "Keep an eye on him for a few minutes, there is something that I need to do."

John looked at Larry. "You okay Lieutenant?"

"Fine, just something that I need to do. I should have done it a while ago, but I got caught up in the moment. Stay here and try not to shoot him. I'll explain everything in a few minutes."

Larry made his way outside and walked about a hundred feet from the building. He removed his backpack and removed his *G.I.*

JOE radio. He raised the antennae and gave it a few cranks. "Mayday, mayday. Calling Eagle One. Anyone read me?" Larry waited a few seconds...nothing. "Mayday, mayday. Calling Eagle One. Is anyone out there listening?" Still nothing. Larry looked up. "What? Did you bring me all this way to abandon me?" He gave the radio a few more cranks. "Mayday, mayday. Calling Eagle One. Lieutenant Rollins of the six-o-eighth Ordinance. Mayday, mayday. Anyone." Larry let go of the button and waited. He was just in the process of collapsing the antennae when he heard a response. He was so caught off guard that he damned near dropped the radio.

"Lieutenant Rollins, Eagle One Nest here. I read you. Please hold your position for a moment. Let me get the Commander-in-chief. He is laying down resting now, but I am sure that he would want to speak with you." Larry looked up and softly let out a *thank you*. A few seconds later, the radio came to life. "Lieutenant Rollins, President Beard here. How you are doing, soldier?"

Larry smiled. "Well Sir, I have been a hell of a lot better. I need to report Sir."

"Sure Son, whenever you are ready, we can go to a secure channel. Do you remember the channel frequency that we were on the first time that we spoke?" Larry paused a moment trying to recall the numbers that he saw on the ham set that he first used.

"I think so Sir. Just please give me a moment and I will be there." To himself, *think Larry, think*. He closed his eyes and spun in a circle. "Six...ahh, six...no, not six, five. Five...six...shit!" He looked up. "You know, a little help here won't kill you." He continued to spin and think. "Five...five, nine...no! Five, nine, six, zero. That's it!" He turned the radio over and gave it a few cranks. He turned it back and he hit the backlight so that he could see the dial. He made the adjustments, "*Five, nine, six, zero*. Here goes nothing."

He pressed the talk button. "Mayday, mayday, Lieutenant Rollins here." He released the button. Nothing. "Shit, I know that is…"

"Lieutenant, welcome back." Larry grinned ear to ear.

"Wow Sir, for a moment there, I thought that I forgot the channel."

"No, you did fine Lieutenant. Now, if you like, you can give me your report."

Larry thought of his wording for a moment. "Sir, I have in custody the remaining terrorist, well, at least I believe that he is the remainder." There was a murmur in the room. "Quiet, quiet! Lieutenant, I am a little confused here. Please explain."

"Sir, for the past few days, I have been on the hunt for the terrorist. I have eliminated about a dozen, and I believe that the individual that I have in custody is the last. I believe that he is the mastermind."

President Beard looked around the room at his cabinet members. They all had a stunned look on their faces. "Lieutenant, I am really quite confused here. How would you know who the terrorist may be that did all of this? Please explain."

"Sir, I would love to sit down with you sometime and go over everything, but right now, I need to get my prisoner some place secure and remote."

President Beard looked perplexed. "Lieutenant, now you are talking riddles. Can you elaborate a little more so that I can follow along?"

164

"Sir, Mr. President, my prisoner, his name is Deval or who really knows what it is. He currently has a device mounted to the back of his neck going down a few inches between his shoulder blades. He also placed a device onto my daughter and another on another man's son. Until I can assess the situation, I need us to be secured and isolated."

"Lieutenant, what is your current location?"

"Sir, we are in a hangar at the Lancaster Airport. I have someone else with me that currently has the prisoner detained. But Sir, like I said, the prisoner has some type of device attached to his upper back that appears to be a remote explosive device. Also, Sir, he has one attached to my daughter and one attached to another child that he had also taken. I need some place to get him and the children to that would be secure and remote. At the present time, I did not see any other people here, but that could all change with daylight coming. I do not want to take the chance of this involving a lot of vigilantes. Sir, I need you to advise."

"Lieutenant, I need to discuss this with my cabinet. Let's say you just hole up where you are and lay low for a little bit. Give me about thirty minutes to discuss this situation and I will talk with you on this channel shortly. Acknowledge?"

"Acknowledged, Sir. Remain here and wait thirty minutes. Lieutenant Rollins out."

CHAPTER SIXTEEN

President Beard asked everyone to please leave the room for a few minutes. "Gentlemen, I need to speak to my man in the field before we all sit down to discuss this. So...if you all would not mind." They all got up and President Beard locked the door behind them. He went to the radio, gave it a few cranks and then he set the frequency.

President Beard made sure that the curtains were drawn and that his back was to the windows. He did not want to take the chance of anyone looking in and possibly reading his lips.

The general and his group was still enjoying a good meal when the radio crackled to life. He stood, "Excuse me please."

As he was headed out the door, it came over the speaker again. "Eagle One calling Groundhog. Eagle One calling Groundhog. Come in Groundhog."

It took about twenty seconds to get a response back. "Groundhog here, go ahead Eagle One."

"Groundhog, are you able to speak openly?"

The general looked around. "Hold on a sec. I am just making my way back outside." After another thirty seconds, "Okay, clear to speak. Go ahead."

"We have a situation that needs immediate response. I just heard from Lieutenant Rollins. His location is Lancaster airport. He states that he is holding the mastermind behind this terrorist attack. General, I do not believe his story. It appears a little too convenient that he alone could track down the head man in a matter of days when we have no idea which way to turn."

"What do you advise Eagle One, am I to retain and bring back. Or am I to detain and hold in place when I get to him?"

"Groundhog, you are to eliminate Lieutenant Rollins and you are to bring back his supposed prisoner."

"Eagle One, did I hear you right John? You want me to eliminate Lieutenant Rollins?"

"Yes, General, that is a direct order. And my title is President, not John. You address me as John one more time and I will have you standing next to Rollins when you get him. Do I make myself perfectly clear General?"

There was silence for a moment. "General, do I make myself clear?!"

The general paused for a few seconds. "Crystal Sir, crystal clear, Sir. For the record, I want it noted that I only do this due to it being a direct order from the current President of the United States. I also want it noted that what you are ordering me to do is just plain murder, no other way to describe it. Will advise situation as I arrive and assess what I am up against. Groundhog out."

"Gen…" The general hit the kill switch before hearing the president out.

*****

Colonel Corde was back in Hagerstown a lot sooner than what was first expected. For safety reasons, all his squad and their equipment went through the decon chamber one more time. As he made his way to the HQ building, he assigned a few personnel to kindly return the bikes that were provided to them for their venture to D.C.

He reported to the base commander, General Harris, and painted a picture that he wished that the general could see. It was a long, somber two hours. The commander questioned him on every angle. Colonel Corde expressed that there was more that he wished that he could have done. "Sir, the destruction was like something that you only see in a Hollywood movie. Hundreds of thousands of people never knew what hit them. But the part that really got me was when I rounded a corner and there stood a pristine cross. It looked as though someone took it off the roof of the Woodrow Wilson House and gently sat it down for us to admire."

The general sat there taking in every word. He did not interrupt one time during the debriefing. When the colonel was done, the general stated that he did not believe that he had any more questions that were not already answered in the colonel's speech.

They sat there for a few minutes while everything soaked in. A knock at the door broke the deafening silence. The general snapped his head up. "Come in." The door opened and his assistant stuck her head in.

"Sir, you and the Colonel's presence is requested immediately in the radio room. There apparently is radio chatter being picked up that you all need to hear."

The two men jumped up and the colonel was quick on the heels of the general. When they reached the room, everyone backed up and made room. The general spoke up. "What's going on? What's the emergency?"

The radio man had one earphone on and one off. He pulled the plug out and turned up the loudspeaker. "Sir, I was picking up traffic between a *Lieutenant Rollins and an Eagle One*. And then from a *Groundhog and Eagle One*. Not rightfully sure who they may be, but they were both on secure limited military channels. Those were not channels that just any Joe Blow could access." The general asked the radio man to please stand so that the colonel could have a seat.

"Corporal, what were the frequencies that you received the calls on?"

The corporal handed his pad to the general. "They are both there, Sir. As you can see, they are a wide range apart. I was just attempting to reach anyone that may be out there when I stumbled across them."

The general looked at the top one that was from Eagle One and Lieutenant Rollins. "Corporal, do you remember any of the chatter between these two?"

"Yes, Sir, I do." The corporal looked around and was a little hesitant to answer.

"Corporal, considering the circumstances, I really do not believe that this is the time to act like everything is of sensitive nature. So, spill it Corporal."

"Sir, the LT was saying that he had detained the mastermind of the terrorist attacks and that he is currently at Lancaster Airport. He was advised by Eagle One to hold his position and wait for his return transmission in about thirty minutes after he spoke to his cabinet."

"And how long ago was that Corporal?"

"Sir, the first one, the one with Lieutenant Rollins was about ten minutes ago and then the other was just when your assistant came in to get you."

The general sat down and took in a thought or two. "Corporal, get the first channel back up. I want us to hear the conversation with Lieutenant Rollins when it comes in."

"Sir, General, may I add some more? Well, mainly what I heard from the second one between Eagle One and Groundhog."

The general looked up. "Sure Corporal, what do you have to add?"

The corporal cleared his throat. "Well Sir, the conversation between Eagle One and Groundhog was quite disturbing." He stood there a second.

"Well Corporal?"

"Sir, Eagle One advised Groundhog that he was to terminate the LT when he reached him."

The look on their faces was a look of pure shock. "What the hell are you saying Corporal? Are you sure that was what you heard?"

The corporal looked around at the rest of the room's occupants. "Sir, we all heard it. That is why I had someone run to you as quickly as they did."

The general and the colonel both looked at each other. The general spoke first. "Well Brad, I say that we wait and see what comes over the air before we make any rash moves."

The colonel nodded. "I agree General, but what we do not know is the position of Groundhog at this moment."

The corporal spoke up. "Sirs, I may be able to answer that question. That is if you give me a couple minutes to do a few things."

They looked at each other. "Okay Corporal, what do you need?"

He cleared his throat. "Sir, I need you to get up so that I can have my seat and access to my tuners."

The colonel stood up. "By all means son, have a seat and do your magic."

"Thank you, Sir. Well, without disturbing the radio set to intercept the transmission when it comes in from Eagle One, I can use this other radio to try to triangulate the signal that we received. Although they are not on the air at this time, I can still use their prior radio signal as a beacon."

"Do what you have to do, corporal. You pull this off and I will do all that I can to bust you right up to staff sergeant."

He got a big smile on his face. "Get that paperwork rolling, Sir!"

The corporal was busy fine tuning his search when he spoke up, "Sirs, may I ask a question here as I am doing this?"

The general answered. "Sure Corporal, and what may that be?"

"Sir, I think that I have the Lieutenant figured out, but who is Eagle One and Groundhog?"

The general chuckled. "Corporal, you really have no clue as to who they really are, do you?"

"No, Sir, I have not."

"Well Corporal, Eagle One is the President of the United States."

The corporal turned and faced the general with excitement. "Really?! I mean… really Sir?"

The general laughed. "Yes Corporal, really."

"Cool! And Groundhog?"

The general smiled. "That would be the Army Chief of Staff, General Leon Seltzer."

The corporal grinned from ear to ear. "This day may be something to write home about."

A moment later the corporal spoke up. "Sirs, I believe that I have the last location of Groundhog." He makes a few notes, stands and turns to the map table behind him and draws a few lines on the map that is laying on the table before them. "Sirs, that would put them right about here."

They move in closer. "Where is that Corporal?"

"Looks like they were in *Barstow*, Sir. Looks like it is just a little bit south and west of Prince Frederick."

The general reaches for the paper map. "Let me see that for a moment. Do you have the map that would connect to this one that would get me to Lancaster Airport?"

*****

Larry waited a few minutes before he went back into the hangar to fill John in on the situation. When he returned to the hangar, John had Deval laying on the ground and his hands were bound behind his back. John looked at Larry and Larry nodded towards Deval. "Just making sure that he stayed put LT. I would not want to be the reason for him getting away." "No problem, John. I need you to hobble him for a few minutes, we need to talk."

John tied Deval's legs together and he looped the rope up and around his wrists and then his neck. "There, that should hold him a few minutes."

He turned to Larry. "What's up Lieutenant?"

Larry made a waving motion. "Come on over here a few minutes." John followed as Larry led them out of earshot of Deval. "John, without giving a reaction, I need to tell you something that will piss you off."

John looked a little puzzled. "Okay, like I could be any more pissed off."

Larry looked towards Deval and then back to John. "Keep your eyes on me John and remain calm. When I was searching Deval, I noticed a lump up between his shoulder blades. When I cut his shirt to remove what I initially believed to be a knife, I saw some sort of device. Not sure what it is, but it appears to be some type of explosive device."

"Okay, LT, what do we do?"

"Well John, that is only part of it." Larry hesitated. "There is one of those devices on both of the children." John started to move, but Larry stopped him. "John, do not show any emotion, just listen to me." John gave his attention back to Larry.

"I am not sure what it is, nor do I know how it is detonated. I did not see a detonator on Deval when I searched him, so I am left to believe that someone somewhere else is pulling the strings. I just do not know who. When I was outside, I scanned the area again for heat signatures, but I did not see any others. It has to be someone away from here that is in charge. I really did believe that Deval was the boss, but now, that thought has changed."

John took a deep breath. "Okay Lieutenant, what is the game plan?"

"Well, while I was outside, I did speak to my commander, and we were advised to remain here and that he would get back to me in half an hour."

"Okay, and when was that?"

Larry could only guess. "I guess that it was about fifteen minutes or so ago. I left the radio on so that I would be ready when they call back."

John told Larry that he would keep an eye on Deval and for him to go do what he must do. "LT, at his present position, I really do not believe that Deval has much of a chance of taking off. He is fine laying there for the time being. Go."

Larry patted John on the shoulder. "Thanks John, I'll be back as soon as I can."

For safety reasons, John had a seat about fifteen yards away from Deval and he asked the children to come sit by him. Bella Marie told John that she is scared and that she wanted to go home. John placed an arm around her shoulder and gave her a squeeze. As she was coming into him, he could not help but feel the device that was on her upper back. He could not fathom why neither one of the children ever said anything about the device.

Larry made his way outside and removed the radio from his backpack. He sat it down and took out his scope. He carefully scanned the area for anything that did not seem to fit. He saw no heat signatures from either bodies or engines. Something inside him just did not feel right. He was in his own little world wondering why there were no signs of life at an airport of this size when the radio crackled to life and snapped him back to reality.

"Eagle One to Lieutenant Rollins, Eagle One to Lieutenant Rollins. Do you read?"

Larry raised the radio up. "Lieutenant Rollins here. I read you Eagle One. Go ahead."

"Lieutenant, are you secure to talk?"

"Yes, Eagle One, I am alone and isolated."

"Lieutenant, I have a squad headed your way. I need you to hold your position. They will relieve you of your duties when they arrive."

Larry sat there a few seconds taking everything in. "Sir, what is their ETA?"

"Lieutenant, they should be there in about four to five hours. They have quite a distance to travel to get to you. Just sit tight and maintain your position. Acknowledge?" Larry hesitated a bit. "Lieutenant, do you acknowledge?"

Larry picked the radio up. "Acknowledged, Sir. Holding position and waiting for relief to arrive."

Larry packed the radio up and went back inside. John saw him coming and Larry signaled him over and away from the children. "There is a squad on the way that is to relieve me of my duties. They will be here in about four or five hours."

"Where are they coming from? Do they know about the devices?"

"Well, first question, not a clue, I was not informed of where they were coming from and for the second, no, I did not mention the devices." Larry hesitated before he continued on. "John, some odd reason, I don't have a good feeling about this. Something inside has got me on point. So, before anyone arrives, we will move."

"And where might that be to LT?"

Larry told John that he scanned the area when he was outside, and he saw no signs of life in any direction. "Not really sure what to make of it, but there was nothing. I did see a few more buildings that appeared to be good vantage points for keeping an eye out for anyone that may be headed this way." He hesitated again a few seconds. "But, some odd reason, this airport is deader than a doornail. There was nothing that even pertained to life. I think that the one building way across the tarmac may be the main terminal. Besides, I am pretty sure that the children are hungry, so, let's head there and see what we can find."

Larry looked over towards Deval. "I say that we move before light. That way, we can serve two purposes at one time. First, we will still have the cover of darkness for about one more hour and second, the heat sigs will still come in handy but only at a better quality."

"Okay LT, game plan please."

"First off, we blindfold Deval as to keep him under control. We should have enough time to get across the tarmac while keeping him semi hobbled. As much as I want to keep my promise to him and skin him alive, at this present time, we really need him alive. So, let's get started."

"Copy that, LT. I'll get Deval."

It took the group about thirty minutes to safely make it across the tarmac. Every so often, Larry would have everyone get down and him and John would scan the area just to make sure that no one was coming up to them.

 Outside the terminal, Larry told John to hold the position while he had a peek inside. Larry scanned and then he slowly made his way in. The power was still out, so he had to pry the sliding doors open in order to gain access. He stayed low and scanned around once inside the vestibule. He made his way to the second set of doors and pried them open as quietly as he could. He slipped through the opening and rolled off to the side.

He propped himself up against the door frame and removed his scope. What he saw both shocked him and answered his question both at the same time. Larry damned near dropped his scope. "Shit!" Slowly, he continued to scan from bottom to top. Once again, there was no signs of any form of life anywhere around. He replaced his scope back into his vest and stood up. Larry pried the door back open, but this time, he slid a trashcan into the opening to hold it open. He made his way through the other and held it open as he motioned for John. John began to stand up, but Larry motioned for him to remain seated. John looked at Larry and Larry made a gesture of a slicing motion across his throat and pointed inside. He then shook his head no. It did not take words to explain what Larry just communicated.

CHAPTER SEVENTEEN

General Seltzer and his squad finished the home cooked meal and was all ready to go. As each one of them rose from the table, they thanked Bea for a wonderful meal. The general did assure her that her hospitality would not go unnoticed. She went to the kitchen and reappeared with a basket. "Here, you boys may get a little hungry later. It isn't much, just a few sandwiches and pie." Once again, they all thanked her.

Bea yelled out the window. "That van ready yet George. These soldiers got a world to save, so get on it." She smiled and gave each one of them a hug as they exited the house. "Hey, you boys take care. May God be with you all the way. Oh, feel free to stop by at any time. My door is always open." The general smiled and tipped his hat.

Just as they were about to the garage, they heard an engine turn over. Mr. Briggs all but broke out in song and dance. "Yes, yes, yes! I knew God would answer my prayers. Now, if only he would answer the one that I really desire."

The general looked at him. "And what might that be?" Mr. Briggs smiled, "I prayed that he heals my ass. It hurts really bad." They all laugh. As the van pulls out of the garage, Bea comes running out.

"Yoohoo, here Mr. Briggs, I almost forgot. Here is a pillow for your bottom." He accepted it and they all laughed.

"Thank you, Bea. As for what the general said about you providing us a meal, this gesture too will never go unnoticed." Another round of laughter.

The general spoke up. "Load up men, we have about a five-hour trip ahead of us." Once again, he tipped his hat to Bea.

The general climbed up into the driver's seat. A few others helped Mr. Briggs up into the elevated van. As they rode along, there were sure signs that the EMP was a little more widespread than originally thought. There were automobiles, big rigs and even an occasional motorcycle scattered along the roadway and the roadside. The biggest hold ups were when they came upon a traffic light. If the light was red when the EMP was discharged, then there was a congestion of autos at the intersection. It was at those times when the four-wheel vehicle really came in handy. The general steered up and over the curb with no problems.

It was bad enough when they were on the road that they could only maintain about ten to twenty miles per hour due to having to constantly swerve around the disabled vehicles. If there had been one in the vehicle that got car sick, then this would not have been the trip for them. The general just found it amazing that the people did not attempt to move their vehicles out of the way.

As he swerved the van from side to side, he called out. "You know, when I was younger, my generation was raised to show respect for others and think of others before we thought of ourselves. Nowadays, the younger generation is all about themselves and what other people can do for them. It is really sad that the world is raising a bunch of pussies that can't even attempt to stand on their own two feet. Instead of going out and earning things, they want to cry until somebody shuts them up by giving them something."

A man in the back spoke up and told the general that he agreed with everything that he just said. "Yeah General, I agree. If you were to see my brother's kid, you would want to bust that little ass of his."

The general agreed. "Yeah Ed, but these days, you can't do that. These days, you can't even bust your own child's ass, let alone anyone else's as it used to be."

Everyone in the back was as comfortable as they could possibly be when all the sudden, the general brought the van to an abrupt halt. A few slid off the seat and hit the floor. Mr. Briggs yelled out. "Shit Leon, what the hell?" He sat back up in the seat and he saw what stopped them. Out in front and appearing on the sides, there was a small militia approaching them. The general placed the vehicle in park, and he placed both of his hands on the steering wheel.

"Gentlemen, we have company. Please do not make any sudden movements and raise your hands to where they can see them."

No one inside or out made any attempt to communicate. The ones outside kept their rifles leveled on the ones inside. The ones inside only moved their eyes and nothing else. Mr. Briggs moved eyes only towards the general. "Okay Leon, what is the game plan here?"

Without moving, the general answered. "Well, at the present moment, until we see someone in charge, we remain still and alive. They have us outgunned by more than I can count, so...sit still."

Someone outside yelled for the general to turn the engine off. Slowly, General Seltzer reached down and turned the engine off. Another command came out for the driver to open the door from the outside and to exit with hands raised. The general called out as loud as he could that this vehicle has a hand crank for the window and that he must lower his hand to crank it down. A response came back that he is to do it, just slowly.

He got the window down and reached out to the handle and opened the door. He called out. "Okay, I am slowly exiting the vehicle." He slipped out as far as he could, then he announced that he had to grab ahold of something, or he would fall out on his ass.

A man came over and grabbed his elbow to assist. "Here General, let me help you."

"You know who I am?"

The man smiled. "Well, I heard that you were coming. But I did not know that it was you until you started to slide out of that hillbilly swamp machine. I was informed that you were coming on horseback."

The general smiled. "Yeah, we were until we were able to get this thing. By the way, who told you that I was coming?"

"An associate of ours, Robert Ridgely, aka, Mr. Bridge."

They both laughed and the man introduced himself. "My name is Venture, Dave Venture." The general returned the handshake. "We were informed that we were to remain vigilant just in case you needed any help along your trip."

"Well Mr. Venture, I would love to stay and socialize, but we really are on a timely mission here. We need to get to Lancaster as soon as we can."

"Damn, Lancaster? General, you have quite a ride with the way that the roads are. So, as you desire, I will not hold you any longer." The man called out. "Let them through and someone get on the horn and inform the others that they are in a hopped-up swamp van that is coming their way. Tell them that no one is to stop them, but to wave them through. Have them attempt to clear the roadway as best as they can."

The man turned towards the general and saluted him. "Sir, in a past life, I was Major David Venture, United States Army. So, I do understand the importance of completing a mission."

The general came to attention, and he returned the salute. "Carry on soldier." He climbed back up into the van and started the engine. He leaned out the window and extended his hand, "Oh Major Venture, thank you for your service."

"Quite welcome Sir, but it appears that my time of service is now back in effect, Sir. Have a safe trip." With that, he stepped back and once again saluted the general. The general returned the salute.

*****

Colonel Corde waited a few minutes for the corporal to retrieve the correct map that would show their location and the location of Lancaster Airport. "Colonel, here you go." He spread the maps out, one above the other. Pointing to the map, "Sir, we are here on Roxbury Road. If you were to work your way back towards Frederick, then you can take route fifteen to just above Gettysburg and then take York Road straight towards Lancaster Airport."

"What are we looking at as in the matter of time and mileage?"

"Well Sir, in a normal world, it would be about two hours or so. But, with the current situations, it is still about one hundred twenty miles, but the time..." He faded off for a few seconds. "Could be three, four hours. Maybe more, maybe less."

The colonel stood there for a few seconds looking at the map. The corporal continued "Sir, you saw more of the outside world than I have in the last few days. I really have no clue as to how far this EMP actually covered. The only thing that I am aware of is that we squirrelled this radio away a few years ago for the *just in case* moment that we are all experiencing at the present. So, Sir, I will leave the travel part up to you."

The colonel thanked the corporal for his input and his knowledge. "Corporal, by any chance, is there a copy of these maps that I could take with me? I would hate to have to detour just to be brought back to where I started out at."

The corporal told him that if he gives him about ten minutes that he could set up the printer and roll off a copy for him. "Sir, I could not tuck away every little thing for that just in case moment, but I did tuck away a few items that I figured would come in use one day."

The colonel told everyone to grab their gear and to follow the directions of Lieutenant McMaster as he gets them loaded into the vehicles that he has ready. There was a little chuckle from a few when they saw that the group would actually be riding in a convoy of old military M151A2 Jeeps.

The general gave a good belly laugh. "Lieutenant, this is totally out of what my mind saw as reliable transportation."

"Well General, the One-five-one A duce has proven reliable in more than one conflict. It has withstood the test of time and climates from World War Two to Korea to Viet Nam to Libya to..."

He cut him off. "Okay Lieutenant, I get the point."

He walked around the vehicle and ran his hand along the contour like it was a fine Italian sports car. "You may have a point there, Lieutenant. I am a little embarrassed to admit it, but I have never been in one of these before."

This time, the Lieutenant gave the belly laugh. "Really General? Oh, that is a good one!" He continued to laugh. "Sorry, I just find that statement quite amusing." He took a deep breath. "I take it that you are a Hummer baby." The general nodded yes.

The colonel arrived with maps in hand. He was impressed when he saw their transportation. "Holy shit LT, where in the world did you acquire these beauties?"

He glanced over at Captain Sheer. "Well, Sir, when the military decided to scrap these, I took it upon myself to mothball a few. You know, *just in case*. So, as you can see, that time of *just in case* did arrive."

The colonel smiled. "Apparently, it has Lieutenant. "

Lieutenant McMasters felt a little out of place. "Colonel, I hope that you do not mind riding in these. I just figured that rather than riding in that old van that we came here in, I would call a few friends and have them deliver these to us. Besides, we are the military, should we not be riding as military?"

The colonel just stood there for a few seconds. "Suppose that you are right LT." The colonel and the captain did the same as the general did. They walked around the Jeep and admired the beauty. "Lieutenant, did you do all the work on these?"

"Yes Sir, from body to modifications. These may look like the old One-five-one A Deuce, but these have more pep. I took the old four banger out and modified the chassis to hold a small block eight. And I gave it better suspension. Less chance of a flip over."

"Well Lt, I am very impressed, but...if you don't mind, can we mount up and get on the road? I would like to get to Lieutenant Rollins before the other crew does. Some odd reason, I have a bad feeling about this whole thing."

"Well Colonel, do you have all that you need to take?"

The colonel looked around. "Believe so. Let's roll."

"Oh colonel, we have about 120 miles to do, so we should be about three hours getting there. Even with the roads being cluttered as they are, these babies can do a good eighty when we can." He stood up on the running board. "Folks, stay up with me and we can do this in good time. Don't be afraid to touch the gas pedal."

Most of the travel all the way to Gettysburg was smoother than expected. Lieutenant McMasters called out to the colonel that they may make it there in less than two hours. "With us doing an average of about seventy, we are doing greater than I originally anticipated." There were a few obstacles here and there, but nothing as major as the squad had witnessed when they were headed to Washington.

Not far from Lancaster, just before East Petersburg, the colonel stood up in the jeep and held his hand up signaling a *halt*. He followed that up with a swirling of his hand to let them know to gather around. The following vehicles did as they were directed. As they were coming together, they already knew what brought the colonel to signal a stop. Off to the left was the charred wreckage of a medium sized aircraft that had come down.

Considering the amount of time and the amount of damage to the aircraft, they all knew that searching for any survivors would be futile. The colonel asked everyone to take a moment and bow their heads in reverence to the victims. "Lord, please receive all innocents that perished on that day. Amen."

All in unison, "Amen."

"While I have you all gathered here, I need to inform you all that we are just a few minutes out from our objective. When we arrive, we will have no idea if the other squad has arrived yet. As you all heard at basecamp, the other squad is coming here to eliminate Lieutenant Rollins. So, when we hit the perimeter fence, Wilson, that is where you come in. I will need you to observe and determine if it is clear for us to proceed. If you determine that there is no threat, then Davis, you are up. You will signal with the hope that we get a response back. A friendly response hopefully. Any questions?"

Captain Sheer raised her hand. "Yes, Captain."

"Sir, let's say that we send a message, and we get a friendly response back and we do go side with Lieutenant Rollins." She hesitated a second. "What...what do we do when the other squad shows up with orders from the president to eliminate the lieutenant? Do we stand our ground or relinquish the Lieutenant?"

"Captain, I am glad that one of you brought that subject up. That part has bounced around in my head since before we rolled out of the base." He stood there a moment. "I would say stand our ground. I do know that the leader of the squad is the Army Chief of Staff and that he outranks me considerably, but I personally am not going to hand the LT over so that he can be executed without even so much as a hearing." They all gave the colonel their full attention.

"So, with those words bouncing around in your minds, I will ask for your vote. I am not going to order any of you to disobey the order of a high ranking general as I am going to do. If any of you want to stand down, then, by all means do it. I will not look upon you any differently if any of you decide to step away from my side. So, before we go in, I would like to hear everyone's vote. Do not vote any differently than what your heart tells you to do. The person next to you is just that, the person next to you. They are not you and they do not have to live inside your head."

The colonel called upon each soldier one by one. After each one said their desire, the colonel asked them just one more time if they were sure that was what they wanted. Each one voted to stand beside the colonel. The colonel smiled. "Wow, you all know how to make an old man cry." A little chuckling sounded. "Okay, mount up soldiers, we are about to enter the battle of our careers."

When they arrived at the airport perimeter fence, the convoy halted. The Jeeps pulled up, side by side. The colonel stood up and looked for a high vantage point. He pointed to an old observation tower just down the road and inside the fence. "Wilson, Davis, there you go. Think you boys can make use of that old tower?"

They looked at the tower and then at each other and shook their heads. "Got it Colonel, we will be there in two minutes." They sat back down, and Davis punched the gas.

The colonel observed the tower awaiting a response while the others kept an eye across the tarmacs. One of the observers saw something in the window of a distant building. "Colonel, there, there in that building! I saw a signal."

The colonel swung around to the building. "I see it too." He swung back to the tower just in time to see Davis signal that they were communicating with their objective. The colonel signaled for the duo to look for an opening to the field and then to return.

Upon their return, the colonel called everyone together. Davis grabbed the map. "Sir, it appears that the closest access that we have is here and here."

The colonel looked up, then back at the map. "Okay. One through three, you take the first service road around the corner to the north." The colonel looked at Lieutenant McMasters. "Sorry LT, I feel the love and time that you put into these babies, but they will have to crash the gate." The LT just looked up and rolled his eyes.

"Four through six, we will go in the gate to our east. Even though we may have received confirmation from whom we believe is that of Lieutenant Rollins, we will still go in locked and loaded and on full alert. Questions?" He looked around. "None? Good, let's roll."

*****

President Beard was in the meeting room pacing like a caged wild animal, he was all but losing his mind being in there. He called one of his assistants. "I need you to call everyone into the conference room before I go nuts."

"Sir...are you okay?"

The president looked at him wild eyed. "Okay? Fuck no, I am not okay! Just do what I told you to do and don't ask questions. Got it?" The man nodded and slowly backed out the door.

A few minutes later, everyone was gathered in the conference room. The president took the floor and began to pace back and forth in front of the room. With hands clasped up under his chin, he was breathing heavy and sweating. After a few minutes of this action, he turned towards the full room and leaned on the table. "I am the President of the United States. I demand that someone get me the answers that I desire. I want to get out of here and I want out now!"

His security advisor stood up. "Mr. President, we..."

The president went off and shut him down rather quickly. "Sit the fuck down Robert! I am running the show here, not you! You all will listen to what I have to say and then and only then, if I ask for a rebuttal do you offer one."

He hesitated and looked around. "If you cannot honor that, then the current position that you currently hold can and will be filled by someone that will do their job. Without speaking a word, but by just the nod of your head, does everyone understand that?" All he saw was a wave of heads nodding.

He reached into his pocket and removed a paper. "Here is a list of things that I desire to have done before the next meeting here in twelve hours. Feel free to pass it around or someone responsible can make copies and pass them out. But, either way, this will be done or as I said, you will be replaced." The astonishment going across the faces in the room was beyond comprehension. The list was first handed to his security advisor.

Robert read the first few lines then passed it on to the person next to him which happened to be the newly sworn vice president, Nicholas Mitchell. Nicholas looked at the list and then at Robert. Under his breath, he spoke to Robert. "He really has lost his fuckin' mind." President Beard heard that comment.

"Vice President Mitchell, is there a problem with what I have written down?"

Nicholas looked at him. "John, are you…"

President Beard turned blood red. "My title is President, and you will address me as such! I am not your friend, so you will not address me as John. Do I make myself clear?" Nicholas looked at him and at that point, everyone in the room knew that he had in fact lost his mind.

He cleared his throat. "Excuse me, Mr. President, but what you have written here is not feasible. We…"

Once again, the president cut him off. He pointed to his security detail. "You, take him into custody!" The men just looked at each other and then at President Beard.

The lead agent looked at the president. "Mr. President, do you mean vice President Mitchell?"

The president grew even more agitated. "Are you stupid also? Do you not understand English? Of fuckincourse I mean the vice president, now do it!"

The lead agent did not rightfully know what to do. He looked at the vice president and then at the president. "Sir, Mr. President, I am not rightfully sure that I can do that. On what grounds?"

President Beard grabbed the sides of his head with both hands. "What grounds? What grounds? On the grounds that I fuckin gave you a direct order, that is what grounds. Now do it!"

The room became so quiet that you could hear a pin drop. Everyone was frozen with disbelief. The president started towards his lead agent. "If you won't do it, then I will. Give me the cuffs."

The agent backed up. "Sir, Mr. President, I cannot do that either. And please do not challenge me. At this moment, I am totally confused on what to do." He looked towards the crowd for answers.

Finally, Chief Justice Joseph Pine jumped up. "John, you are totally out of control. I have the authority to remove you from power if you are deemed mentally incompetent to hold your position." He pointed to the lead agent. "Agent, please take appointed President Beard into custody."

President Beard rebuked the chief justice's desire. "You can't touch me Joe, I am the president, what I say goes."

The lead agent felt as though he was between a rock and a very hard place. "Mr. Chief Justice, I am totally without the ability to understand what is going on here and as to what I am rightfully to do."

President Beard jumped in. "What you are to do is this. You are to listen to me and to me only." The agent still stood there looking between the president, the vice president and the chief justice.

Finally, the president's personal physician stood up. "Okay everyone, let's take a moment and calm down." All eyes went upon him as he approached the president. "John...excuse me, Mr. President, you are currently experiencing a meltdown. You need to be sedated and placed on bedrest."

"Fuck that! I am still the president and you all will abide by my commands. I am not having a meltdown. What I am having is treason in the ranks."

The doctor leaned in and took a hold of the president's arm, "John, come on."

The president jerked away. "Don't you ever grab me like that again. I am not your ragdoll."

The chief justice nodded to the lead agent and to the physician. The agent started towards the president as the physician pulled out a syringe and injected the president. The president jerked away. "What the hell Mike. What did you do that for?"

"Well John, you are out of control, and you need rest." The president started to wobble just as two agents caught him. The physician told them to take him to his quarters. When the president was out of the room, the cabinet came together to discuss what they were going to do. The chief justice suggested to remove President Beard and swear in the vice president.

"Under the act of war, the vice president could become appointed president if we all cast our votes to remove a president that has been diagnosed as incompetent and unstable by his personal physician and confirmed by at least three high ranking officials. In other words, John could be removed, and Nicholas could become acting president."

They all talked about it among themselves for a few minutes. Nicholas finally spoke up. "You know, to be totally honest with you all, just the thought of being president scares the hell out of me. Not too many days ago, I was biting my tongue as Speaker of the House, now, today, you all want to make me president. How in the hell did I slide three positions in about the same number of days? Right now, my mind is just blown that I am about to take on the top position of what we all woke up to just a few days ago as the *free world*. What the hell did I do to get here?" They all looked at him. "Sorry, I am just rambling. I am not actually looking for answers." There were a few sighs of relief.

"Okay, if we are going to do this, then we will need a vote from everyone. Should we attempt to cram everyone in here or do we go out into the hall and do this?"

The Chief Justice spoke up and asked everyone to gather in the hall around the podium. "Well gentlemen, if we are to vote and the vote goes for Nick becoming president, then we will already be at the podium. So, if you all would not mind." He made a gesture towards the door.

Once everyone was gathered, the chief justice called the room to order. "I am pretty sure that everyone in this room is aware that our current acting president, President Beard, is apparently having a breakdown and we need someone stable in the position of president to carry on the tasks that are at hand. So, by a unanimous vote, we can make the current vice president which just a few days ago was former speaker of the house Nicholas Mitchell, President of the United States." He looked around to see a few shocked faces along with a few pleased faces.

"What I will ask from each of you is for your vote and then after that, please step off to your left for a 'Nay' vote and if you vote 'Yea', then please step off to the right. That way, it will be easier to keep track. Any questions?" He looked around and saw no objections. "Well, good now. Let us begin."

CHAPTER EIGHTEEN

Both gates were hit the same time. The gunners kept watch over the tarmacs as they headed towards the terminal building. Once they were near the front entrance, Colonel Corde told all the gunners but one to stay vigil on the tarmac. "If any of you see anything so much as a squirrel move out there, I want you to fire a warning shot." He turned toward his own Jeep and pointed toward his gunner. "You keep your barrel trained right over my shoulder at all times. If the least little thing looks like it is about to go sideways, then you fire over my shoulder, not through it. Got it?" The man acknowledged and the colonel exited the vehicle.

Colonel Corde looked around. "Captain Sheer, you are with me, and I also want you three with me. Let's go." Slowly, they made their way towards the sliding doors. Right before the first set, the colonel saw Larry coming towards them with his weapons at the ready. They stopped. "Hold on men and Captain Sheer. Captain Sheer, step up please."

She made her way to the door and Larry pointed for her to open it. She began to open it when two of the men with them grabbed the doors and Larry backed up. "Hold it, where is General Seltzer?"

Captain Sheer spoke up. "Lieutenant, General Seltzer is a while behind us, he is with his own squad coming from a different direction. We intercepted the transmission that he had with you, and we felt as though we should get here first."

Larry looked a little puzzled. "What are you not telling me?"

The colonel jumped in. "Lieutenant, I am Colonel Bradley Corde, we do not have a lot of time. Do you mind if we step in, and I can brief you?"

Larry did not like the sound of that. He stood there holding his ground. "Sir, I do believe that it would be best if I waited for the General to get here. He was the one that I communicated with. So, Sir, if you would not mind, maybe you can just wait back outside in your..." He looked hard around them and outside. "Just wait outside in your vintage *A-Deuces* and we can get this straight when the general arrives."

Colonel Corde did not want to do it this way, but he was running out of time and options. "Lieutenant, as your superior officer, I am ordering you inside so that I can brief you. Now soldier, retreat back inside and hear me out. Trust me LT, you will thank me in a few minutes. Now, lower your weapons and back up." Larry hesitated a few seconds, "Lieutenant, now!"

Larry holstered his weapons and motioned for them to come in and he led the way. The colonel motioned for Captain Sheer to enter first before the other three soldiers. Once they passed through the second set of doors, the three soldiers quickly came to arms and began quickly scanning their surroundings. One of them shouted. "Colonel, stop right there! Casualties Sir!"

The colonel and the captain both took up arms. The colonel yelled out. "Lieutenant Rollins! Freeze where you are."

Larry stopped with his back facing them. "Colonel, it is not what it appears to be. You wanted to come in to tell me your story, well Sir, how about you also coming inside to hear mine." Larry slowly turned to face them. "I was as shocked as you were when I first set foot in here a few hours ago. If you are truly a combat veteran, then you should be able to determine that this carnage is at least a few days old." They all looked around. "Do the math Sir, this had to happen sometime around the time of the attacks. So, how about you all lower your weapons, and you all follow me." Larry turned and continued to walk inside.

The colonel looked at Captain Sheer and made a gesture with his weapon for her to follow Larry. He looked at the three men. "Lower your arms but stay on alert. Stay behind us."

They made their way through a little corridor and up a staircase to the second floor. Before they appeared around a corner to a well-lit room overlooking the tarmac, where John was at the ready with his weapon, Larry called out. "John, we are coming in. There is six of us."

When John saw Larry emerge, he lowered his weapon. "Nice to see some new and friendly faces. Come on in."

As they entered, the colonel saw Deval hog tied and laying on the floor. "I take it that is the one that you claim to be a terrorist that you are holding."

"Affirmative Sir. He is the one. He is not going anywhere anytime soon. But Sir, I do not believe that is why you are here. What is the briefing that you claim to be here for?"

The colonel looked around. "Lieutenant, is it just the two of you men here, well, besides the one tied on the floor that you claim to be one of the *terrorists*?"

"Well Sir, we each have a child here that was taken by the one that you like to bite your tongue on when saying the word *terrorist*. There were two others, Sir. Those two, you will find in the hanger on the far side of the tarmac. One has two rounds in his chest and the other has one in his chest."

"Lieutenant, I do not have a lot of time to stand here and reminisce about the past situation. What I do need to do is to brief you on what is about to happen here as soon as General Seltzer arrives here. Is there a chance that I could speak to you in private for a few minutes? I really do believe that you will thank me real soon."

"Sure, Sir. John, could you give us a moment?"

"No problem, Lieutenant. I got this."

They started over towards the other side of the room when the colonel's radio crackled. "Sir, we have a large four-wheel van headed this way. From what we can gather, the front seat occupants are in cammo field dress. The passenger appears to have a few stars on his bar."

The colonel responded quickly. "Do not allow them inside the fence. Repeat do not allow them inside the fence. Use force if you have to. My orders! If that is General Seltzer, tell him that I am here with Lieutenant Rollins and that you are ordered to await word from me before you can allow him to proceed. Understand?"

"Got it, Sir. Will hold at entrance."

The colonel stopped Larry where they received the message. "Lieutenant, I need you to listen to me and listen good." Larry acknowledged. "Lieutenant, back at base, we intercepted a message between Eagle One and Groundhog. Are you familiar with those call signs?"

"Yes Sir, President Beard and General Seltzer."

"Good, that is good. What is bad is this." He hesitated a few seconds. "The bad part is that General Seltzer is not only coming to relieve you of the prisoner...he is also coming to eliminate you at the orders of President Beard."

Larry jumped for a second. "What?!"

The colonel looked him dead in the eye. "You heard it right Lieutenant, he is not here to save you. So, I suggest that you listen to what I am offering. That is if you would like to make it out of here walking."

Larry was still somewhat in shock. "What's going on Colonel? Why would President Beard order me eliminated?"

"That, Lieutenant, is the one question that we do not have the answer for. That is the reason why we raced up here hoping to beat the general here. If he had gotten here first, then Lieutenant, I am sorry to say it, but he may have greeted you with a round rolling out the chamber. I am hoping that I can talk to him before he decides to do something that may haunt him for the rest of his life."

The radio came to life. "Colonel, Sir, General Seltzer would like a word with you."

Colonel Corde looked at Larry. "What's it going to be Son? You in or out?"

Larry sort of chuckled. "Sir, what do you think? I did not track this asshole down and come this far just for someone to put a bullet in my head. Let's go see what the general wants."

198

The colonel smiled and slapped Larry on the shoulder. "That's the spirit LT." The colonel turned towards Larry. "Oh, Lieutenant. Keep no more than two steps near me."

"Got it, Sir. No more than two steps."

*****

General Seltzer sat there fuming for a few minutes. "David, put that window back up." The driver did as he was instructed. The general continued in a low even tone. "Listen up. Without any more movement than necessary, I would like you all to lock and load. I do not know what they are planning, but whatever it is, I want to be ready." Slowly, they each kept an eye on the two soldiers that kept them at the gate as one by one, they slowly removed their weapons and made sure that a round was in the chamber.

"I have something to tell you all that I have been holding in and allowing to eat at me." He took a deep breath before continuing. "I am under orders from President Beard to eliminate Lieutenant Rollins and to bring his prisoner back to..." He let his words fade out for a second as he thought about it.

Mr. Briggs jumped in. "What did you just say Leon? John did what?"

The general slowly turned in his seat to face all that was in the rear. "You heard me correctly, he has ordered me to eliminate the lieutenant and he wants me to bring the prisoner back."

"Back to where Leon?"

"Bobby, that is the one question that just bombed in my mind. Back to where?"

"So, Leon, what are we doing? Personally, I think that John had lost his mind quite a while ago. I was absolutely floored and terrified at the same time when he was sworn in. If you are planning to go through with this, then I am out. I will have no part of killing an innocent man on the order of a lunatic." The general was going to continue on when a tap on the window startled them all. The driver rolled the window down and the soldier on guard told them which door to enter.

"General, Sir, I was told to advise you all to leave your weapons behind if you would like to enter the building. There will be someone at the entrance that will confiscate your weapons. Sir, I was also advised to inform you that there is a sniper beaded on each of you just in case you all are planning on doing any more than just talking. Sir."

The general did not say a word for a second. He just stared at the soldier standing there attempting to keep his composure and breathe all at the same time. "Very well soldier, we will abide. Tell them that we will proceed." The soldier stepped back a step and spoke on the radio. As the van rolled past him, the guard all but peed himself from nerves.

*****

Newly appointed President Mitchell was up and pacing trying to figure out how to begin his new task as president. He had often thought of the day that he may desire to run for the position, he just never dreamed that day would arrive when he would be placed in that post. Now, life was different.

Nicholas had to sit down a minute and attempt to figure just what the new line of presidency was, so that he would be sure to call on the right person when their new position was required. First one that he called was his new vice president, Cameron Glass. She arrived at the conference room and Nicholas asked everyone else to leave so that they could speak in private for a few minutes. When they were all gone, Nicholas rose from the conference table and walked over and pulled the shades. He went back to the table and sat on the edge next to Cameron. He just sat there for a moment with his eyes to the ceiling.

"You know Cam, I don't know about you, but I am scared to hell and back. I really, really do not know what to do." He stood up and started pacing. "What the hell do I know about being president, about running a country or as far as that goes, literally commanding an army? I can't even get my kids to..." His words fell silent when his mind went to this area. He stood there frozen for a second before he made a wobbly attempt to get himself in a chair.

Cameron stood and assisted him with sitting down. He sat there in shock. "My...kids...my wife..." Silence for a moment. He lowered his head, and he began to weep uncontrollably. Cameron sat there consoling him the best that she could. She also tried to keep from allowing her own mind to think of what she had just a few days ago and what she had to contend with now. That control lasted but a minute. She too could not hold it back any longer. She hung her head next to Nicholas and they wept together.

It was a knock at the door that brought them both back to reality. They each wiped their nose and Cameron was the one that answered the door. The lead agent on duty wanted to know if all was good and if they needed anything. Cameron assured him that all was good and that she would notify him if they needed anything. She closed the door and returned to the table. "You know Nick, for the record, I too am scared to hell and back and beyond. Like you, I wonder what the hell it is that I know about being a vice president. One thing that I do know though." She made an attempt to cheer him up. "Care to know what that is?"

He raised his head. "What might that be?"

"I do know that if you do something stupid to make me president, I will find some way to beat the hell out of you and fuck you up beyond recognition. Got it?"

Nicholas did cast a small smile. "Got it."

"Okay Mr. President, let's say we do something to try to get everyone out of this tomb and back to the living."

"Got any plans there…Miss Vice President." He looked at Cameron. "Did I say that right? Or would it be Madam Vice President? Either way, whatcha got?"

She sat back a moment. "Well, best thing that we have going for us is the knowledge that no one, I mean *no one* up above us knows who the heck is actually in charge. They have not a clue if it is still CJ, John or Santa Claus. So, with that, we need to make an attempt to get out in a civil manner, not as that maniac John was trying to do. We have had confirmation that there is still a habitable world out there. Although we have not received any word about what is directly above us. I personally believe that D.C. is no longer there. Well, at least not as we remember."

Nicholas agreed with her on every aspect. They did have an advantage to a certain degree. "Okay." He stood up and puffed out his chest. "As acting President of The United States, I do believe that I need to call an emergency cabinet meeting."

She smiled. "Okay peacock, put your feathers back down."

He smiled. "Let's get Jerry in here so that he can round everyone up and get them in the meeting room. Tell him to round all security personnel up and bring them. They too, will need to be in on the game plan as well. Tell him to have everyone there in ten minutes."

"Gotcha Boss, ten minutes."

Nicholas and Cameron were there seated by the time that anyone began to filter in. As they entered, he asked them to sit anywhere. "Just have a seat and make yourselves comfortable. At this present time, it does not have to be formal seating."

The one that was attorney general when everything happened said that he looked at that statement as a reprieve. "Thanks Nick. Oh, sorry, can I still call you Nick, or do I need to address you as Mr. President now?"

Nicholas looked at him and chuckled. "Anything Adam, just don't call me late for dinner."

When everyone was in the room, Nicholas asked to have the door closed. The lead agent closed the door and stood in front of it. Nicholas looked to him and stood. With a sweeping hand as a welcome. "Jerry, please, you and your team, please have a seat. This meeting includes all of you also."

Jerry looked puzzled. "But, Sir, I am…"

Nicholas held his hand up to cut him off. "Jerry, I really do not believe that we have anything down here to keep us on guard." He hesitated a second before adding. "Well, nothing but what we have locked away in the other room." A round of chuckles went around the room.

Jerry L. Lucky has been a part of the Presidential security staff for almost twenty years. He and Nick got to know each other through the years as Nick was climbing the political ladder. Nick always promised Jerry that if he ever became high enough in office, that it would be him that he would desire to be by his side. Well, it looks like Nick gets to keep his word.

"No, on a serious note, there is a matter that is a critical point that we all..." He hesitated and made a sweeping motion across the room. "When I say, *we all*, I mean everyone in here in this room. Although I may have been casted into this position beyond my control, I am still me. I seek answers and you all here are the ones that will help me, more so help us, to get them." He looked around and saw no objections.

"I, along with Vice President Glass here..." He stood and stuck his hand out for her to take it. She accepted and stood. A loud round of cheers and whistles went out. She took a bow and sat back down. "I, along with Cam. Oh, by the way. Please do us a favor and continue to address us as you did a few hours ago. We still have a lot of getting used to for the titles, so please, be easy on us."

She raised her hand and pointed to Nicholas. "What he said."

"As I was saying, we talked about it, and we firmly believe that we all need to come up with a civil manner in getting out of here." A few murmurs went around. Nicholas spoke up. "Please, if you have something to say or add, please speak up so that we can all be involved."

A hand went up. "Yes Jeremy, take the stump."

He stood up. "Sir." Nicholas gave him a stern look. "Sorry… Nick. I do agree with the fact that we all need to devise a means of getting out of here, but at this present time, besides what Jim was able to ascertain the few minutes that he was out there a few days ago, we do not know if there is even a place to house the government. What if we get out there and there is not a building standing for a hundred miles?"

"Well Jeremy, that is a good point to ponder. But, as with General Seltzer, we will need to send out a scout party before we all go out there like gangbusters. Besides, from what we learned from when John attempted to escape, it will probably take a few days to dig ourselves back out. I, along with no one else in here has the foggiest clue as to how much earth was blown back over the entrance when the general's crew sealed it up."

Another hand went up. "Yes Alex."

She stood, "Now, correct me if I am wrong, but didn't Leon, General Seltzer, make contact with a police chief on the outside? You see, what I am getting at is this. If we could get a hold of him, then there may be a chance that he may know more about what is available for us to use as a secured facility to reestablish our government and get it up and running. Besides, maybe his officers could also offer additional security if we need it."

Nicholas smiled. "You know Alex, you are not wrong, that just may be a very good idea." She gloated for a moment.

"Oh, Alex, where are you on the ladder now?"

She smiled and chuckled. She held her hand up and started counting on her fingers. "Not rightfully sure Nick, I think that I am at Secretary of Defense. Glad that it isn't my job to do payroll."

They all laughed at that statement. "Don't worry Alex, I will personally make sure that you get all of your raises."

"Anyone else have any input?" Slowly, Jerry's hand began to go up. "Ahh, Jerry, Jerry, Jerry. What took you so long buddy?"

"Well, Sir." Nicholas gave him his infamous glare. Jerry glared back. "Sir. As lead agent, I am not sure that I can allow you to exit the safety of this bunker without a large security force in place ahead of time."

"Jerry, I totally agree with your sense for security, but...we need to take all the factors into account. Although we have in fact established that that there is life beyond these walls, we still have not a clue as to the extent and or damage that has been done both psychologically and structurally. We need to find out just how far these attacks have actually reached out and to how many people that have been affected." He paused a second. "As for a security force, we have quite a few people here and our arsenal is quite extensive. If we were all armed, then we would have the large security force that would be under your direction Jerry."

He paced for a few seconds before continuing. "Besides, beyond that old ham radio set that we have here, we have not a clue what, if any communication that may still exist out there. So, before we can attempt to reestablish our government, we need to get out and see exactly what we have left. Who knows, we may only be a handful that has actually survived." He looked around. "Anyone else?"

Jerry slowly raised his hand. "Sir."

"Yes Jerry, are you going to tell me that I alone cannot go?" Jerry smiled. "Not at all Sir. I just have one very important question."

Nicholas gave a bow and a welcoming roll of the hand gesture. "By all means good Sir, what might that be?"

Jerry stood tall. "Sir, I have no problem assisting you all in getting out of here. I was just wondering what we were to do with President Beard? He is still locked in his suite, and I received a message a few minutes ago that he is quite riled up." Everyone got a little chuckle out of that.

Nicholas smiled. "Thanks Jerry, I sort of forgot all about him." He sat there a second in thought. "Well, not to be like pin man in balloon land, but we could take him with us."

Just about every hand in the room shot up. He looked around. "Then again...we could leave him here with a volunteer guard." All hands went down. "Wow, and I thought that you all loved your president."

Someone in the back yelled out. "We do. And you are it."

Nicholas smiled. "Thanks. I feel the love." He looked around. "Jerry, you have any volunteers to stay behind? Whomever stays will not be in need of anything but fresh air. There is enough food, water and medicine to last for about twenty years. Any takers?"

One hand went up. "I will stay."

CHAPTER NINETEEN

The van pulled up outside the main set of doors. There was one soldier at the door with weapon at the ready and one came down to the van. The soldier opened the general's door and the rear door. She shouldered her weapon. "Sirs, please step out, one at a time and surrender your firearms." The general was first. He stepped out, opened his coat to reveal two side arms in a shoulder holster. "Sir, I will remove them. Do you possess any more weapons? Knives, claymores, fingernail clippers?"

The general smiled. "No Ma'am, just what you see here."

"Next. Step out from the rear."

Mr. Briggs was next. "I left my MP5 on the seat, but feel free to search if you like."

"Sir, that will not be necessary. Like you were previously informed, if you do not abide, then the sniper that has you in sight will act accordingly."

He looked at her very seriously. "Understood."

"Good. Step up with the general. Next." The others did as they were told and like Mr. Briggs, they each decided to leave their weapons behind in the vehicle. When the last one was done, the soldier at the door told them all to please enter.

General Seltzer was the first in line. When he entered the main lobby, Colonel Corde was there to greet him. The colonel saluted. "Sir, General, welcome. Glad to finally make your acquaintance."

The general returned the salute as he looked around at all the carnage. "Colonel, kinda nice to see more people in uniform. Just sorry that it has to be under these conditions." He looked around some more and made a hand motion. "All this…"

"Sir, this was not any of our doing. Lieutenant Rollins was the first here and this is none of his doing either. All that we can assume is that the terrorist did this in order to eliminate any and all witnesses to what they were about to do. And what else…that is totally beyond my knowledge."

"Where is Lieutenant Rollins?"

"Sir, before we go to Lieutenant Rollins, may I have a private word with you?"

"I suppose." The general looked around. "Lead the way Colonel." They went off to the other side of the lobby to a small office next to the service desk. The colonel motioned for the general to enter first. He then entered and closed the door.

The general turned to the colonel. "I do believe that I already know the subject but go ahead anyway Colonel."

The colonel hesitated a moment before he started. "Sir, I have some of the best soldiers that there is on this planet. With all that has been taken away from us, they still retained the ability to do what they were trained to do. And that is to track and intercept messages. Whether it be coded, direct or on a secure channel, like I said, I have the best under me. Actually, they are better than the best, they are the greatest."

The general just raised an eyebrow. "I think that I know where this is going. So, say what you may Colonel."

"General, Sir, I, well, we more than I, know why you are here. And Sir, no disrespect meant, but we cannot allow you to do what you came to do. If you feel the need to court martial me after all of this is over, then Sir, you do what you must do. But right now, I cannot allow you to terminate Lieutenant Rollins as President Beard has ordered."

The general looked around in the dim lighted room and saw an extra chair. "Let's have a seat a moment Colonel. I have lots to say." He sat there a moment carefully collecting his thoughts. "Colonel, I will clue you in on something. I just informed my men about why we were here not ten minutes ago. When I did tell them, I thought that they were going to shoot me." The colonel did not say a word. "Mr. Briggs out there made it very, very clear that he wanted no parts in this. He was shocked that we came this far without me ever saying anything about what President Beard ordered me to do. Frankly Colonel, I never had any plans on carrying out his order. Like you, I just felt as though he could court martial me when this was all over. The choice would be his. But...I was not going to kill someone when there was no evidence of anything amuck pointing to the Lieutenant."

They sat there and chatted for about another thirty minutes attempting to come up with a game plan before they both stood and shook hands. All eyes were on the door when it opened. As they emerged, the colonel gestured for his soldiers to lower their weapons.

The general took the stump. "Listen up everyone." He first focused his attention on his men. "What I told you all at the gate. Well, that is not going to happen. Colonel Corde and I have come up with a new plan. We will run it past everyone. If someone does not agree or if they have something better, than please, speak up or forever hold your peace. Also, after we lay everything out here, if there is any of you that feel as though you do not want to go along with us, then I can promise you that there will be no repercussions from backing out. Understand?" No objections were noted.

They were all unaware that Larry was around a corner when the meeting was going on. After all the votes were in and there was none to walk away, Larry stepped out into the light. With a weapon at the ready and resting on his hip with muzzle up in the air, he announced himself. The colonel and the general turned to face him.

The general snapped to attention and made an announcement. "Attention, officer on deck." The whole room came to attention as the general saluted Larry. "Lieutenant, General Seltzer reporting for duty." Larry looked at the colonel. The colonel saluted also, smiled, winked and tipped his head towards the general. Larry returned the salute, and they all dropped their arms and continued to stand at attention. "At ease men. Relax"

They all did as were told and the general approached Larry. Once again, he quickly saluted Larry. "Lieutenant, may I shake your hand?"

Larry looked a little perplexed. "Okay, Sir, if that will make you feel better." Larry extended his hand and received the general's hand. "Okay, Sir. Not sure what all this about, but I will go along with it."

After a few minutes of small talk, the general got right to the point. "Okay Lt, where is this prisoner of yours?"

"He is being held upstairs, Sir. He is under guard at this present time with another gentleman that was also dragged into this nightmare."

The general motioned for a few of his men to join him. "Please show me the way Lieutenant."

When they arrived upstairs, they found John standing guard over Deval. Deval was still laying on his stomach hog tied, and his mouth was taped. Larry went over and ripped the tape off his mouth. Deval let out a little squeal. "You bastards have not a clue what is going on here. You can bring the whole Army before me, and you know what? I will destroy you all. Either one at a time or all at the same time. I will be so kind to leave that up to you." Deval started to laugh.

The general looked to Larry. "LT, got more tape?"

Larry smiled. "Coming up, Sir."

The general saw something move off to his right rear and it startled him. "What the?"

"That is a part that I did not get to yet. And then there is more." He motioned for Bella and John Jr to come on over. "Kids, come on over and meet General Leon Seltzer, he is the Army Chief of Staff." They came over.

Bella motioned for Larry to bend down. In a child's whisper that could be heard a mile away, she asked away. "Daddy, does that man outrank you? Is he your boss?"

General Seltzer smiled and then bent down. "Well Sweetheart, for the moment I do. But, in a few days." He looked at Larry. "Your daddy may be my boss."

She smiled and not understanding, she answered. "I like that idea Daddy." They all got a little chuckle out of that. Well, all but Deval. He started to speak just as John was applying a new piece of tape.

Larry asked John Jr. and Bella to stay with one of the soldiers a few minutes while he spoke to the general. Off to the side, Larry laid the rest out for the general. "Sir, I said a few moments ago that there was more. So, here it is." Larry hesitated a second. "When I was searching Deval, I noticed a device. Not rightfully sure what it all entails, but I do believe that it is some sort of wireless explosive device that is somehow attached to the base of his neck."

The general looked towards Deval. "Did you locate any type of detonating device?"

"Negative, Sir. I, along with Mr. Meyers searched the surrounding area and the aircraft that they were about to take, and we came up empty handed."

"I see. And there are no other individuals that you are aware of?"

Larry took a deep breath. "Well, Sir. There were others in a residence in Zooks Corner, but they have all been eliminated. I do believe that it was seven others."

The general looked at Larry kind of strangely. "Been busy, haven't you Lieutenant? Are you trying to tell me that you handled a band of terrorist all by yourself?"

"No, Sir, I am not. There was a small armed group of us that mainly consisted of relatives of Mr. Meyers that made the raid."

"Lieutenant, I have a million questions and I hope you have the answers to give me."

"Sir, I would gladly answer your questions, but I do not believe that this is the time nor the place to do it. I have my own

213

questions that I need answers to. But first, I need to find out how to get one of those devices off my daughter and Mr. Myers' son."

The general looked more confused than he did two minutes ago. "Okay Lieutenant, time to back up. What do you mean that the children have devices too?"

"Well Sir, I noticed them after I had Deval secured. Both Bella and John Jr. each have one mounted to the back of their neck. Funny, I noticed them, but not one time has either of them said anything about something attached to them. Besides being an explosive device, it must also be delivering some type of numbing agent to where they do not notice it. I really do not know."

The general waved for Mr. Briggs to come over. "Yes General, what can I do for you?"

"Mr. Briggs, I need you to get Andersen and..." He points his thumb towards Deval. "Drag that piece of shit into that office over there. Before you do all that, please have the children taken away from this area. I would prefer them not to see this."

"Yes Sir. Give me a few minutes to get everything ready."

John said that he would take the children for a walk to explore the terminal. "Hey Johnny. How would you and Bella Marie like to go and see if we can find some snacks somewhere?" When you are a child, it does not take much convincing to get you motivated by the sound of *snacks.* The three of them started to head down the corridor. John looked back and gave a thumbs up.

Once he was sure that the children were out of the area, the general gave a nod and Deval was moved to the office. After a moment, the general waved for Larry and they headed towards the office to where Mr. Briggs, Colonel Corde and Andersen were now standing guard over Deval. He told one of Colonel Corde's men to stand guard outside the room. "If anything looks like it is turning shady and Deval starts out that door before anyone else, then I order you to shoot him before asking questions. Got it?"

"Yes, Sir. I understand."

The general entered the office. "Clear that table and lay him up here where we can see what we are doing." Mr. Briggs took his arm and swiped everything off the desk. They all grabbed a body part and they slammed him down on the desk face down. Deval tried to say something, but the duct tape was well placed.

General Seltzer reached for one of his side arms but felt an empty holster. "Shit! I forgot."

Larry removed a Glock and tapped the general on the elbow. "Here Sir, use mine."

The general smiled. "Thanks Lieutenant." He took the weapon, cocked it and placed it to the temple of Deval. Deval started to breath heavy.

"Calm down asshole. I am not going to shoot you just yet, I just wanted to know if I had your attention. I see that I do, good. In a moment, I will remove the tape. You will give me the answer that I desire, or I will have Lieutenant Rollins get busy taking you apart, piece by piece. If you understand, blink quickly and tightly three times. If no answer, then the Lieutenant will begin. Understand?" Deval just laid there. Larry removed his knife and started towards Deval. Deval started to grunt and blinked his eyes rapidly. Larry placed the point to Deval's cheek and nicked it. Deval flinched and breathed heavier.

The general backed up. "Mr. Andersen, take a look at that thing on the back of his neck."

Andersen removed a headlamp and put it on. Slowly, he spread the back of Deval's shirt to expose the device. "Would someone please hand me the magnifying glass out of my bag?" Larry handed it over. Anderson leaned in and made a better assessment. "Lieutenant, any idea where a cafeteria or fast food joint may be? I need some aluminum foil to block any type of signal that may decide to come in and set this thing off." Deval gave a little chuckle.

The general did not like that, and he slapped Deval in the side of the head with the Glock. "Now asshole, that was funny. Go ahead and laugh at that." Deval just breathed heavy and tried to wrestle out of his restraints.

Larry sent word out that he needed aluminum foil. After a few minutes, there was a knock at the door. Larry opened it and a hand appeared through the door with a handful of foil sheets. He passed them to Andersen, and he quickly began to pack the device. "Since no one has any idea as to where the detonator may be, then I do believe that it would be best if we were to neutralize this thing until we do locate such a device."

The general leaned in. "So, Mr. Andersen. What do you suppose that the detonating range for something like this may be?"

"Well General, considering that this has not been set off yet, then I would venture to say that someone would have to be within a quarter mile to set this off. It appears to be just powerful enough to kill the one that it is attached to and maybe maim someone within a few feet of them. It is no WMD, Weapon of Mass Destruction."

The general stood there a few seconds. "Okay I know what WMD stands for. Time to get the answers that I desire." He slapped Deval in the head again. "Hey asshole, you still awake?" The hatred that could be seen in Deval's eyes was immense. "I am going to remove the tape, if you say anything besides the answer that I am after then the Lieutenant here will step in. Nod if you understand." Deval nodded. "Good, see, we can work together." The general removed the tape in one quick painful motion. Deval yelled out. He knew that the general was old school like Larry and that it would be best if he did not speak out.

The general pulled a chair up next to the desk, spun it around backwards and sat down to be eye level with Deval. "Okay now, question number one. What is that device on the back of you and the children? Shit, I forgot all about the children!" The general stood up. "Mr. Andersen, don't you think it best if the children also had theirs wrapped in foil?"

Mr. Andersen was shocked to learn that the children also had a device on them. "Damn it General, why didn't you say something? Of course, it would be best. The children need to be found and their devices wrapped. I am really surprised that they never said anything about them being on their neck. Please, someone locate the children and get those devices wrapped. I really need to take a closer look at what we have here. We need to move him out into better light."

Four of them grabbed Deval and carried him face down out into the terminal and placed him by the window. The general had a few men grab the desk and bring it out to where they were. "Put his sorry ass up there on the desk so that Mr. Andersen can get a better look." Four of them grabbed him and ever so roughly tossed him on the table. Deval was about to say something when

217

the general gave him a stern look. Mr. Andersen removed the foil and grabbed the magnifying glass. As he was examining it close, he saw a small reservoir on the underside that was about half full. "Not rightfully sure, but there is a light green liquid in a tube that is either being distributed as a numbing agent or it is a timing device or acting as both." He stood up and looked to the general. "Sir, can you get the answer for me?"

"Gladly Mr. Andersen. It will be our pleasure. Ready Lieutenant?"

Larry removed his knife and stood at the ready. "Whenever you are ready, Sir."

The general grabbed a chair and as before, he spun it around and had a seat. He tapped Deval on the head with the Glock. "Okay asshole. I believe that you are aware of the question, so start squawking." Deval just lay there and that told Larry that he was up.

Larry raised one of Deval's pant legs and made a small incision on his calf. Deval flinched, but he did not say a word. Larry took the blade and got a hold of the skin and started to slowly remove it. That got a reaction from Deval. "See Deval, if you remember, I did promise that when I caught up to you that I would skin you alive. Well guess what dickhead? Here we are?"

Deval squirmed a little, but he refused to speak. The general sat back down, and he once again gave Deval a smack in the side of the head with the Glock. "Well asshole, got anything to say? Or do we continue to have the LT here take you apart piece by piece?" He just lay there defiant and quiet. "LT, he is all yours."

Larry raised another pant leg and did about the same as before. But this time, he made a longer incision and was a bit rougher.

Deval fought to get loose, but all that did was to make him bleed more. He attempted to roll off the table, but the men around him stopped that action. The general looked around to the colonel. "Any of your guys happen to have any rope or straps. I would hate for this one to get away without enjoying his slow execution."

The colonel nodded his head and one of his men quickly disappeared down the terminal and out the door. He returned a few minutes later with a couple camouflage ratchet straps. "Sir, will these do?"

The general smiled. "In more ways than one."

Two men held Deval still while two others wrapped the straps around the desk and across Deval. Once they were done, the general gave it another ratchet or two just to make sure that they were tight.

Deval was having a hard time breathing and he finally spoke up. "Hard to breathe. Hard to breathe."

The general pulled his chair back up and had a seat. "Tell you what asshole, as soon as you hear me, and tell me what I want, then I will hear you, and give you what you want. Agreed?" Deval just stared at the general.

The general stood back up and moved his chair out of the way. "LT, looks like you are up again." Larry took his knife and slashed the pant leg halfway up to Deval's thigh. He was just beginning to make an incision when Deval called out.

"Wait! Ask your question."

The general smiled and nodded to Larry. "That's better asshole. I knew that it would only be a matter of time."

He sat back down and placed the Glock next to Deval's cheek. "The device. What is it?"

Deval just stared at the general. The general was about to stand again. "You already know what it is. General, why don't you ask the question that is really going through your mind. That one big question that everyone wants to know." This time, it was the general's turn to stare at Deval.

Deval gave a slight chuckle. "What's wrong General? Cat got your tongue?" The general kept his cool and did not respond as Deval had hoped. "Tell me about the device. Tell me all about the device and don't leave anything out or Lieutenant Rollins will not be stopped once he starts."

"General, there is only so much that I can tell you. It was all a surprise to me when I was told about it."

The general looked serious. "Okay asshole, I'll ask the big question and I want a big answer." The two locked eyes as the general blurted it out. "Who the fuck is behind this device? Who had this placed on you and why?" Deval gave a big laugh and began to cough due to the straps restricting his airway.

"General, soon enough, you will all discover who is behind this. As for why, I do believe that you already have this answer, but I will tell you anyway. It was placed to ensure that I did what I was supposed to do. Just as each of those two children have the same device on them so that their parent would do as they were assigned. Once their obligation was fulfilled, they would have had their devices removed and deactivated. But Lieutenant Rollins and Mr. Meyers had to go the extra mile and try to play hero. That is why their children still have their devices on. Oh, for the record, if you attempt to remove them without the deactivation code, they will literally lose their heads. There is a failsafe switch that is connected to their spine."

The general reached up and gave the ratchet another few clicks. Deval blurted out. "What the fuck, General!"

"Well Deval, that was an exciting story, but I want to know who you are working for. I figured that if I squeeze you hard enough that the answers would eventually come out. So, can we continue while you can still breathe?"

Deval laughed. "You just don't get it, do you? You still don't have a fuckin' clue. I know that it has only been a few days since your entire world had been flipped upside down, but I figured that a man of your caliber would be a lot more aware of what we have here." The general reached for the ratchet again. "Hold on General, don't get your stars out of line."

General Seltzer got really close to Deval's face. "Who the fuck is at the top? What is his or her name?"

Deval hesitated. "General, if you loosen the strap on my chest and sit back, I will tell you something that is going to be a story that you may want to tell your grandchildren one day."

The general hesitated a few seconds, then he reached for the ratchet. He loosened it a few clicks. "Okay asshole. I showed good faith, now it is your turn."

"General, I wish that I could have a good cup of coffee while I tell this, but...I guess that it is what it is." He smiled, "Ready General? Hold on, you are going to love this."

"You can spare us all the theatrics and spill it out or I will have Lieutenant Rollins spill your blood out."

Deval smiled. "Fair enough General. But I must warn you. What I am about to tell you will in no way change any of the events that have already taken place, nor will it change the events that will and must happen. This is bigger than your mind can possibly comprehend." He took a deep breath and then began again. "I, along with many others are a part of an organization that is so far up the ass of American society that you may not sleep another full night for the rest of your life after you hear this." Deval had the attention of everyone around him.

Deval looked around. "Well now. Now that I have everyone's attention, it is time to get interesting." No one said a word. "I arrived here in the spring of 1996. Around that time, my commander arrived, and he set everything in motion. We were all given assignments and different fields to train in. I became Leonard Bloom and I worked my way up and into the Department of Homeland Security. The same department that I made my way into was supposed to be the same department that was to keep people like me out." Deval took a few seconds to let out a slight laugh. "We became doctors, lawyers, police officers, military leaders and even politicians that worked their way up the ladder."

The last job description really got all ears perked up. "The one that I answer to has been my leader since I was a teen in the Middle East. He came here and we all came together as we promised to do so many years ago as we sat in the sand in a poor ass country. His original name is Sergio Alverna." All attention was on Deval now.

"What the hell, I want to see the expressions when you hear this. General, the one that I answer to is the same one that you answer to."

The general's eyes got big and wide. "What are you trying to say asshole?"

Deval laughed. "Really? And you call me *asshole*." He laughed again. "For an intelligent man, you really are fuckin' stupid." General Seltzer started to get quite red, and he raised his hand up to slap Deval with the Glock. "Hold on, General, my commander is your commander. He is what you may commonly call the *mastermind*." The general almost fell as he jerked up off the chair. Deval laughed so hard that he started to choke from lack of the ability to breathe.

CHAPTER TWENTY

Jerry pulled all his men together and had a meeting before they all headed towards the tunnel to get out. He informed them that he would most likely hold point all the way until they were at their objective. "I know that all of you guys are more than qualified and willing to hold point, but, if we are to venture out into a world that we know absolutely nothing about, then if anything goes sideways, well, I want that to be on my record, not yours. If we get to a point where we feel one hundred per cent confident that we are in safe territory, then and only then, I may relinquish point and fall back to the president. The main thing that we have as an advantage on our side is the knowledge that Nick is now the president. No one on the outside is aware that John had to be removed. Any questions?" No hands raised.

Jerry called for a few of his men to take charge in gathering the weapons for their adventure. He realized that they had enough firepower to hold off a good-sized army, but he also knew that they would be on foot and very limited to what they could physically carry. "Small arms and large power. We should not need any more than a few LAWS as a high-power source. MP5's and nines should be good for everyone. It really would not hurt to have some of the cabinet members carry also. Can never be too safe and too secure."

Jax Black was the man that volunteered to stay behind and keep an eye on the now sedated President Beard. Jax extended a hand to Jerry. "Jerry, I will hold the fort down as you all get out there and get us back up and running. I will keep a radio with me so that you can keep me informed of what is going on."

Jerry accepted his hand and he pulled Jax into him. "I have all the confidence in the world in you." He whispered in Jax's ear. "Sorry you raised your hand. I was hoping that you would accompany us."

Jerry called everyone together in the room. "We roll out to the tunnel in about ten minutes. If you take it, then you carry it. Try to go as light as possible. Anything that is left behind will be safe. But, just in case." He scanned the room. "If you think that it is of utmost importance, then we lock it in the vault." He hesitated a second, "Once we hit the tunnel, the first wave of diggers will be the first to ride down the tunnel. Everyone one else will begin to walk. The second wave will be the first in the parade. When the first are dropped, the cars will come back and pick up the second wave and so on. I realize that it is a fifteen-mile hike, but due to the limited transportation that we currently have, I am doing the best that I can to get everyone there as quickly as possible." He looked around for any hands that may object. He saw none. "Ten minutes folks. Clock is running. Get going." Everyone scattered like roaches when the light is flipped on.

Jerry stood at the barrier door with Jax as everyone flowed through. "Keep rolling, keep rolling. We have a long way to go, and I would like to move as much as possible in the daylight. If need be, once we break through, we will remain inside until daylight. If we had the luxury and the safety to move under the cover of night, then I would just bust out. But...we don't."

After the last body was through the opening, Jerry turned to Jax. This time, he extended his hand. "Take care Brother. I will see you soon."

Jax took his hand, but this time, it was he, that pulled Jerry in for a hug. "You take care too Brother. I too will see you soon. Just remember one thing."

Jerry raised an eyebrow. "Yeah, what's that?"

Jax smiled, "If you leave me with a crazy man, then don't expect me to be normal when you return." They both got a laugh at that.

Jerry stepped through, turned and saluted Jax. "Take care my friend and make sure that this gets locked. Oh, under no circumstances does John get out of his quarters until we return."

Jax saluted back. "Got it. In his cage he stays." He grabbed the chamber door and pulled it shut.

When the first wave of diggers arrived, they were overwhelmed at the sight of what was before them. There was so much earth that was blown back into the tunnel that they had no idea as to how thick the earth between them and the outside was. The only guide that they have to go by for direction in digging were the sides of the tunnel. No one present has ever been down here before, so they were not aware of how much or how long it would take to reach the outside. One man took charge and started grabbing shovels to pass them out. "Alright Gentlemen put all your New England upbringing away and lend a hand. Trust me, it won't kill you. Your hands were made for more than groping your understudies." He asked a few if they would not mind taking the other pedal cars back that were left when General Seltzer and his crew first came through.

It took about an hour for the second wave to show up. They were all pretty anxious to get out of that tunnel that they all pedaled like hell to get to the end. One man claimed that if he survives that he would not mind having one of those pedal cars. "I could see me and the wife putting down the NCR bike trail along the Gunpowder enjoying the day. Well, that is if it is still there. I guess that we will all know in a day or two if the world still does actually exist out there."

*****

Jax passed by President Beard's suite and put his ear up to the door. "Quiet as a church mouse." He continued to the kitchen area. He swung open the double doors on the huge climate-controlled cabinet. "Damn, I feel like a king all alone in his castle." He scanned the shelves. "What to eat first, what...to...eat...first." All the food that was in there has been there for years. It was still good, and it was plentiful. The cabinet along with the storage bins had been stocked for many years for that *just in case moment.* There were some C-rations from the mid to late forties. The most recent date that he could see on the roster was 1961. "Damn, Kennedy was in his first year of presidency when this was stocked." He saw something that he recognized. "Ahh, a canned glazed ham. Guess what Daddy is having for dinner!"

He located a medium sized can of sweet potatoes and some asparagus. He heated everything up and made a nice sized plate for dinner. When he was done, he slid the chair back and kicked his feet up on the table. He removed a cigar from his inside jacket pocket and lit it up. Blowing out smoke rings, he was in heaven. "This isn't all that bad. I could get used to this for a few days."

Jax was zoned out in his own little world when he heard a banging sound. He jumped up and tossed his cigar on the plate. "What the hell! Damn you Beard. What the hell does he want?" He made his way to the president's suite and yelled out. "Yes, Sir, how may I be of service?"

President Beard screamed out as he beat on the door. "Who the fuck are you? Open this fuckin' door, now!"

Jax called back. "Sorry Sir. I am under orders not to let you out under any circumstances."

He kicked the door even more. "Who gave you those orders? I am your president; I am demanding that you open this door. Now!"

"Sorry President Beard, but President Mitchell gave direct orders to not open the door." There was silence for a few minutes. Jax figured that he had finally come to terms that he is not to be allowed out of the suite. He began to walk away when he heard a crash in the suite. He went back to the door and put his ear to the door. "Sir, are you alright?" No answer. He tried again. "President Beard, are you alright Sir?" Still no answer. Jax was torn between opening the door and just walking away. He called out one last time, "Sir, are you okay? Sir, unless it is a medical emergency, I cannot open the door." He placed his ear up to the door. Nothing.

He was about to open the door when he heard some shuffling inside. "Okay Sir, it appears that you are fine, so I am going back to my dinner now." Jax slowly walked away, all the while keeping a keen ear to the presidential suite. When he made his way back to the kitchen, he started for the dessert cabinet. "Gotta be some pound cake somewhere in here. That and a little powdered sugar would hit the spot right about now."

*****

The digging crew was making pretty good time. The earth was not settled, so that made digging a lot faster than expected. When the second wave arrived, they did not replace the first crew as was first expected, rather they all worked together to get out as fast as possible.

After everyone was now present at the end of the tunnel, someone asked if they had any clue as what time of day that it may be. Jerry removed his Faraday pouch and pulled out his watch. "Well, it says here three-forty-five. Not rightfully sure if that is A.M. or P.M., but it is nonetheless three-forty-five."

Someone called out. "Good job Jerry, keep up the good work." They all stopped digging long enough to clap and laugh it off.

About an hour later, a digger on top pulled a shovel full of dirt away from the ceiling. "Shit! Holy shit! Light! I see light!"

As many as could scrambled up to the top. "Son of a bitch! It is light!" That little bit of light gave off more hope than any have had for days.

"Come on boys, let's get this thing cleared." They all but ran over each other in an effort to get the mound down to where they could get out. Nicholas stood there with a tear in his eye. He thought, 'If only the world could work together like these men were at this moment'.

Although they saw light, it was still about three more hours before even the skinniest body would have been able to slither through and touch the ground outside. The thickness of the earth covering the opening was over forty feet long, the apparent back pressure of the charge that sealed the tunnel kept a small void near the ceiling. It was like seeing hope without the possibility of reaching it. When there was enough room to squeeze the smallest person through, it was the receptionist from the Department of Defense that was chosen and called to the top of the mound to squeeze through and report back what she encounters.

She climbed up to the top of the mound and peered down the long narrow opening that was her hope of ever reaching fresh air. She looked back. "Ah, excuse me, you think that I am supposed to be able to squeeze through there? Explain that one please."

The man that was on top of the mound with her held out his shovel. "Well...you may have to dig a little bit along the way, but Lydia, we all have faith in you that you will get through. Honestly, not to add any pressure, but the lives and the sanity of everyone here depends on you getting through. Just keep focused on the light and keep moving forward. As you are getting through, we will all be bustin' ass in here to get the opening bigger. So, what do you say?"

She had a tear rolling down her cheek. "I guess that it wouldn't mean a thing if I was to tell you that I am claustrophobic. I...I don't think that I can do it."

The man looked her dead in the eye and with a smile. "Sorry Miss, but you have a whole group of people that would love to do what we need you to do. So, take a deep breath, focus and get the hell through there. If you lose hope, how much morale do you think that these people will have in making an attempt to get out?"

She gave the evil eye right back to him. "Well, how about this. Get the next skinniest one up here and let them play the tunnel rat. I really do not believe that this is for me."

The staring contest went on for about two minutes until the man cocked his head towards the light. "Daylight ain't going to wait."

She took a deep breath, looked at the opening and reached for his shovel. "Give me that damned thing." In a loud voice, she let everyone know that when all of this is over, that she deserves a big ass raise.

Nicholas yelled up. "Lydia, you do your part, and I will make sure that you get your *big ass raise* and I will even throw in a corner office."

She smiled. "Deal!"

*****

Jax had his belly full, and he was just about asleep when he heard banging coming from the president's suite. Slowly, he made his way to the door. "Sir, are you okay?" He could barely make out what President Beard was saying. He asked again if he was alright. This time, he placed his ear to the door in order to hear better.

In a low faint gruff tone, he heard, "Can't breathe. Can't breathe."

"Sir, President Beard, are you okay?! Do you need me? Sir!" No answer. All that he heard was a sound of someone in distress and gasping for air. "Hold on Sir. I will be back in a moment."

Jax ran and grabbed his radio. He pressed the button. "Jax Black here. Anyone read me?" He waited a few seconds before repeating. He was torn as to what to do. Does he go against orders and help the president, or does he stick to his orders with the belief that the president could die if he did not go to his aid. He moved to another room and tried the radio again. "Mayday, mayday, can anyone hear me?" He banged the side of the radio. "Mayday, mayday, please, anyone!" Still nothing.

He paced for a few minutes until a low banging brought him back to reality. "Shit! Shit! Shit! Damn it, John!" He made his way to the lock box and located the key to the president's suite. As he ran towards the door, he grabbed the AED that was in a cabinet outside the suite. There were seven keys on the key ring for the president's suite. Of course, it was the last key that he tried.

As he got the door unlocked, he picked up the AED with one hand and turned the knob with the other. As he was going through the door, he called out. "Hold on Sir. Hol…"

Before he could finish his statement, President Beard quickly stepped from behind the door with a small fire extinguisher raised above his head and swung down as hard as he could resulting in crushing the side of Jax's head in. Jax was dead before he ever hit the floor. Just to make sure that he was no longer a threat, President Beard landed a few more blows to his head. He tossed the extinguisher and stepped over Jax's body. He stopped and turned back to retrieve the radio from Jax. "Sorry buddy, but I will need this more than you."

*****

General Seltzer was white as a sheet. He raised his Glock and moved back to Deval and shoved it in his mouth. "You bastard, what the fuck are you saying?!" Deval tried to laugh. All that did was piss the general off even more. He shoved the barrel even farther in Deval's mouth which made him gag. Blood began to come out of the side of Deval's mouth. The general cocked the weapon. "Mother fucker, you will answer me, or you will eat this fuckin' bullet!"

Colonel Corde quickly approached the general. "General, don't do it! We need him to talk."

232

General Seltzer hesitated a few seconds, "You're right. I almost lost it. Sorry." He removed the weapon from his mouth, wiped it on his shirt, then pointed it towards Deval's backside and pulled the trigger resulting in shooting him in the ass. Deval screamed out. The general looked to Larry. "Where is that duct tape?"

Larry picked it up and handed it to him. "Here Sir."

The general pulled off a piece and slapped it over Deval's mouth. "Whenever you decide to act like a man, then the tape comes off."

General Seltzer stood up and walked away. He stopped a few feet away and turned to face Larry and the colonel. "Gentlemen, if you would not mind, I would like to speak to the two of you for a moment. Please follow me." Slowly, General Seltzer walked with his head down until he was in the office once again.

The colonel entered second and Larry was last. In a soft tone, "Lieutenant." He waved his hand towards the door. "Please close the door."

They all had a seat and not a word was said for a few minutes. Finally, it was Larry that broke the silence, "Sir, I am not sure as to what Deval meant by that statement a few minutes ago, but I can only hope that it is not what it sounded like."

The general finally raised his head. "Lieutenant, I too hope that what I heard is not what I believe that it means. But Lieutenant, it appears that you have had more experience with this whole situation than any of us others. Not rightfully sure as to how or why, but you have. I am sure that one day, everything will flow out. But, for the time being, we need to focus on what is in front of us at this present moment. We can beat on Deval all day and I believe that all we will get out of him is what he wants us to know. I feel as though he may eventually give us all that we desire, but it will be in bits and pieces, and it will be up to us to put the puzzle together."

Colonel Corde spoke up. "Gentlemen, how about I take a crack at him. Apparently, it appears that between the three of us, I am the only one that he cannot or has not gotten to. The lieutenant here had possession of him when we got here and General, he seems to be very familiar with you also. But me, I am just a reserve colonel that plays army one weekend a month and two weeks in the summer. He has no knowledge of me and nothing over me. I do believe that he may be more open to me while feeling that I am an outsider."

General Seltzer let that sink in for a moment before offering an answer. "Colonel I..." He changed gears a second. "By the way Colonel, what is your first name? That is if you would not mind."

"I do not mind. Bradley, Sir. My first name is Bradley."

"Okay, Bradley. I believe that you may be on to something. Maybe you, by being a reservist and not active. Well, not active until a few days ago. Deval may be more apt to opening up to you and slipping up. What the hell do we have to lose? That is right, absolutely nothing. So, how do you want to get this rolling?"

"Well." He thought for a second. "I could somewhat come on as the buddy that he needs. I could use reverse psychology on him. Just allow me to keep an eye on him while everyone gets some grub. Let him think that it is just him and I against the rest of the world. I think that I will be able to make headway. Like you said, what have we got to lose? Nothing." Silence for a moment, then the colonel stood up. "Well Gentlemen, no time like the present. We are burning time that we so preciously need."

The general opened the door and held it as Larry and the colonel left the room. He thanked each one and patted them on the back as they exited the door. "Thanks guys, we really need to make headway as soon as possible."

The colonel left the office and went straight for Deval. "Listen up folks. It is getting late, and I am pretty sure that most of you may be pretty hungry by now. I was informed that chow is being prepared down the hallway in the cafe. So, if you all would care to, please feel free to go eat."

One of his men spoke up. "But, Sir, what about him? Who will watch him?"

Colonel Corde looked at Deval and then at the soldier. "Honestly son, does it appear that he can go anywhere? Hogtied and a bullet in his ass, trust me, he is safer than your grandmother. You all go, I will stay."

"Well, okay Sir, if you say so."

The colonel waved. "Go. Go, enjoy your dinner. I got this."

When the colonel was sure that no one else was in the area, he pulled a chair up next to Deval. He leaned in and smiled. "Comfy?" Deval gave an evil stare. Now it was the colonel's time to laugh. "What's the matter, ah...what was it that the general called you? Oh, that's right, asshole." Deval was getting more pissed every second.

"Well now asshole, what's the matter, cat got your tongue?" Deval struggled in his restraints and attempted to say something that was being blocked by the duct tape. "Oh, sorry. Would you like me to remove that so that we can have a few minutes of conversation?" The colonel reached over, securely grabbed the tape and forcefully ripped it off. Deval let out a yell.

In a low, gruff tone. "What the fuck is wrong with you? Take these bindings off me and treat me like the leader that I am."

The colonel laughed that statement off. "Really? Leader? You call yourself a leader? Look at you. Look at the mess that you got us into. How in the hell am I supposed to follow someone that has allowed himself to get in the predicament that you are currently in? You should be calling me Sir. At least I am still out and about and moving forward as we have planned for so long."

The colonel looked disgusted. "As soon as I can figure a way into the bunker to free our great leader, then I will be greater than you. At that time, I will ask for permission to execute you. But, until that time comes, you will remain silent, or I will go above orders and silence you myself. Before they return here, I will tape your mouth back up and I will feed them some type of bullshit about the device." The colonel stood and retrieved the duct tape.

"You know, things would have been a lot smoother if I was in your position. There would have been no way that I could have been taken, but...we all make mistakes." As he was placing the tape on Deval's mouth, he leaned in closer. "Just don't make another mistake that will get you a bullet in the forehead. You understand asshole?" Deval struggled and was about to say something just as the colonel placed the tape over his mouth.

It was not but a minute later until the first began to arrive back from the café. When Larry and the general arrived back, Larry slowly made his way over to the colonel and Deval. "Well Colonel, any luck?"

The colonel took a deep breath. "As a matter of fact, Lieutenant, I did get a bit of information that may work to our advantage."

Larry asked the colonel if they could take this into the office with the general. He agreed and asked his men to keep an eye on Deval. Larry motioned for the general and pointed towards the office. When they were all present, Larry closed the door and asked everyone to have a seat. "General, apparently the colonel has something to offer." He had a seat. "Hit it Colonel."

The colonel smiled. "Thanks Lieutenant. I feel like I'm on a gameshow."

He repositioned himself in his seat. "According to asshole, there is a handheld device that controls the attachment that is on his neck and that of the children. It has a very short range and yes, it is an explosive device. It can be lethal to anyone within about ten feet when it is set off."

Larry took a deep breath. "Okay, thanks Colonel, but what I want to know is one thing. How do I get that off the children without it going off?"

"Lieutenant, that there is the million-dollar question. He told me that there is a failsafe tamper switch installed that will set if off at the least amount of prying. So, for the children's sake and your own, if I were you, I would leave it alone until we find who may have the remote or at least the knowledge to disarm them."

Larry and the general locked eyes for a moment. The general took the stump. "Now Colonel, didn't you tell me that you have one of the best electronic guys in your unit? Didn't you tell me that he could hack, find or access anything?"

The colonel sat there a second in thought. "Well, I do vaguely recall something along that line. Let me get him and we can see what kind of insight he can offer."

CHAPTER TWENTY-ONE

After about twenty minutes of crawling and digging, there was an ear-piercing screech heard coming over the top of the mound, everyone stopped digging and looked up. Lydia let out a yowl. "I did it! I did it! I'm through! Yippee!!"

As if it were well rehearsed, there was a loud 'Yeah' called out in unison. Just the sound of her words gave additional gumption. Nicholas screamed out as he pointed his shovel up towards the opening. "Onward men! We have a world to get to."

The dirt was continually being discharged backwards. Every so often, the lead digger would be replaced by a fresh body. There were a few that oversaw the hydrating process. As the tired came down off the mound, they would have a seat for a few minutes and down a bottle of water.

Nicholas finally made it to the top as front digger. As he peered over the mound, he could see Lydia furiously digging on her end. He yelled out. "You know Lydia, you may even have your own staff as you are made the head of the Department of Transportation."

From a few bodies back came a response. "Hey Nick, what the hell?! That is my position."

Nicholas laughed, "Relax Roger, you seem to forget that you climbed the rungs just like me. You are somewhere around Labor and Human Services, not sure. But, once we get out of here, we will get all that straight. Besides, nobody, not even you wanted the job that you had."

He thought for a second. "So, so true Nick. Just keep throwing that dirt this way."

It took about another two hours until the lead digger was able to lay his shovel down and lay on top of the mound. Lydia lay down on the mound also and smiled. "Hi there Timmy Ringo." He smiled back. "Hi there yourself, Lydia Hite." He peered past her. "Nice place you got out there. Mind if I check it out?"

She blushed, "By all means, please join me."

Someone from the rear yelled out. "Hey, we would like to come out too. So, the two of you, just get a room will ya? But first, get the hell out of the way, President Mitchell wants to come through."

Everyone moved to the side to allow Nicholas to make his way through. There was enough room to crawl out, just not enough room to walk out. As he made his way to the other end of the mound, he paused. Closing his eyes, he turned his face upwards, "Please dear Lord, please guide everyone here safely on our unknown journey that is about to be before us, Amen."

Over the top of the mound, he heard quite a few say, 'Amen'.

Right behind Nicholas was Jerry. No matter what, his position was to be by the president's side no matter what. Before Nicholas slid down the mound, Jerry put an arm up across his chest. "Hold on Sir, let me check it out before you go out."

Nicholas looked at him with a surprised look. "Really Jerry? Do you expect the natives to be hostile? Besides us, there probably isn't a single person left on this planet out there that actually knows just who the hell the president actually is at this present moment. Hell, I am it and I am still telling myself that. So, unless you want to shoot me, then, last one down is a rotten egg!" With that statement, Nicholas gave a jump and began down the mound.

Jerry was still able to make it down before Nicholas and he quickly made his way out to the opening. He looked around and saw that all was calm. Nicholas joined him out in the open. "Jerry, check it out, do as I do." Nicholas leaned his head back, closed his eyes and took a deep breath. "Ah, never smelled so fresh, huh Jerry?"

"No Sir, never so fresh." They stood there a few moments in their own world. The others filtered out one by one and they also joined Nicholas and Jerry. They all stood there feeling and listening as if they were children experiencing all of this for the first time. All they heard were birds singing, an occasional pesky fly and the sound of the slight breeze blowing through the trees. The smell of spring was ever so present in the air.

Finally, Jerry nudged Nicholas. "Sir, this is all lovely, but I think that we need to move and attempt to make friendly contact."

Nicholas looked at Jerry. "Damn Jerry, this may have been the very last moment of solitude that any of us may ever experience. A real fuckin' *pin man in balloon land*, are we?"

Jerry showed no emotion, "That I am Sir. Now, let's move. You stay in the middle of us." Jerry called for the other security detail to fall in accordingly.

Someone called out, "Billy, hey Billy!" Everyone looked around. They called out again for Billy. "Anyone seen Billy? He was right behind me when we were crawling out. Hey Billy!"

Jerry had two men go back in the tunnel and take a look around. They emerged a few minutes later. One man got Jerry's attention.

The man shrugged his shoulders and held his hands up while shaking his head. Jerry looked around. "What the hell."

Jerry pulled everyone together for a brief meeting. "Alright folks listen up. Not sure what happened to Billy, but we do not have the luxury, nor the resources to waste the time to conduct a search party. So, with that thought in mind, until we know what or who we may be up against out here, I need to express that everyone stays together. Even if you need to pee, pee in the buddy system, no one strays alone. Got it? Any questions?" No hands were raised. "Great, I will lead. So, let's roll." They attempted to keep to the same route that they believed that General Seltzer may have taken. It took a few hours until they were able to reach route 210, Indianhead Highway.

There were a few fast food joints that came into view. One man looked, "Oh my God, what I wouldn't give for a cold cut sub right about now."

Jerry took the post. "I believe that it would be best if we were to hunker down here and send a few down to scout the area ahead. Since we still have not a clue as to what is before us, we still need to proceed with caution." Jerry looked around. "Bobby, you the one with the radio?" Bobby gave a thumbs up. "Good, see if you can raise anyone."

Bobby pulled the radio from the Faraday bag and gave it a few cranks. "Mayday. Mayday. Anyone read me?" Silence. He looked at Jerry and Jerry gave him a signal to keep rolling. A few more cranks and he looked at the gauge, it showed full power. "Mayday, mayday, anyone out there." Silence. Bobby shook his head and stood up.

A few seconds later, "Mayday caller, Marine One here, you are on a secure channel, identify yourself." Everyone got really quiet, then cheered. They all looked at Bobby as he stood there frozen with disbelief.

Bobby reached for the radio and all but dropped the receiver. "Quiet, quiet!" He had a big grin on his face. "Marine One, Marine One. This Secretary of..." His words faded for a second as he looked at Nicholas. "Nick, what am I secretary of?" They all laughed.

"Just use labor."

Bobby gave a thumbs up. "Marine one, this is Secretary of Labor Robert Vander. I have Eagle One with me." They waited for a response. Nothing.

He looked at Nicholas. "Try them again Bobby. Maybe he did not hear you."

Bobby raised the handset. Just as he was about to speak, the response came. "Sir, please confirm your response."

Nicholas stepped over to Bobby. "Here, let me have that." Nicholas stood tall and puffed out his chest. "Let me show you how it's done." He cleared his throat. "Marine One, Eagle One here. Ready for confirmation?"

"Eagle One, whenever you are ready Sir."

Nicholas looked around. "This is how I do it." They all chuckled. He raised the handset. "November Echo Mike Tree Six Niner Att Fower."

It did not take but about three seconds for a response to come back. "Sir, Eagle One. We are locked in on your signal. How many in your party?"

Nicholas asked everyone to count off one at a time. A moment later. "Marine One, we have forty-two. Repeat, we have fower two."

Ten seconds later. "Eagle one, ETA for dispatch is three minutes. Birds are revving up now for extraction. If all is secure, hold tight and remain in position." The cheers could be heard a mile away.

Nicholas stood tall. "Quiet, quiet. Listen up folks, looks like a few hots and some cots tonight." The cheers and slaps on the backs were deafening.

A minute later, the sound of blades hitting the air was heard off in the distance. Bobby yelled out, "Listen! Listen! Choppers!" Another round of cheers.

Nicholas called out to the ones that would ride with him in Marine One. "Hey everyone, if it is still there, then chances are, we will be headed to Camp David." Nicholas looked up and he saw a squad of choppers headed their way surrounding Marine One.

He lowered his head and shed a few tears. Lydia approached him and put a hand on his shoulder. "Sir, are you okay?"

Nicholas raised his head and wiped his eyes. "Yes. Please excuse me."

"Nothing to excuse Sir. You are human."

He looked at Lydia. "Please do me a big favor Lydia."

"What is that Sir?"

244

"Please stop calling me Sir and please call me Nick."

She had a sheepish grin and turned a little rosy color. "Wow! Ah, okay Sir. I mean Nick. Wow! I can call the President of the United States Nick!" She did a little jig. "Cool!"

Nicholas did his own Jig. "She said Okay, she said okay!"

She jabbed him in the ribs. "Stop mocking me...Nick"

There were six Apache attack helicopters facing in different directions that sat still hovering above the landing sight of Marine One and the five Hueys that were for the extraction of the rest of the group. Against the direction of Jerry, Nicholas remained outside and made sure that everyone was on board their crafts before he entered Marine One.

As he was headed up the steps of Marine One, an all too familiar voice yelled out. "Nicholas! Don't you dare fuckin' board my craft!" Everyone that was still on the ground turned with weapons drawn to see President Beard standing there about twenty-five feet away to the rear of the craft with a handgun pointed at Nicholas. "I am still the President of the United States. All of you will obey my orders. Lower your weapons and take that man into custody." Everyone just stood there.

Nicholas slowly made his way down the stairs. He made a motion with his hand. "Stand down men. We can straighten this out." He made it to the ground. "John, what the fuck is wrong with you? You have been removed by a deciding vote."

President Beard took two steps towards Nicholas. "Deciding vote? You all drugged me and locked me in that room like some kind of fuckin' animal. Then you all decided to commit mutiny and make yourself president. Isn't that the way that it really happened?"

Jerry stepped in with weapon raised and pointed at President Beard. "Sir! Drop the weapon! Now!"

President Beard laughed and turned towards Jerry. "What the fuck are you going to do Jerry? You going to shoot me? I don't think so! I am still your boss; I am your Commander in Chief. You work for me, remember?"

"Sir, you have been relieved from your duties due to mental illness."

President Beard laughed. "You think I'm fuckin' nuts Jerry? Really? I'll show you fuckin' nuts." What President Beard did not know was that as he was carrying on with his tirade, an Apache slowly swung around and kept a vigil on what was going on. He turned back towards Nicholas and raised his weapon. At that moment, the thirty mm M230 cannon on the chin turret of the Apache let out a quick three round burst right over his head. That really got his attention to where he almost fell forward. He regained his balance and was about to point the weapon at Nicholas again.

"Really John? Is this how you want to go out? I can guarantee that the next burst will be quite lower."

President Beard stood there stunned for a moment before talking. "What the hell Nick! After all that I did for you as you were coming up. And this is how you repay me? Maybe you are the one that is fuckin' nuts."

"John, for everyone's sake and safety, we need you to place that weapon on the deck." President Beard stood there looking around. "John, there is nothing to think about. Place the weapon down and you will be escorted onto Marine One." He remained as he was. Nicholas slowly approached him. He reached his hand out. As he did that, there were many weapons that were trained on President Beard. Standing there with his hand out. "John. Come on. Give me the weapon."

President Beard stood there frozen in both fear and disbelief as he looked down to see red dots settled all over his chest. "Come on John, let's not go out like this. Hand me the weapon." Finally, he looked up, let the weapon fall and spin on his finger and handed it to Nicholas. Nicholas removed the weapon from his hand and put his other hand on his shoulder. Some of the security started to move in, but Nicholas waved them off.

As they entered the doorway, a marine snapped to attention and saluted. "Welcome aboard Marine One." He looked back and forth between the two. "Sirs." He gestured towards the seating area. "Sirs, make yourselves comfortable. We will take you to Camp David to where you can begin your command Sss..." His pronunciation and completion of *Sir* fell silent. He was not sure how to complete the sentence.

Once aboard, Nicholas asked if they had heard anything from either Groundhog or Lieutenant Rollins. The commander of Marine One came into the seating area. "Sir, if you desire, we will attempt to raise both of them for you. As far as I am aware, Sir, we have not had any contact. Sorry to sound ignorant to the fact Sir, but we have monitored the airwaves since the attacks, and I have not been informed of any such activity. The first activity that we encountered was from your man today."

When they first boarded, Nicholas had President Beard taken to the lounge area so that he could lay down and be examined by the doctor on board. A few minutes later, the commander was called to the lounge. "Excuse me Sir. I will be right back."

When he returned, he told Nicholas that President Beard has been sedated and that he will be resting comfortably for a bit. "Thanks, Commander."

"Anything else, Sir?"

"No. No, I just want a moment to myself, thanks."

"Yes, Sir."

Nicholas looked out the window and he was able to see people milling about attempting to put their lives back together. He spoke to no one in particular, but he was hoping that the Marine commander would offer some input. "What the hell happened out here? We need to get back up and running so that maybe we can get to the bottom of this all and find out who all was involved."

He sat there a moment in deep thought wondering where and what may have happened to the agent that was watching the president. He also wondered about Billy. Did Billy take off or did he and the agent meet the same demise. Only President Beard could answer those questions.

He sat quiet for the next few minutes until the commander called out to him. "Sir, Mr. President, we will be touching down in Camp David in approximately two minutes, Sir."

He looked up. "Thanks Commander."

"Sir, the doctor would like to know if you would like to keep President Beard aboard or should we have him transported to medical."

He thought for a moment. "Commander, how about we leave him where he is and place one guard in the lounge, two outside the lounge and at least two outside the craft."

"Sir?" Nicholas gave him a direct stare. "Roger, Sir. One in, two out and at least two outside." He began to leave when he stopped and turned. "Sir. May I ask a question?"

"Of course, Commander. Anytime."

He carefully gathered his thoughts before speaking. "Sir, is there something that I should be aware of?"

Nicholas took a deep breath. "Commander, something just isn't right, and I do not want to take any chances, okay"

"Quite okay, Sir. On it."

CHAPTER TWENTY-TWO

Colonel Corde called out for one of his men to retrieve Specialist Leatherwood. The soldier hurried down the hallway towards the café that they all ate at to retrieve Leatherwood. About five minutes later, they all turned to see the men scurrying towards the office. "Yes Sir, Colonel, what may I be of assistance to?"

"Specialist Leatherwood, I told the general here that when it comes to electronics that you are the absolute best. Was I lying?"

The specialist just stood there for a moment being unsure as to the best way to answer this question. "Sir?"

"Okay, now is not the time to be modest Specialist Leatherwood. We need you to take a look at a device and we need your expert opinion and maybe your expertise in disarming it."

"Sir?"

The general looked at him. "Specialist Leatherwood, is that all that you can say?"

He looked at the general, "Sir?" The general gave him a death stare. "I mean, no Sir. I can say a lot when I have to. I am just a little foggy on what you all are asking. What is this device?"

The general spoke up. "Now we are getting somewhere."

He stood up and walked over to Specialist Leatherwood. "Son, it appears that asshole out there along with the two children have some type of explosive device attached between their shoulder blades."

"Sir?"

The general turned towards the colonel. "Colonel Corde, if he gives that fuckin' response one more time, I will personally shoot him along with asshole out there! Get your *expert* here a larger vocabulary. That is a direct order."

The colonel asked for a moment with Specialist Leatherwood. They went out into the hall and the colonel closed the door on the way out. "Look here Leatherwood, if you don't say anything besides, *Sir*, then chances are, the general will act upon his threat. Got it?"

"Got it, Sir. I am just a little fuzzy as to what you expect of me. Do you want me to examine it, defuse it or what?"

The colonel looked at him. "Really Leatherwood? You couldn't say that in there? All you could say was just Sir, Sir, Sir?"

"Sorry Colonel. He just makes me nervous. That's all."

The colonel looked at him. "Nervous? Why is that?"

"Sir, he is the Army Chief of Staff. He is the top man."

Colonel Corde looked at him. "Well, you did say the key word, *man*. That is correct, he is just a man, and he is no God or anything. Just be yourself around him. That is all that he asks of you too. Besides, he wants you to look at an explosive device. I am pretty sure that he too would desire that you be you and not be nervous. Got it?"

Leatherwood took a deep breath and exhaled. "I suppose that you are right Colonel. I'll give it a chance."

"Oh, want to know a little trick that I always use?"

"Sure Sir, what is that."

The colonel smiled, "When you confront someone that makes you really nervous, just picture them in their underwear."

"Sir?"

The colonel smiled. "When you go back in there, every time that you look at the general, do not see the uniform or the man, just see him in a pair of pink underwear. With frilly lace if need be."

They both laughed. "Okay. Okay Colonel. I can do that."

"Good, let's go."

They went back in, and the general gave them both the evil eye. "You two ladies good now? Or do you need another few minutes of together time?"

The colonel chuckled. "No. We are good. All that I ask is that you stop making him nervous."

"Colonel?"

Colonel Corde chuckled again. "Now you sound like he did a few minutes ago."

This time, the general chuckled. "Well hell, I guess I do."

Specialist Leatherwood also gave a few chuckles and then turned towards the general. He smiled, "General, I am ready. Where is this device?"

The general was a little perplexed at the sudden change in the demeanor of the Specialist. "Okay, Specialist Leatherwood, let's get out there to the device."

The general motioned for everyone to exit. As they did, Specialist Leatherwood chuckled and the colonel gave him a slight push on the shoulder and whispered, "Stop that."

They approached the desk that Deval was still laying on all bound and gagged. The colonel took the platform. "There you go Specialist, your subject."

"Okay, where is this device that you were talking about?"

Larry removed his knife and slit the back of Deval's jacket open far enough to lay his jacket open and expose the device.

The specialist moved in closer. "Interesting. Very interesting."

The general moved in and whispered in his ear. "Back to a limited vocabulary, are we?"

Leatherwood chuckled. "No, no Sir. You just interrupted me before I could finish." He turned towards the general and smiled. The general did not smile.

"If at all possible, I am going to need a few things."

The general spoke up. "Well, if we have it, then you can have it. If it is anything that we need to go to the mall for, then we are screwed. What is it that you need?"

"Thanks, General. I need a small mirror, like a dental mirror."

Someone spoke up. "You may be in luck. On the way to the café, I noticed that this airport has a dentist office down the corridor."

The general looked at her. "You shittin' me? A dentist office in an airport? Who the hell has that much time before their flight to have dental work?"

She shrugged her shoulders. "Do you want a mirror or not?"

The colonel chuckled. "Go Sergeant." He placed a hand on her shoulder. "Hold on a sec. Leatherwood, anything else special?"

"Well, maybe cuticle cutters, a Leatherman tool, small flashlight, preferably LED, bobby pins or paper clips, magnifying glass, peroxide, gauze, tape and...colored alcohol."

"Colored alcohol?"

"Well, if you can only get clear alcohol and maybe some type of food coloring...that should work."

"Anything else?"

"Besides prayers and space...nope." The colonel told three of them to hurry out and get what was needed. "Oh colonel, hold on! One more thing. Canned air."

The general spoke up. "What? Canned air? This ought to be good."

"General, the butane in the canned air will help freeze the circuit if I can get to it. May as well get a few cans."

The general looked at the colonel. "Butane?"

Specialist Leatherwood smiled. "I know Sir and using butane on live electronic circuits to cool them down can be risky, well, more like very flammable. But...unless you have access to either liquid nitrogen or Freon, then I will have to make do with what I can get."

The colonel made a gesture and the three soldiers started to take off down the corridor in search of the needed items. "Hold off! One more thing Colonel. I need a can of starting fluid."

"Okay, I'll bite."

"Sir, I need the ether to knock him out. I'll be damned if I will lift a device and take the chance that he moves and blows us all up."

The colonel looked at the runners. "Okay, now go."

The general looked at the colonel and in a low voice. "This kid is good, huh?"

"General, I would want him to have my back any time that I could. This kid is beyond good. He is the best. Just wait and watch. When he succeeds and all of this is over and done with, we should make him at least a Lieutenant."

It was a long fifteen minutes before the final runner made it back. The specialist had a few others drag a table over to him so that he could lay out his tools. The general looked at his layout. "Damned kid shoulda been a doctor." Leatherwood gave the general a thumbs up and a smile.

"Anything else Leatherwood, or are you good?"

"Well, I would ask you all to vacate the area, but that is just my opinion. Like I said, butane and live circuits can be a bad nightmare."

The general looked at the colonel. "What do you want to do Brad?"

"Well General, my thought is to run, but I personally will walk at a brisk pace. So, no disrespect, but every man for himself." At those words, everyone around them started moving in different directions.

The general was the last to leave. He looked at everyone scrambling. "Shit! Why me?" He was about to go when Leatherwood told him that he could really use a hand.

The general looked around and all were now invisible. "Like I said a second ago, '*Shit! Why me*'? Being the highest rank, I should have been the first out of the area." He turned to Leatherwood. "What can I do to assist?"

"Well, I really could use you to take that Leatherman and grab that thing and pull it up off his skin just the slightest bit so that I can get a look under it. I will let you know when to stop. Not too far Sir, or we will both know that you went to high."

"Smartass."

The general looked at Leatherwood, "I bet you got beat up a lot as a kid, didn't you?"

He laughed, "No. No, Sir, no one was ever around long enough to pay attention to me. Hell Sir, I was in the Army eight months before anyone noticed that I was gone. By me having to do most everything for myself, I learned a lot of neat stuff to do. I learned electronics and built metal detectors, solenoid locks for my room and an occasional explosive."

That last description raised an eyebrow. "Really? Explosives?"

He laughed. "Nothing big Sir, just stuff that would blow a trashcan lid to scare either the raccoons or an occasional bear." Another raise of the eyebrow. "Don't worry Sir, pyrotechnics never was my desire to create, just my desire to disarm, remove and study. Just don't make me nervous."

The general leaned in.` "Leatherwood, you have me beyond nervous. I am about to shit my pants."

"Okay, Mr....Ah, what is his name Sir?"

"Asshole. His name is Asshole."

Leatherwood looked at him and smiled. "Okay, Mr. Asshole, time for you to go to sleep." Leatherwood sprayed the starting fluid on a part of Deval's shirt that Larry sliced, and he placed it over Deval's nose and mouth. Deval tried to fight the moment, but being bound as he was, he did not have much choice. "Please hold still Mr. Asshole, this will only take a minute or two. Well, then again, it may be for eternity. We will all see in a few minutes."

When he was calm, Leatherwood left the rag lay by his face to keep him under. "Ready to raise that thing Sir?"

"Ready. But if I survive this, I am retiring. Okay, where do I grab it?"

"Let me have the tool." He retrieved it and showed the general where to grab it. "Just don't squeeze too hard, okay?"

"Okay." He took a deep breath. "Here I go. And you said that you would let me know when to stop lifting, correct."

He smiled. "General, for what it is worth, I have not lost an assistant in five years." The general looked even more nervous. Leatherwood chuckled. "My assistant ETS'd, that is how I lost him."

This time, the general chuckled. "You had me on that one."

"Okay, just a little lift, Sir." He got a grab on it and started lifting. "Hold it! Right there." Leatherwood took the flashlight and the magnifying glass and did his examination. "Wow! This dude is good."

"Okay, good being good or good being not good?"

"Sir, I mean good as to where I would love to study under him. Well, him or her. This is beautiful. From what I can see, I do believe that this is Middle Eastern design."

The general was more curious than nervous. "What brings upon that conclusion?"

"Sir, the design and the older version of components. These are still readily available and used in the lower countries. Don't get me wrong, these may be outdated to us, but they work just the same. Just keep that pressure for a moment."

He grabbed the alcohol and the food coloring. He poured some alcohol under the device and then squirted the food coloring. A few seconds later, more alcohol. "Okay, just another moment or two, Sir. Give the color a chance to work under the skin and I will have a better idea as to how I can remove it." He looked with the little exam mirror. "Huh, interesting."

"Okay Leatherwood, after all this time, you decide to find something else interesting? What may that be?"

"The reservoir appears to be what I would presume to be some type of numbing agent. Not sure if it is a timed-release liquid and when it is gone, the patient is gone or if it was just designed to last so long while allowing no discomfort. Or is it a liquid switch that will set this device off when it finally runs out? But, either way, we do not have a lot of time to try to figure this one out. So...before we get started, I have one question."

"What is that Leatherwood?"

"Sir, before we begin, I need to know if I am really getting Lieutenant after all of this is over."

"Really Leatherwood?"

"Sir, it is just you and I at this moment. So, by me knowing what my future may hold may have a great impact on what your future may hold."

"Leatherwood, I am not sure if that is a bribe or a threat."

"So, that is a yes then?"

The general gave him a gruff look. "Okay, deal. I will personally place the bars on your shoulders."

Leatherwood smiled, "Thanks, Sir. I feel a lot better now." He grabbed the mirror again. "Okay, Sir, need a little lift again." The general remembered the force that he needed before and did not need to be coached when to stop.

"Okay Lieutenant, what do you see?"

Leatherwood smiled. "Thanks Leon." The general did not like that. Leatherwood was examining the connection. "Aw, lighten up General. We should be best buddies by now. Because, if this goes off, I will be the last person that you spoke with here on this planet."

"Well, I will lighten up, but you do that again and that will be the end of your career. Is that understood Specialist Leatherwood?"

The glow of the moment went south real fast. "Understood, Sir."

Leatherwood used the LED to try to pinpoint the travel of the clamps that retained this device to the spine. "Wow General. There is a hooked effect on the attaching. It is almost like the way that staples are administered after surgery."

"So, the answer to removing it is?"

"Well, we only get one shot at removing this. Like I said, this is very old school and very old technology. What I believe that I can do is this..."

He picked up the mirror and placed it under the device in an attempt to use it as a leverage device. "Okay, Sir. I will be in need of that Leatherman tool. That is if you do not mind." The general released the pressure that he had on the device and allowed it to rest on the mirror handle. "I am going to pinch the fingers off the best that I can in a fashion that the flow of the liquid should be halted. Once I do that, I will snip each end of the finger right below the pinch and hope that it works without me shitting my pants." The general gave another eyebrow raise.

"So, what is your long-term plan?"

"Well, General. If and I mean it as a big *if*. Stay with me here, Sir. If the first crimp does not set it off and I am able to crimp number two and then I snip the first and that does not set it off. Well, then I will continue to do number two snip and so on. I do believe that by that time, we should both have learned if my plan was successful or not."

The general was starting to have a few beads of sweat come up on his brow. "Okay...and then *if* all goes good and we get this thing off, what then."

Leatherwood sat back a bit. "Well, Sir. About three milliseconds after the last snip, that is if we make it that far, I plan on launching that bitch as fast and as far away from us as I humanly can and hitting the floor all in one swell swoop." He almost thought that the general smiled and tried to chuckle.

"Okay, General. This is where I will ask you if you would like to leave. It is about that time that it is to get a little dicey. So, if you abandon me from here out, I will totally understand and respect that decision."

He grunted. "Leatherwood, before you talk me to death, do what you planned on doing, and get that thing off of him."

Leatherwood smiled. "Aw shucks General, I knew that you loved me. Let's do this."

Before he made the first crimp, he looked up. "You too, please don't abandon us either." He grabbed the mirror handle and lifted ever so lightly. He got the Leatherman seated on the first finger. A few deep quick breaths. "Here we go." He closed his eyes, gritted his teeth then squeezed as hard as he could as he tried not to shake the device as much as his hand was shaking. First crimp, no problem. He exhaled. "Whew! That was intense. Let's try number two." He took another breath and made the second crimp. "Son of a bitch! I may be onto something." He looked at the general and chuckled. "What are you sweating for? I'm the one taking all the risks." Slowly and safely, Leatherwood made all the needed crimps and cuts but the last two. Although he was pretty sure that his method was a good one, after each crimp and especially after each cut, he exhaled sharply and damned near had a heart attack. At the last set of fingers. "General, one more set and we may be free and clear." He looked at the general, "Ready, Sir?"

He nodded. "Hit it, Seymour." Leatherwood looked at him strangely, but then shook it off.

Second to last cut caused Leatherwood to start sweating like he was in the desert sun. "Sir, I really am glad that I am sweating like this."

"Yeah, why is that Leatherwood."

He smiled. "Because Sir, the way that I have been pissing myself, I can blame it on the sweat."

"Wanna know a little secret?"

Leatherwood held the device with just one finger holding it to Deval's back. "What's that Sir?"

"I too can blame the sweat on the same thing."

Leatherwood let out a laugh. "Sir, no offense, but please don't make me laugh right now. In about sixty seconds, we can share a drink and tell jokes, but now..."

"Affirmative."

Leatherwood repositioned his hold of the device. He took a deep breath and exhaled slowly. "General, one last crimp and snip and we should be home free. You ready for the big finale?"

"Ready as ever Lieutenant."

Leatherwood smiled. "Damn that sounds good. Wait until I call Mom and tell her."

He was reaching to the last finger to make the final crimp when the situation changed dramatically. They both jumped. Leatherwood almost lost his sweaty grip. "What the fuck!" The device started to beep, the blue and red lights started to flash then it went into a whistle mode that started to intensify.

The general jumped in on this one. "Crimp the fuckin' thing and cut it!" Leatherwood was shaking uncontrollably when he attempted to hold it and crimp it. After he managed the crimp, he went to spin the Leatherman for the cutter and his sweaty hand lost the grip and the tool fell to the floor.

"SHIT!" The general quickly retrieved the tool and opened it for the diagonals. Leatherwood was screaming. "Cut it! Cut it! Fuckin' cut it!"

The general was shaking uncontrollably as he went for the finger. He made the cut and Leatherwood kept to his word. Within three milliseconds, the device was airborne and whistling towards the far side of the room. They both dove to the floor behind the desk that Deval was laying on still hog tied and with the ether rag at his face.

The device hit the floor and it bounced a few times before coming to rest behind a row of seats next to the window. The whistling stopped. They both stayed there for about thirty seconds bent over on their knees with their fingers in their ears. Finally, it was Leatherwood that made the first move. Slowly, he rose his head above the desk. With his fingers still in his ears, he peeked over in the direction of where he launched the device to. Nothing.

He took one finger out of his ear and reached over to the general and tapped him on the back. The general picked his head up a little, fingers still in the ears and looked at Leatherwood. "I think that we are okay. It never went off."

Before removing his fingers. "You sure?"

"Well, for the moment I am."

They both slowly rose to their feet and stretched their necks in the direction of the device. The general looked. "Humf, son of a bitch. Maybe you did good. Let's just leave it where it is for a bit just in…." A loud *BOOM* was all that they heard. The general yelled. "God damn it Leatherwood! What the hell?"

"Well Sir, at least it went off there and not here. Maybe that is some sort of indication as to what we can expect when we remove the ones from the children." The general looked shocked. "Damn, I almost forgot that the children had one on them too."

"But Sir, we also need to look into getting the pieces out of asshole so that we will know what to do on the children."

"Yeah, that we do." Apparently, the slight blast was enough that it caused the rag to move that was under Deval's nose and he started to stir. The general grabbed the can of starting fluid and sprayed the rag again. He quickly pushed it under Deval's nose, and he fell back out. "Night, night asshole."

After the blast, there were a few faces that appeared around the corners. Larry called out. "Is everything okay?"

The general called out. "Come on in folks, the show is about over."

Larry was the first to get to the desk with Deval. "How did things go?"

Leatherwood pulled the back of Deval's shirt open. "Device is gone, but we need to see how we are to get these barbs out."

Larry asked for the Leatherman. He reached down and got a good hold of one. "Like this." He ripped it out as hard as he could and tossed it. Although Deval was unconscious, he apparently felt the removal.

Leatherwood looked at the general and then back to Larry. "Sir, I was hoping that we could find a less painful way to remove them."

"Yeah? And why is that?"

"Sir, I do believe that we will use the same technique on the children."

Larry lay the tool down. "Copy that Specialist."

"Ah, pardon me Sir." He looked at the general. "My title is Lieutenant. I was a specialist. My good friend here, General Seltzer field commissioned me to Lieutenant."

Larry looked at the general. The general sort of grinned and nodded. "Not official yet, but it is at least in the works."

Leatherwood smiled. Leatherwood had a seat next to Deval. He used Deval's shirt to clear some of the blood away from where Larry removed the first barb. He asked Larry if he could please locate the barb that he removed. When he located it and brought it back, they all looked at it and they could see that it was shaped like a fishhook with a barb on the end to hold it securely in place. They also noted that there was an opening in the point. "Okay, at least now I have a better understanding of how it is attached, how the liquid is administered and hopefully how to remove it."

He lay the flashlight on Deval's back and used the magnifying glass to get a better look at the ones that were still attached. He stuck his hand out. "Hand me the tool please." Larry handed him the tool. Leatherwood followed the curvature of the hook and he pushed it in. A second later, he saw the tip pushing up against the skin. "A little more and..." The point popped through the skin, and he was able to grab it with the tool. "That's how we will do it. Just like that."

The general patted him on the shoulder and looked at Larry and winked. "Good job Lieutenant."

Larry smiled. "Leatherwood, whenever you get ready, I will go get one of the children."

"Copy that Sir."

CHAPTER TWENTY-THREE

Once everyone was taken to their temporary quarters, Nicholas sent word out that he would like his cabinet to come together for a meeting. He looked at his watch and direct his speech to his assistant. "Currently fourteen hundred hours. Let everyone know that we will meet at seventeen hundred. Okay?" He made a note and was headed out the door. "Mickey. Please ask the commander to come in. Thanks."

A moment later, a knock at the door. "Come on in."

The commander entered. "Sir. You called for me?"

"Yes, I did." He waved his arm around towards the screen and all the controls. "Would you have any clue as to how I may bring this to life so that maybe, just maybe I could see what has happened in the world? Well, that is if this works at all."

The commander smiled. "I can get you up and running in just a few seconds." He stood there a second. "Sir, my I speak openly?"

Nicholas looked at him. "By all means Commander."

As he was getting the screen connected to the outside world. "Sir, I do know that the main destruction was aimed and isolated at the White House. There was the initial attack on the east coast infrastructure that was very successful. Well, successful on their part. Once we got past the EMP strike that caused catastrophe upon catastrophe, we were able to learn that the rest of the world, while in total shock, was still functioning. Not rightfully sure how much you were able to establish, Sir. So, if you have any questions, I will try to give you the answer, Sir."

"Commander, could you brief me on what all happened? We were all in our posts at the White House when word came through about some sort of bombing and we were all rushed down to the bunker. The last word that we had…" His words trailed off as he thought about CJ. He hesitated before continuing. "The last word that we had was that President Wolford and his family was headed to Marine One and we thought that they would wind up here." He looked up at the commander with pain in his eyes. "Any ideas Commander?"

"Sir, may I sit down?" Nicholas gestured for him to sit. "Thank you, Sir." He sat a moment to collect his thoughts and attempt to put the words in the right order. "Sir, it all began and ended in a matter of minutes. The initial strike was to the infrastructure over the Susquehanna River and to the Conowingo Dam between Harford County and Cecil County in Maryland. Thousands upon thousands died in just the matter of minutes."

He shifted in his chair. "Sir, as that was happening, an aircraft that was reported missing a few years ago over the Indian Ocean somehow made it into the airspace above Washington, D.C. and struck the White House. There are confirmed reports that there was some sort of small nuclear device on the craft. At the moment of impact is where we believe that President Wolford and his family perished."

Nicholas got up and slowly walked toward a window. He stood there silent for a few minutes with his head hung low before returning to his seat. "Sorry Commander. I just needed a minute."

"Understood Sir. I will continue when you are ready."

Nicholas took a deep breath. "Okay Commander, please."

"Sir, from what investigators have been able to gather is that this was a well-planned, organized attack. Like I stated, the bombings on the Susquehanna and the White House attack all occurred over a period of just a few minutes. There are unconfirmed reports that there was a mortar attack on the White House just before the craft came in. Oh, also Sir. There was an EMP that was released that resulted in hundreds of aircraft and satellites falling from the sky and many major auto accidents on the roadway for a forty-mile radius from D.C. Sir. It has not been a pretty sight out there the last few days."

Nicholas sat there taking it all in for a moment. "Commander, has there been anyone that has taken responsibility for all this?"

"Sir, there has been little to no available communication in this general area since the attacks. We have reached out to outside organizations, other world leaders and news agencies and we have had no one step forward."

Nicholas just stared with a blank look on his face. "Doesn't that seem to be a little odd Commander? I mean that no one has stepped forward. Hell, if I pulled this off, I sure as hell would claim responsibility. I would want the world and all of my followers to know what kind of power that I have."

The commander sat there. "Sir, I have got nothing. Sorry. Sir."

The commander picked up the remote and the big screen came to life. National Cable News was live on the scene of the perimeter that was setup not too far south of the rest area on I-95 in Savage, Maryland. The reporter was just one of hundreds from around the world that were covering the chaos twenty-four hours a day. Nicholas asked the commander a few more questions, then he requested that he call his cabinet for a meeting. The commander stood, saluted and left the room. Nicholas sat there a few minutes switching from one channel to another just to witness the same thing over and over again. Within ten minutes, the cabinet was assembled, and everyone was seated around the table. Nicholas entered and they all stood up. He looked at them all. "Really? Sit back down." He smiled. "Must admit, that was impressive." He asked that one of the estate staff to be summoned. When they arrived, he asked everyone to order what they desired so that they would have lunch available as they held the meeting. When all orders were taken, Nicholas stood up. "First off, I just want to apologize for having to have you all here today. Personally, I was enjoying life a few days ago just being Nick. Now, I have been thrusts into the position and the title of President of the United States. I admit that this is not a post that I ever saw myself in, not even in my worst nightmare." That broke the ice a little and there were a few chuckles.

"Before we go any further, and before I fall down and cry, please, let's all lower our heads in reverence and say a silent prayer for our families that are no longer with us. As for me, the reality of that fact has yet to hit me. I am sure that as time comes along, I will sit somewhere, quiet and alone and I will let it all out and cry like a baby. But, as for this moment, I need to keep my composure and begin the post of free world leader." He looked around. "Let's all take a moment, shall we."

All fourteen people around the table sat there with their heads hung low and not a word was spoken. The security staff participated also. There were a few sobs that came about, but no one rose their head to see who it was. The moment turned into minutes. The longer that the silence went on, the more sobs that came out. It was not until about fifteen minutes until the knock that came at the door broke the silence and anyone lifted their head. The security agent nearest the door grabbed the knob to keep the door from opening. When all had their eyes dried, he too wiped his and opened the door to allow the staff to enter with the food and drinks. Once everyone had their food, Nicholas stood and began. "Keep eating while I deliver my spiel." He could see that everyone was enjoying what they ordered. He realized that it has only been a few days, but some of them that were gathered acted as though they had not had a good meal in months.

"Okay, remember, I am new at this, so, if I say something wrong or out of order, then please speak up. I am not perfect, and I do not intend to begin to portray that I am. Okay?" He looked around and saw no one that disagreed with him. All he saw was a group of people totally indulged in their food.

"Okay now. First order of business should be to get to the media and go on camera so that the rest of the world can see that there is a president in charge." No response, just everyone still eating. "Okay, how about first order of business will be all of us getting naked and dancing on the tables." Two of the fourteen stopped eating in mid bite and paused. They then looked at Nicholas with uncertainty. He smiled, "Well, at least the two of you were listening to what I said. I think I will wait for everyone to get done stuffing their faces." The two nodded in agreement and continued to eat. Nicholas exhaled sharply and slowly sat down to his own food.

*****

When Leatherwood was ready, Larry went to the lounge room where the children were napping. He approached John Jr. and told him to come with him. "What about Bella?" Larry put his finger to his lips. "Shh, let Bella sleep for now. When we get ready for her, we will come get her."

"But...where are we going?"

"I am taking you to see your Daddy. He will tell you everything when you see him. So, come on." Larry held his hand out and John Jr. took his hand. He looked back at Bella as she lay there sleeping.

Once they reached the terminal, John Jr. saw his father and he let go of Larry's hand and took off running towards his father. John Jr. hugged his father so tight that John's face was turning red. "Easy now Son, don't squeeze my head off."

"But Daddy, I missed you and I miss Mommy. When can we go home? I want to go home."

John peered up to the other men standing there. "Soon Junior, soon." He had him release his grip so that he could look at him.

"Johnny, I need you to listen to me for a moment." He was not sure where to begin. He paused to collect his thoughts. "Johnny, some bad men did something to you that we need to fix."

He looked at his father like he had two heads. "What's that Daddy? Nobody did anything to me." Now it was John's turn to look at his son like he had two heads.

John reached up behind John Jr. "Don't you feel this, Johnny?"

John Jr. reached up and felt the device. He scowled, "No Daddy, what is it?"

John looked at him shocked. "You really don't feel that?"

John Jr. started crying. "No Daddy. What is it? Take it off."

John hugged his son real tight. "It will be okay Son. Daddy will take care of it." One more squeeze. "Okay, listen up." He turned John Jr. to face Leatherwood and the general. "Johnny, I need you to go with these two men here. Okay? They will get that thing off your neck."

He started sobbing again. "But Daddy, I'm scared."

John looked up at the general. "So am I Johnny, so am I. Now, go with them, okay?" John Jr. slowly let go of his father and the general reached out his hand and Johnny took it.

John stood up and walked up close to Larry. "How could he not know or feel that thing on his neck?"

Larry shook his head. "Not rightfully sure. Must be some good numbing agents." They watched the duo walk away hand in hand. "Hopefully all will go well with this one. Then..." He paused and took a deep breath. He felt a few tears escape his eyes. "Then, I have to get Bella and put her through that. I just wish that we had a surgeon that could get that thing off them instead of a computer nerd."

John looked at Larry. "Maybe all those hours of playing video games did Leatherwood some good."

Larry nodded in agreement. "But right now, we need to get outside for the *just in case*.

Since they were more familiar with the attached device now than they were an hour ago, it did not take as long to get this one removed. As before, when they were at the last finger, the device started to arm itself. And as with the first one, Leatherwood had a hold of the device as the general made the final crimp and cut. As before, Leatherwood threw it as fast and as far as he could. But unlike the last time, they had the child on the floor behind the desk when they performed the removal. And that is where they remained until the device went off.

After the explosion, they both raised up on their knees, looked in the direction of the explosion and then at each other. The general held his hand up. "High five Lieutenant."

Leatherwood returned the high five. "Okay, General, a little too early to celebrate, but it did feel good."

The general agreed. "Well Lieutenant, let's carefully get these barbs out of this here child and send him with his dad."

"Copy that, Sir."

They carefully removed the barbs and got the holes cleaned and covered with a bandage. The general stood up and saw John looking. He waved for him to come in. John sprinted in and around the backside of the desk. Johnny was just coming out of it when John knelt next to him and cradled him in his lap. "Hey Buddy. How you doin'?"

Johnny was still a little groggy. "Daddy? Daddy, is it gone?"

John smiled and cried at the same time. "Yes. It's gone Johnny. You are safe now."

"Can we go home now Daddy? I want to see Mommy."

John held him and rocked him. "Hopefully soon Johnny, hopefully soon."

Larry looked towards Leatherwood and the general. "You guys ready for the next patient?" The general stood up. "Ready when you are Lieutenant. We will be more than thrilled to get this over with." Larry agreed and left to get Bella.

Colonel Corde finally made his way in. "So far so good?"

The general looked up. "So far, Colonel. We have one more to go." He looked up at Deval. "Kinda wish that I had left that device on him for a bit. If we had known more about it, then maybe, just maybe we could have gotten some answers." He took a deep breath and exhaled sharply. "But Colonel." He looked him dead in the eye. "No matter what, I will get what I am after. One way or another, I will get my answers. And that statement, Colonel, you can stake your life on."

The general retrieved the remains of the first two devices and brought them back over to where Leatherwood was located. He held each up and they examined them.

The general started. "Interesting. Look how this opened up rather than ripping apart. The main charge would have literally blown the victim's head off." From the shell of the first two devices, they saw that the device would send the charge inward to the spine rather than exploding and sending shrapnel all about. It appears that they were only designed to kill the person that it was attached to and maybe someone that may be within about ten feet, not so much others around them.

Larry returned carrying Bella Marie. She may have been a little heavier than anticipated, but she was still *Daddy's girl*. "Daddy, what are they going to do to me?"

"Sweetheart, that is something for Daddy to worry about, not you. See that man over there?" He pointed to Leatherwood.

"Well, him and that other man, they need to fix something that some bad people did to you."

"What did they do Daddy?"

Larry smiled. "One day, I will tell you and your little girl all about that."

Bella smiled and giggled. "My little girl?"

Larry kissed her on the cheek and put her down. "Yes."

The general called her over and had her lay down on the makeshift bed. "Hi there, little lady. We meet again, you must be Bella Marie." She nodded yes. "Well, my name is Leon. But if you like..." He looked up to Larry. "You may call me Lee if you like."

She smiled and giggled. The general smiled and looked at her, "What's so funny?"

She giggled again. "My girlfriend's name is Lee. But you are not a girl." Larry and Leatherwood burst out laughing.

The general looked at them both. "Specialist Leatherwood." He glanced at Larry. "Sergeant Rollins, you guys find something funny about that?"

Bella laughed, "I do."

The general smiled at her. "Sweetheart, you can laugh at whatever you so desire." He gave one more death stare at the other two. They both kept a smug look on their faces.

For some odd reason, the general was feeling bad about having to do this to Bella, but he grabbed the rag and the starting fluid. He leaned into her. "Sweetheart, I am going to have to put you to sleep for a few minutes."

276

She looked at Larry. "Daddy?!"

Larry walked over to her and knelt down. He took her hand, "Honey, Mr. Lee will take good care of you. When you wake up, Daddy will be right here. Okay?"

She looked back and forth between Larry and the general. "Lee?"

He smiled. "It's okay Sweetheart, I will be right here the whole time." He reached up and made an 'X' on his chest, "Cross my heart and hope to fart."

She laughed. "Fart? No silly, it is *cross my heart and hope to die*, not fart."

He smiled. "Oh, okay. I will save the fart for when you wake up." She laughed again and the general put her to sleep.

Larry and John stayed for this one. Leatherwood and the general learned a lot from the first two. One main thing that they believe that they learned was that the fluid has to have a free-flowing pressure, or it will begin to arm itself. On both devices, as soon as the second to last finger was severed, the device came alive. This time, they were more than ready.

As with the one taken off John Jr., the two part time surgeons made relatively good time. Leatherwood was getting better at launching the devices. They were all just happy that they were as small as they were, or his arm may not have been good enough to keep them clear of the explosion.

They all crouched down behind the desk and waited for the device to go off. About two minutes went by before anyone was brave enough to poke their head up. The general kept one finger in one ear and raised his head. Nothing. He lowered his head.

"Hey guys. What went wrong? Shouldn't it have gone off by now?"

Leatherwood looked at him and smiled. "Go get it and check it out, I'll be here waiting for you."

When they were sure that it was safe to get up, the general tapped them both. "Come on. While the gittin' is good, we need to be gittin' the hell out of here." The general looked toward Larry. "Lieutenant, would you mind if we put asshole in your vehicle?"

Larry gave a little chuckle. "Sir, I have no vehicle."

The general gave him a puzzled look. "No vehicle? How the hell you get all the way here." Larry smiled, puffed his chest and responded. "General, Army Ranger, second seventy-fifth, Fort Lewis, Washington. We rangers walk everywhere."

The general smiled. "Well Lieutenant, this time, we may have to find space for you in one of our vehicles. We really do not have the time or the fuel to keep up to or down to your pace."

"Sir, I may know where to acquire another vehicle. The vehicle that two men were in that located Deval. That vehicle should be around the hanger on the far side of the tarmac."

Larry thought for a moment. "Sir, if we have any pilots among us, then there may be a craft that can fly. Well, at least it was in the process of getting fitted to fly when I came upon them in the hanger."

"Where do you suppose the pilot is Lieutenant?"

He took a deep breath. "Sir, I do believe that he is in the hanger with a couple nines in his chest." He attempted a smile. "Sorry."

"Well, either way, we need to get out of here and try to make some type of contact with our side." He looked for Colonel Corde. "Anyone seen the colonel?" Everyone shook their head no. "Someone locate the colonel and inform him that we are bugging out in thirty minutes." He slowly turned in a circle, then called out. "Load up people! Train leaves the station in thirty. So, let's move."

As the general went back to the office and had a seat so as to have a few minutes of peace to think, Larry left for the far hanger to retrieve the car that the men with Deval was driving. As he was nearing the building, he heard someone talking. He stopped and attempted to catch what was being said. Since the atmosphere was filled with dead silence, with not even a bird chirping, Larry was careful not to get too close to the door or to step on anything that would give him away. He could hear someone talking, but he was unable to make out what was being said. He knew the language was not English. As his best guess, he thought that it was a Middle Eastern language. Not one that he was familiar with, but he recognized the dialect. To himself, "What the hell?"

He slowly moved back about thirty feet and acted as though he was just arriving. He purposely gave out a few coughs to warn whoever may be inside the hanger. Not ten feet before the opened hanger door, Colonel Corde popped out. Larry acted surprised and just for show, he reached for his Glock. "Damn Sir, I almost shot you."

The colonel smiled. "Sorry, Lieutenant, didn't mean to startle you. And besides, I would have had the jump on you. I heard you coming a mile away. Your cough gave you away."

Larry looked at the colonel. "So, Sir, what brings you over here? You know, so far away from everyone else?"

At first, the colonel had a blank look on his face, then that changed. He smiled. "Lieutenant, I was looking to see if there was another vehicle available that we could possibly salvage. All I saw was an aircraft that was apparently being worked on before the mechanic died of sudden lead poisoning."

Larry just stared him down a moment. "Colonel, there should be a sedan on the other side of the hanger. There was a vehicle on the highway ahead of me that picked up Deval and brought him here. It was running a day or so ago, so, as long as I can locate the keys in a timely fashion, then it should run again now. If need be, I will jump the ignition." They kept their eyes locked. "Colonel, care to join me in getting the vehicle?"

He just stood there a moment, not sure how to answer. Finally, "Sure LT, lead the way."

CHAPTER TWENTY-FOUR

The commander was able to get the big screen up and running in the meeting room. While everyone was still eating, Nicholas took the remote and changed the channel to WNEW to see if Lenny Woods was anchoring the news that day. When the picture came up, it was on a commercial that was apparently filling the spot that it paid for. But the commercial was for the Washington Zoo. He shook his head. "No matter what, the media would never change. I am pretty sure that they are aware that D.C. no longer exist. But, just as with any other commercial, you can see a Fourth of July sales commercial weeks after the fact. If you pay for the spot to run *X* amount of times, then no matter what, it runs. Well, it appears that the attack did not hamper the media."

Just then, there was a knock at the door. An agent opened the door, received a piece of paper and handed it off to Nicholas. He looks up with a smile on his face. "Hey folks! We just received word from the outside from General Seltzer. It appears that they are well and that they have completed their mission. Now, they ask where to return to." Cheers went out all around the room. Nicholas smiled. "I knew Leon would get through. Praise the Lord!" More rounds of applause and cheers.

Nicholas asked Jerry to get the radio in with them so that they could all hear what was going on. "Affirmative, Sir. Give me a few minutes and I shall have someone return with the radio." Now, it appeared that everyone in the room was paying attention. There was a series of small talk that was going around when there was a knock at the door. The agent opened the door and was presented the old-style GI JOE radio and pack. He passed it off to Jerry which in turn presented it to Nicholas.

Nicholas chuckled. "That thing was working before I was born." He took it and looked it over. "I feel like an idiot. Ah...anyone here close to a hundred that knows how to work this?"

Jerry chuckled this time. "Sir, let me have a go at it. All we need you to do is speak."

Nicholas smiled. "Hell, ask anyone of them, they will tell you that I can talk nonstop all day."

The agent gave it a few cranks and handed the receiver to Nicholas. "Sir, when ready, press this to talk and release to receive."

Nicholas looked at it, "Okay, seems innocent enough. Ready or not, here we go."

He looked over the room with receiver held up like a trophy. "Eagle One to Groundhog, Eagle One to Groundhog." He released the button and waited. He looked at Jerry. "You sure you know how this works? It sure..."

"Eagle One, Eagle One, Groundhog here."

The room went wild. Nicholas was thrilled also, but he needed to maintain control. "Shh, quiet! Hold on a second."

Once again, he held the receiver like a trophy and held it up. Some chuckling went on for a few seconds. "Groundhog...Leon?"

"Yes Sir. Whom do I have the pleasure to be speaking with Sir?"

"Leon, it's me, Nick."

"Nick?"

Nicholas smiled, "Yes General, this is President Nicholas Mitchell."

Silence. "Groundhog, still there?" More silence.

He looked at Jerry and shrugged. Jerry smiled. "Give it a second Sir, Groundhog may be in shock." They all laughed, well, all but Nicholas.

A minute later. "Ah...Nick?"

"Yes Sir, General."

"Sorry for the delay in response. Between shock and moving to a more private area, it took a moment." Nicholas looked towards Jerry and Jerry gave him a smile and a thumbs up.

Nicholas mouthed 'asshole'. Another smile, and, another thumbs up from Jerry.

"Nick, is this conversation private or public?"

"Well, I am at David with all that was left in the bunker. Well, everyone but Billy and Jax. We are currently in the conference room. Just the cabinet members here at the moment. Why, what's up?"

"I really would appreciate it if maybe it was just you, and I for a moment. Oh, and maybe Jerry. Is he there?"

Nicholas smiled, "Leon, Jerry follows me to the shitter." The room chuckled together. Well, all but Jerry. "Okay, give me a moment to get the room clear." He asked everyone to exit for a few minutes.

Once the room was clear, Nicholas informed the general that they were secure. "Nick...you sitting down?"

"I can, why, what's up?"

"Sit down Nick before you fall down."

Nicholas had a seat, "Okay Leon, some odd reason, I feel as though another nuclear blast is about to hit."

"Oh Nick, this is a good one."

Leon looked around to make sure that there was no one in the area. "Nick, it is John. He is behind all this." Silence.

"What are you saying Leon? Please explain."

"Nick, John is not who we thought that he was. He is the mastermind behind the attacks."

Nicholas was now glad that the general told him to have a seat. "Are you sure Leon? I mean, how did you come up with that idea?"

"Long story short, John had me come here to eliminate the person that tracked down and found the terrorist that he believed was the mastermind. Turns out, Beard is the mastermind."

"Leon, are you one hundred percent sure about this? I mean, could there be another side to this?"

"Nick, I along with a man from Colonel Bradley Corde's Guard unit out of Hagerstown just removed three explosive devices. One was on the terrorist and the other two were mounted on children. So, Nick, this is the only side to this."

Nicholas sat there in thought for a moment. "Where are you located now?"

"We are at Lancaster Airport. When we arrived here, I witnessed the aftermath of what was done here. Apparently, Lieutenant Rollins foiled the plot to use this airport as an escape route.

Everyone here was murdered to keep them silent. Bodies were strewn about the terminal and the shops."

Nicholas sat in silence for a moment. "How does John fit into this Leon? He was…" He allowed his mind to drift back to the bunker and the performance that President Beard had held. The more that he thought of it, the more that he realized that maybe the general was correct.

Nicholas turned ashen and turned to Jerry. "Get a detail to check on President Beard! Have everyone come back in here where it is safe." Jerry acknowledged and made a mad dash to the door. As he ran out the door, he yelled out for a few men to follow him and for a few others to get everyone back in the room. They rounded the corner to the helipad, and they all stopped suddenly. They could see two agents laying on the ground that were stationed outside the craft. They drew their weapons and Jerry gave hand signals for which direction that each was to take.

Taking no chances and keeping vigil to their surroundings, they made their way to the underside of the craft. Jerry took the lead and slowly made his way up the service ladder on the back end of the craft. Once inside, he signaled down to the agent below him to come up and to have the others enter the main door. Jerry waited for the agent to signal a go. Slowly, Jerry and the other agent made their way through the back of the craft clearing it as they went along. When they reached the lounge, they found the agent that was stationed outside the lounge lying dead on the floor. President Beard was not there. They waited for the duo that came in the main door before they moved any further. Once they all met up, the duo told Jerry that they encountered no resistance on the way in. They told him that they did find the pilots dead in their seats. "Shit! He is headed to the president! Move! Move! Move!"

They all scrambled down the main stairs and ran as fast as they could to get back to the meeting room. When they turned the last corner, there was an agent laying there on the floor dead. "Hold up!" Jerry slowly made his way to the door alone. He stood off to the side and quietly tried the doorknob. Locked. He looked up to his men and signaled for one to come to him.

Jerry whispered that he wanted one agent to go outside and see if he can see anything through the window. The agent quietly went back to the others and dispatched one for the mission. They waited about five minutes before that agent returned. Jerry motioned for him to proceed. "Sir, I could see everyone in the room including President Beard. He has a weapon in one hand and a small box that appears to be some sort of remote control in his other hand."

"Remote? What? Like the television remote?"

"No, no Sir. Almost looks like the old-style slide phone."

Jerry thanked him and asked him to go back up the hallway with the others. He stood there a few minutes trying to figure things out. Finally, he whispered, "What the hell." He knocked on the door. "Agent Lucky here, open up." No response. He knocked again. "Agent Lucky here, open the door." Nothing. "President Mitchell, can you acknowledge me?" Nothing. "President Mitchell, I am coming in. I am about to break the door down." Nothing.

He called for an agent down the hall to retrieve the ram. As the agent was coming down, there was a voice that came over the intercom system throughout the compound. "Agent Lucky,

President Beard here, if you value the lives of anyone in this room, then please do not carry out your desire to enter this room by force. There will be a time for you to enter, but Agent Lucky, now is not the time. I will inform you when that time is right."

Jerry asked two of the agents to keep an eye on the door and he sent another two outside. "If anything changes one of you hightail it out to the chopper and get me. Do not attempt to play superhero here. Got it? I am going to attempt to get some help here."

Jerry and the rest made it to the chopper, and he went for the weapons cabinet in the arms room. When he arrived, for some odd reason, he was not surprised to see the keypad destroyed. "Damn you Beard!" He went for the Faraday box. That too had the keypad smashed. "Beard, you fuckin' asshole! I'll kill you myself when I get to you." He looked up and all but screamed. "Can it get any worse?"

Just then, one of his men came in the room. "Sorry Jerry, but yes. The cabin radio is destroyed too." Jerry was furious.

He sat down for a moment before he said *fuck it* and stormed in to kill President Beard. "Ray, isn't there a toolbox on board for emergencies?"

He thought for a second. "In the belly, hold on." He went halfway down the back ladder and stepped off to the maintenance bay. He looked around and found what he was after. He opened the box and there it was. "Alright, a wonder bar! They sure named that thing right. It is a wonder that you can ever get by without it." He grabbed it along with a claw hammer and made his way back up the ladder.

When he entered the arms room, he displayed them like trophies. "Jerry, let's get some work done."

Jerry took the tools. "Let's go for the Faraday first, that should be a lot easier than the arms cabinet." It did not take too much effort to break into the Faraday safe. Besides, this case was in one of the safest and most guarded crafts on the planet. Jerry handed the tools to Ray, and he grabbed two radios. "Here, see if you guys can get into the weapons case. Don't think that it will be as easy as this one was. But I will see if I can raise someone on this radio to get some help here."

Jerry knew that using the frequency that was being used in the meeting room would be out of question. He also knew of another frequency that agents used for emergencies that was outside of the president's knowledge. Jerry changed the dial and made an attempt to reach assistance. It took a few minutes of fine tuning of the old-style radio, but he finally made contact. He felt like he hit the lottery.

"This is Agent Gerald Lucky, shield number three zero four two zero, authentication Alpha Niner Two India Romeo Zulu."

A response came back. "Hold a second Sir, so that I may verify." About three seconds went by when the response came in. "Sir, authentication valid, response gearing up." A few second pause. "Sir, is this correct? I have your location as Charlie Alpha Mike Papa, Delta Alpha Victor India Delta? Confirm."

Jerry pressed the button, "Affirmative Sir, Here with Eagle One."

"Sir?" Another pause. "Sir, do I read you correctly? You have Eagle One on presence?"

"Affirmative, actually two Eagle Ones. One is holding one hostage."

This time, about ten seconds lapsed on the other end. The radio crackled to life. "Agent Lucky, this is General Wheeler, commander of Patuxent Airbase. Is what I was just informed accurate? You have two Eagle Ones, and one is holding the other hostage? Confirm please."

Jerry took a deep breath and gave a little smile. "Yes Sir, General, you have that correct." Jerry knew what was coming.

"Agent Lucky, please elaborate."

Jerry took a few deep breaths before answering. "Sir, Long story short, President Beard has taken sworn in President Mitchell and his cabinet hostage in the main meeting room here at David. President Beard is armed and unstable." More dead airtime.

"Agent Lucky, we have Delta dispatched and en route. Hold your position and wait for assistance."

"Copy that Sir. But Sir, due to the situation, may I advise to sit down in Sabillasville and auto in."

"Agent that can be arranged. Will advise and get confirmation back to you. Copy?"

"Copy Sir."

Jerry sat back and exhaled sharply. "We may be getting to the end of this after all."

The radio crackled to life. "Agent Lucky, confirmed, Delta will set down before objective and come in stealth. Copy?"

Jerry smiled, "Copy that General, thank you."

"Quite welcome Agent, just looking out for the best for Eagle One." He paused a second, "Whichever one that is. Godspeed in your mission Agent Lucky. Patuxent out."

Jerry sat back and called out. "Cavalry on the way gentlemen. Let's go out and be the welcoming party at the gate."

By the time they got to the gate, the Delta team was already coming down the service drive on their black stealth motorcycles. Jerry looked. "Cool, I want one." The commander of the unit stopped and was briefed by Jerry. A layout of the building was presented, and the Delta Team took it off to the side to get their game plan.

The commander returned to Jerry. "Agent Lucky, we will take it from here. You and your men are more than welcome to observe, but you may not interfere. Understood?" Jerry acknowledged and he informed the commander that there were two agents on the backside keeping guard.

With precision timing, the team dispersed and took their positions. The two agents on the backside were relieved and they joined Jerry and the others. "Well gentlemen, as much as I hate to pass the torch when we are still standing, I had no choice."

One agent spoke up. "So, what do we do now? Do we just hang out here or do we stick around them?"

Jerry smiled. "They know more about what is best than we do. We are good at up close, but they are good at all positions. So, we may as well go inside to the dining area and wait."

The team set up their surveillance equipment on the outside of the window as well as all along the walls in the corridor outside the meeting room. They had eyes and ears on everything in that room. Through the walls, they could see the faint images where everyone was seated, and they could see what they assumed to be Nicholas and President Beard standing. President Beard never stood still. He was constantly pacing and most of the time, his arms were flailing with weapon in one hand and device in the other.

The commander had the prints to the building in the corridor with him and he located a weak position in the wall. He removed a marker and made an X on the wall. One of the team joined him and removed a razor knife. With earphones on listening to the rants of President Beard, slowly, he drew a small square of about eighteen inches for an incision in the wall at about chest height. When he cut, he was careful to cut through slowly and quietly while President Beard was carrying on. When President Beard stopped talking, he stopped cutting.

After about ten minutes of work and he was through the double thickness of the drywall. Now to get through the lead lining and the sound proofing. When he reached the backside of the interior sheetrock, he stopped and motioned for the commander. The commander held up a heat signature scope. He nodded, then motioned for another team member that arrived with a tripod. He quietly opened the tripod and mounted his weapon. He fastened the scope and brought up the screen. Once he had his target located, he pushed the lock button. The weapon was now staying with the movements of President Beard. "Sir, target acquired and locked. Waiting for directions."

Although the image was a lot clearer with the lead removed, the commander was attempting to figure out just what the device was that President Beard was holding. He whispered something to the other man, and he quickly disappeared. A minute later, he returned with a third man that had a small case.

The commander explained the situation then stepped aside to let the man do his job. He opened the case and removed a small scanner with a pop-up screen. He held it up and pointed it in the direction of the device that President Beard was holding. As he followed the device, his screen was continuously flashing a series of nine digits in red. In no particular order, as each number to the device code was located, the number would lock and turn green.

It seemed as though an hour went by between the eighth and the ninth digit locked. The man whispered, "Sir, we got it. Permission to scramble signal." The commander kept an eye on both the screen showing the movements of President Beard and the screen of the locked numbers.

The commander whispered to the men. "We have to do this in one motion. As soon as he detects that the device is locked, he will respond." He paused a moment. "When he turns, and his weapon is in no way a danger to anyone…" He paused again to make sure that what he is about to order is correct. "You have permission to simultaneously scramble and execute."

Both men whispered together. "Copy that, Sir." One man took control of both instruments. They all kept vigil for almost ten minutes until President Beard started to turn. Just as the man was about to push both buttons, President Beard went off again, turned back to the group and headed towards Nicholas.

Under his breath, the man whispered. "Damn it! Should have taken it."

The commander patted him on the shoulder. "Just give it a moment. You see an opening, you take it. Copy?"

"Copy Sir."

President Beard went straight for Nicholas and placed the weapon under his chin. Some in the room gasped at this movement. "Well now Nick, looks like we may be having the head of state losing his head." He got right up in Nicholas' face. "I AM STILL THE FUCKIN' PRESIDENT. GOT IT?!"

Nicholas did not say a word, he was not sure what would send President Beard off. He stood there frozen with the muzzle shoved tightly into the underside of his chin. "Nothing to say now President Mitchell?" President Beard laughed and removed the weapon. He began waving the weapon towards the other hostages. "Any of you want to save your president?"

He continued to wave the weapon at random. When he did stop the wave. "How about you Delbert? You want to save your president?" Delbert just sat there. President Beard kept the weapon pointed on him as he made his way around the table. He placed the weapon to Delbert's head. "What's the matter Delbert, cat got your tongue? I do believe that I asked you a question. Now fuckin' answer it!" Delbert started shaking uncontrollably.

"Not the time to get scared now, Delbert!" He grabbed the back of Delbert's collar. "Get up! Walk with me. Maybe I can kill two birds with one stone." He chuckled a bit. "Sorry gentlemen, no pun intended." He dragged Delbert over to Nicholas and stood them side by side. He told another to push a chair around to the end of the table. "Here, both of you sit down." He pushed Delbert into the chair. "Here, just like that. Maybe I can get you both together."

President Beard reared his head back and laughed. He yelled out, "What a wonderful day" as he allowed his arms to flail out to the side. In a split second, there was a loud bang and President Beard crumpled to the floor. As he was falling, the sound of the door being blown off the hinges made everyone jump and focus their attention away from the body.

Nicholas jumped up and Jerry made his way straight for him. "Sir, are you okay?"

He remained silent for a few second. "Ahh, fine Jerry. I am fine, just a little in shock, but fine."

"Sir, we need to get everyone out of here."

Nicholas agreed. "Gentlemen, we need to vacate. Let's roll." Some were so much in shock that they had to be assisted in standing and being ushered out of the room.

As Jerry was guiding Nicholas to another meeting room, Nicholas asked to get the media in there. He needed the world to see that the United States did have a governing body. "Sir, as soon as we get you secured, I will personally contact them and have them here. Agreed?"

Nicholas stopped in the hall and turned towards Jerry. He stuck his hand out. "Thank you, Jerry. I mean it from my deepest inner being. Thank you."

Jerry accepted and shook his hand. He smiled, "Just doing my job, Sir. Just doing my job." He smiled and cocked his head towards the direction they were traveling. "Now get."

CHAPTER TWENTY-FIVE

The general saw Larry returning to the terminal after getting the car. He yelled out from the office. "Lieutenant! Get in here, I need to run something by you. Something ain't right."

Larry made his way over to the general. "Yes, Sir. What's up?"

"Lieutenant, I was just on the horn with President Mitchell when..."

Larry cut him off. "President Mitchell? I thought..."

The general looked at him. "Me too, I was as shocked as you are. Apparently, it is a long story. One that was abruptly cut off."

Larry gave a quizzical look. "What do you mean?"

"Well, while you were gone, I was contacted by Eagle One and President Mitchell came on." More strange looks from Larry. "Anyway, as I was talking to President Mitchell, the communication stopped dead. I tried to reach him, but to no avail." He paused. "Not sure what to make of it."

Larry looked around to make sure that they were alone. "Sir, I have my own dilemma going on. I should have said something earlier, but I wanted more proof before you threw me in the brig."

"What are you saying Lieutenant?"

"Well Sir, when we were in the office earlier discussing about having the colonel take a crack at Deval, I glanced over, and I thought that I saw a bulge on his upper back, about the same location as Deval."

The general sat there deep in thought and not hearing a word as Larry carried on. Finally, "General, General, still with me?"

The general gave Larry a real ashen look. He too looked around to make sure that they were alone. "Lieutenant, close the door, would you?" He looked again. "I think that I felt what you are talking about."

"Sir?"

"Earlier, as we were leaving the office. Remember that I patted each of you on the back?"

"Yes."

He hesitated. "I did feel something on his upper back between his shoulder blades."

Larry took a deep breath. "Sir, I am afraid that there is more."

"How so?"

"Well Sir, when I went over to the hanger to get the car that Deval was picked up in, well Sir...." He collected his thoughts. "Sir, I am not by any means a linguist, but I heard the colonel talking to someone in what I believe to be was Arabic. I do know that it was some sort of Mid-Eastern language. Sir, I did spend enough time in country to pick up on that much." He took another look around. "Sir, I hope that we are wrong and that we are just building a paranoid scenario. I am at the point that I do not trust anyone anymore." After that, they sat there in silence for a moment.

"So, Sir. What's the game plan?"

The general sat there a moment. "Lieutenant, I hate to make you the babysitter, but I need you to keep an eye on the colonel. Not sure if you could convince him to ride with you or not, but, if you can, that would be great. That would allow me time to try to reach President Mitchell to see what is going on. Sound good?"

Larry smiled. "Do I really have a choice?"

The general smiled back, "Of course you do Lieutenant. But if you say no, then I will just order you to do it and it will be done. How does that sound Lieutenant?"

Larry chuckled, "Sounds like a plan Sir. I can stick asshole in the trunk while the colonel and I can become good friends really quick. If my calculations are correct, we should be about one hundred miles from David."

"I do believe that your calculations are correct."

The general flipped back the flap on his watch. "Time to roll Lieutenant. Get a couple guys to grab asshole and get him in the trunk."

"Copy that." Larry went outside and called a few men to come inside. He asked them to load Deval up." No need to be gentle, he can no longer detonate on you."

The guys gave him a concerned look before one answered. He stretched his answer out. "Oookkaaay, Lieutenant." They carried Deval to the car with Larry and the colonel right behind them. As they were placing him in the trunk, Deval tried his best to scream something out. As he was lying there bound and gagged, he continued to give a death stare to Colonel Corde.

General Seltzer stood up on the running board of the Jeep and called out. "Mount up folks, we have a few hours ride ahead of us." He pointed to two different Jeeps with a main gun mount. "You, the one with the 30 cal, you take point. You with the 50 cal mount, bring up the rear. Anything looks like a threat, light it up. Got me?" They acknowledged and the gunners took their positions.

The general made sure that Larry was placed at least three vehicles behind so that he could be out of sight of the colonel as he attempted to raise Nicholas. After a few minutes, the general cranked the pack and called for Eagle One. Nothing. He waited a few minutes and tried it again. Still...nothing. He spoke to the tech in the backseat. "Not sure if this thing is broke, or if something happened at David and we are in for a surprise when we get there."

Surprisingly, there was little to no dead vehicles along their travel route. They did occasionally acquire an obstacle to avoid. But otherwise, it was smooth sailing with them being able to maintain an average speed of about thirty. The driver called out. "Sir, I must admit, I have been doing this for eight years now and not one time have I ever been this close to an A-Deuce let alone driving one. I have heard a lot of horror stories about these babies, but I just don't see them. This does run pretty good and pretty smooth."

The general chuckled. "Well Sergeant, at the speed that we are maintaining and the smooth road that we are on, well..." He paused and chuckled again. "Don't let it fool you. You are on a smooth course. Try doing thirty when there are holes and ruts. Usually anything over twenty on rough, uneven ground and you know where you may be?"

"Ah...no, Sir. Where?"

"Upside down Sergeant. These do flip rather easily." He turned to the driver. "And Sergeant, I do believe that the Lieutenant that owns these babies would be quite pissed if you tried out my theory."

The gunner in the lead Jeep raised his hand to let everyone know that they are halting. The general had the driver swing out a bit so that they could see around the lead Jeep. They observed a roadblock ahead that was made up of debris of vehicles and trees. The lead gunner locked and loaded as they came to a halt and the general's Jeep pulled up next to the first. The general stood up and used his field glasses to get a better look.

The gunner also had his glasses out and he was looking around. "Sir, movement at ten o'clock."

The general swung around to get a look. "I see him. We need to get someone up there."

Just then, a call from the rear. "Sir! Civilians approaching your six!" As the general was turning to look at the rear, he noticed armed individuals emerging from the sides also.

He yelled out. "Everyone hold your position and remain calm. I will handle this." The general exited the Jeep and removed his sidearm. He walked out in front of the lead Jeep. He was not sure who was the lead of this group, but he would soon find out. As loud as he could, he called out. "I am General Seltzer, United States Army, who is in charge here?" All the advancers suddenly halted, no one said a word. Again, the general called out. "I am General Seltzer, Uni…" He never got to finish his sentence before he was interrupted by the sound of one person clapping.

He looked to his left and he saw a man approaching him clapping. "Bravo Leon, bravo."

The general looked shocked. "Billy? That's really you?" He paused a second. "Where the hell did you come from? Nice to see you again."

Billy laughed. "Hold off on that feeling a few minutes, Leon. You may change your mind." He looked at the general's convoy. "Wow, impressive Leon. Where in the world did you find the ol' one-five-one A Deuces? Did you start your own little army?"

The general knew that this was not a friendly social visit. But, until he had it figured out, he decided to play along. "No, no Billy. These are actually the prize possessions of the LT in the rear vehicle."

Billy looked back to see Lieutenant McMasters acknowledge and salute with his MP5. "Okay, okay, good for him." Billy took a deep breath and cocked his head a little to the side. "Well Leon, by now, with you being the smart man that you are, you are probably aware that I am not here for reminiscing hour. So…let's cut to the chase, shall we?"

The general knew what was coming, but he continued to play along. "What can I do for you Billy?"

Billy gave a slight laugh. "Well Leon, first off as a good faith gesture, I will have my people lower their weapons and I ask you to have your people do the same." Billy made a motion indicating to lower all weapons, and all his people did as directed. The general just stood there giving no directions. Billy cocked his head. "Well?" The general just stood there. Billy laughed and raised his arms in disbelief. "Really Leon? It's going to be like that, is it? A one-sided affair again that shows no trust. Wow! Feels like we are right back in the bunker."

The general looked at him puzzled. "Since you brought up the bunker, just how in the hell did you get out of there and up to here?"

Billy smiled, "Damn Leon that is the main reason that I am here. You have never had any faith or confidence in my abilities. Any time that I had an idea, you either dismissed it or you never even listened." Billy began to pace. "You are the leader of a many thousand-man army, but you never listen to the point man. Sad Leon, very sad."

The general has heard about enough., "Okay Billy, spill it. What do you want?"

Billy walked over to the general, put an arm around his shoulder and smiled. "That's what I wanted to hear Leon." He stepped away, folded his hands and tucked them under his chin. "Leon, I do believe that you have a package for me." He looked around. "And since I do not see it sitting in any of the Jeeps, then I would venture to say that it is either in the van or in the trunk of the car."

He gave a big grin. "So, which is it, Leon?"

This time, the general laughed. "Billy, I really don't think that I have anything that you may desire. We are on a timely mannered mission. So...you and your people just step aside and let us through, and I will deal with you later."

Billy stood there a moment, blank look on his face. Without warning, he burst in laughter. The general just held his ground. Billy stopped laughing and got a real serious look on his face. "Listen up, General. I really do not believe that you are in any position to haggle." He looked around. "In case you failed to notice when you drove up." He waved his hand in a sweeping motion. "This is my show, and I am the emcee." All of Billy's men laughed along with him. "So, you see Leon. There is no time for you to deal with me later."

From the rear came a call. "General, we will handle this. You take your package and move along." The general turned around and to no one in particular, "Who in the hell is that?"

John smiled and called out. "General, they are with me. Sorry for the surprise, but I like to keep family close. As you will notice, they are all around us." Billy swung in a circle noticing that all his warriors were surrounded and outnumbered.

Larry and John welcomed the group. John walked over to the one that called out and embraced him. "General, come on over. May I introduce my brother, Clemon?"

The general approached him. "Nice to meet you." He looked around. "How in the hell did you all get out here?"

Clemon smiled. "General, we are not just family, we are mountain folk. We have our ways. We have communication that you would never understand."

John thanked Clemon for catching up so quickly. "Well brother, I hate to cut the family gathering short, but I really do believe that the general has to git." Clemon told the general that his people would take care of Billy's marauders and that he should be going. The general thanked him and his family for their timely service.

The general asked for one thing. "What may that be Sir?"

He points over his shoulder. "Would you please get that piece of shit bound, gagged and in the trunk with his partner?"

Clemon smiled and saluted. "Would be my pleasure Sir." A few of his relatives grabbed Billy and he protested all the way.

Once Billy and his men were idle, the general thanked John and Clemon and he stepped into the Jeep. He turned to face the convoy and with a big smile, "Let's roll boys!"

From one of the Jeeps came an 'Ahem'.

The general looked and saw Captain Sheer standing there with her hands on her hips. He turned a little red. "Sorry Ma'am." He smiled, "Let's roll boys and…" He pointed to her and finished what he was saying, "Girl." She gave a thumbs up.

CHAPTER TWENTY-SIX

Once they were all located to another conference room away from the other, Nicholas asked Jerry to get the radio. Jerry did as he was asked and came back a few minutes later with the radio. "Sir, do you want it in here or do you want a private setting?"

Nicholas looked at him and smiled. "Seriously Jerry? After what we all just encountered, I would prefer to keep everything out in the open with a group vote."

He looked around. "How does that sound to everyone?" No real verbal answers, just head nodding. "Well Jerry ol' boy, looks like the public has voted. Set it here on the table."

Jerry did as he was told. He cranked up the box and listened for static. When he was sure that it was alive, he handed the receiver to Nicholas. "Here Sir, ready when you are."

Nicholas took the receiver and once again held it up like a trophy. A few smirked and did a two-finger applause. Nicholas smiled. "Thank you, thank you. Please keep it down."

"Well, God be with us and let us get through." He took a deep breath. "Groundhog, Groundhog, Eagle One here." He waited a few seconds. "Groundhog, Groundhog, Eagle One. Come in." Silence. He looked at Jerry. "Are you..." The look in Jerry's face answered that uncompleted question. "Okay Gerald, I get it."

Jerry gave a smile. "You got this, Sir."

"Groundhog, Groundhog, Eagle One here." No response. "Groundhog, Groundhog, Eagle One here. Come on Leon, where are you?" He looked at Jerry. "Before you say anything, take a look at this thing." Jerry looked at the settings. Good. He lifted the receiver, looked it over and listened. Good. He pressed the button. "Groundhog, Groundhog, Eagle One here. Do you read?"

A second later. "Eagle One, Groundhog here. Is everything okay on that end?"

Nicholas looked at Jerry. "What did you do differently than me smart ass?"

Jerry smiled, "Sir, I hit the transmit button rather than the mute button that is for locking on receive only."

Nicholas turned a little red and smiled. "Give me that damned thing!"

"By all means Sir." The snickers went around the room.

Nicholas looked at them. "You know, you all can be replaced along with Gerald here." Snickers stopped.

Nicholas pressed the correct button this time. "Leon, have I got a tale for you."

The general came back. "Bet yours can't top mine!"

Nicholas laughed, "A twenty says that I can."

"Well Nick, I got a hundred that says differently."

Nicholas sat there a second. "Okay Leon, what do you have?"

The general took a few seconds to grasp the correct ideas in his head. "Nick, I have one terrorist and I also have Billy." The murmurs went around the room.

"Billy? Our Billy? Where in the hell did you find him? The last that anyone saw of him was when we all exited the bunker."

"Yes Sir, Nick, I got Billy."

Nicholas was really confused, his words were spaced and elongated. "But...Billlly...wass...with...usss. He...came..." He never finished his sentence before going into deep thought.

"Nick, not sure how in the hell he got out of the bunker and got up here in PA, but he had a group that was all hell bent on taking this asshole terrorist that Lieutenant Rollins tracked down."

Nicholas had no response to offer. His mind was still back at the mouth of the bunker right before they rolled out and they were calling for Billy. He finally snapped out of it. "Leon, I am lost for words. I am having a hard time getting this picture in my head." He paused. "Billy? Are you sure? Our Billy? What does Billy have to do with any of this?"

"Well Leon, I have him bound, gagged and riding in a trunk. When we meet up, I will let you open the trunk. That way, you can see for yourself, and you can ask him that question." Nicholas stood up, placed the receiver down and began pacing. Every so often, he would look up and see the ones around the table looking at him.

He went back and sat down. "Well Leon, John is dead."

"What?! I mean, how? When?"

"When we were speaking last, it appeared that he escaped the med suite on Marine One, eliminated all that was guarding him and made his way into the conference room and took us all hostage."

The general screamed. "WHAT?!" Nicholas did not expect that. That response hurt Nicholas' ear drum.

"Thanks Leon. Next time, scream into a bag."

"Sorry."

"Jerry had to have Delta come in and take control back. Leon, John was out of his mind. I knew that he had a few issues, but he was about to execute Delbert."

The general thought for a moment. "Well Nick, I guess we all have to do what we have to do." He pulled the flap off the top of his watch. "Nick, we should be arriving in about two hours. We can all sit down and try to figure this mess out together."

There was a knock at the door and Jerry answered it. The agent on the other side handed something to Jerry and Jerry closed the door. He went over to Nicholas and leaned in. "Sir, this was recovered from President Beard's hand."

Nicholas looked at it. "Hold on a moment Leon, Jerry just brought me something." Nicholas examined the device. It looked like an older style slide phone. He turned in over and over. He squeezed the side and it popped open a little bit. "What the hell?" He slid the side panel open, and a keyboard appeared. He picked up the receiver. "Ah, Leon. I was just handed something that was recovered from John. It apparently is some sort of remote device that Delta jammed before executing John. It looks like an old-style slide phone. Besides the Glock, I was not sure what he had in his hand. But apparently, this was it."

The general came back quickly. "Nick, whatever you do, *DO NOT PRESS ANY BUTTONS*! Please! Nick that may be the remote for a series of explosive devices that we've encountered."

Nicholas did not even close it up, he just carefully placed it on the table. "Okay."

*****

It took about another three hours for the group to arrive at David due to them encountering many vehicles still abandoned on the roadway. Before they arrived, Jerry contacted the media and informed them that there was in fact a sworn in president in office and that they would hold a press conference later that day.

When the general's group turned onto Park Central Road, the convoy was halted by men in camouflage and a pretty good size arsenal. The lead vehicle pulled to the side to allow the general's vehicle to encounter the man standing in the roadway.

As the Jeep stopped, the man in camo snapped to attention and saluted. The general saluted back and told the man to stand at ease. "Sir, President Mitchell has been anticipating your arrival."

The general smiled. "Probably not as much as I have been..." He looked at his insignia. "Excuse me. Did not see your rank at first, Colonel."

The colonel smiled. "Quite alright, Sir. I surprise a lot of people by being out here still playing with the big boys. Many think that I should be behind a desk pushing a pencil."

After he said that statement, he saw the eyebrows on the general crunch a bit. He realized that it did not come out as he intended. "I apologize, Sir. I did not intend for it to sound as though you were one of them."

The general laughed, "You know Colonel, a little embarrassing to admit, but it took this incident for me to actually realize that I too miss being out in the mist of things. After all of this is over, hell Colonel, I may spend more time out here than behind the desk."

The colonel just stared ahead. "Yes, Sir that may be good." Another fumble. "I mean..."

The general stopped him. "Quite alright Colonel." He pointed to the backseat. "Care to join us Colonel?"

The colonel looked shocked and impressed at the same time. "Ah...sure Sir." He saluted again.

"Get in the Jeep Colonel."

"Yes, Sir." He climbed in, smiled a big smile and gave his men a thumbs-up and mouthed, *'Yeah'*.

When they were coming up to their turn, the general looked off to his right and saw the sign for the campground. To no one in particular, he called out. "Back in my younger days, my wife and I stayed there once. The cabins may be drafty and old, but we were young, and we didn't give a damn. Sure would like to do it again, sometime before I die."

After turning, they were only about at the tree line when they were confronted by men in camouflage that appeared to come out of nowhere. The men saw their colonel and the general and stepped to the side. They snapped to attention and held their salute as the convoy rode past.

As they were approaching the main house, there was Nicholas and Jerry standing there waiting their arrival. The general hopped out of the Jeep and went to Nicholas. He embraced him as if he were his own son that just returned from afar. He released and stepped back. He looked at Jerry. "Come here Jer, I got one for you too."

Jerry tried as hard as he could to remain professional, but the human part took over and he returned the embrace. "Nice to see you again too, Sir. Welcome to Camp David."

The general pointed over his shoulder with his thumb. "Jerry, I got two in the trunk. Please place them in custody."

"Will do, Sir."

"Oh, Jerry."

"Yes, Sir."

"The one, he may have to be carried, he has been bound like that for a couple of days. Pretty sure that his legs may not work for a bit."

"Affirmative, Sir. Carry it is." Jerry called a few agents, and they went to the car to get the two out. When they approached the car, Larry tossed them the keys and he headed towards the general.

General Seltzer looked over and saw him coming. When he arrived, the general introduced him. "Nick...oooppss. Excuse me, President Mitchell, this is Lieutenant Rollins. He is the one that is responsible..." At the word responsible, Larry thought that his heart would leap out of his chest, and he failed to hear anything else clearly.

The general stood there waiting for a response from Larry. "Lieutenant." He nudged him. "Lieutenant, this is no time to be modest. Shake the president's hand."

Larry snapped out of it and extended his hand. "Sorry Sir, just a little exhausted."

Nicholas shook his hand. "No problem, Lieutenant, we will make sure that all of you get some good food and definitely some good rest. After that, when your mind is fresh, we can debrief you."

Four agents each had a hand on Deval as they carried him. As Billy was passing Nicholas, they just locked eyes and not a word was exchanged. Nicholas turned to the general. "Wow Leon, I am still blown away that Billy had some hand in this. I...I...." He stood there a moment trying to find the words. "I really have not a clue where to begin Leon. I am numb." He shook his head. "Billy...we, I mean him and I, we came up together. I remember when he first reached the hill. He was so gung-ho to make a difference. He wanted to learn it all, he..." Nicholas stood there with so many memories flashing through his head.

The general placed an arm around him. "That's alright Nick. We will get this straightened out as we move through it, and we will find out just how far and how deep this all goes. I will make it a personal interest to find out who all was involved, and I will have them hanged. Hell, I may even put the rope around their necks myself!" Larry was now not too thrilled to be there at that moment.

Nicholas took all the brass into the meeting room and introduced everyone. He especially paid attention to Larry and his uncanny ability to track and capture one of the terrorists. "Folks, what we have here is a real American hero. When we get back up and running, I want to pin the highest medal available on this young man. I will also promote him a couple ranks and find a cabinet position for him. Hell, if I have to, I will create one."

Larry stood there both humble and scared to death. He had so many thoughts going through his head that he thought that it would explode. The general took the floor. "Mr. President, you said that the media was on the way?" Nicholas nodded yes. "Great, when they get here, I would like to personally take Lieutenant Rollins out and introduce him."

One of the gentlemen in the room raised his hand. "Mr. President, not to sound like a reporter, but may I ask Lieutenant Rollins a question? I mean if he does not mind."

"Sure Sam, but he is right here, you could have asked him if it was okay."

A few chuckles went out. Sam felt a little embarrassed. "Right Sir, sorry."

Sam took a deep breath and exhaled slowly before asking. "LT, would you mind?" Larry answered by shaking his head no. "Lieutenant, just how were you able to track down the supposed terrorists? How did you know which way to start? Sorry, but I am fascinated in things of this nature. As I am sure that many others in this room would like to hear it."

Larry stood there a moment trying to figure out if he should run, or does he face the music. He raised his head and looked to the heavens. Inside, he heard a voice saying, 'Larry, you never ran from a thing before, so don't start now'. "Before I answer your questions, would you all please have a seat? This is going to take a bit and when you hear it all, you may wish that you were seated so that you wouldn't have fallen down."

Everyone in the room found somewhere to sit, whether it be chair, cabinet or floor. Larry began slowly pacing back and forth. He had his hands folded and tucked under his chin as he did so. He came to a stop and faced the group. "I want you all to know that I am not trying to make any excuses for myself nor am I seeking any pity. I am not sure if I should sit or stand."

One man stood up and offered his chair. "Here Lieutenant, sit."

At first, Larry was a little reluctant. After the man insisted a second time, Larry sat. He sat with his hands folded on the table out in front of him. "Wow, where to begin." He took a deep breath and looked up. "I would like to clear the air and my conscience. I am not all the hero that you all think that you see."

The general interrupted. "Humble, isn't he?"

Larry looked at him. "Please Sir, let me get this out."

Larry stood and began pacing again. He stopped at the head of the table, moved the chair out of the way and leaned on the table. He looked upon the group. "I am the one that placed the charges on the bridges and the dam on the Susquehanna." The looks of shock and the expressions that came out brought the room to a roar.

The general jumped up. "Just what the hell are you saying Lieutenant?! You are one of them?" He was quick to act. "Agents! Secure that man!" Three agents grabbed Larry and placed him in handcuffs. He gave no resistance. The general walked over to Larry. "Well, Lieutenant, thanks for giving us a heads up before we made asses out of ourselves before the media." He gave Larry a hard stare. "Get him out of here. Place him with his comrades."

Nicholas jumped in. "Hold on a second General. Something inside tells me to hear what he has to say. Something does not feel right." The general was a little reluctant, but he gave in.

Larry looked at Nicholas. "Thank you, Mr. President." Larry collected his thoughts once again before starting. "I did not do it willingly. I, along with John Meyers had no choice. Our children were taken from us and if we did not carry out what was presented to us, we would have received our children back in

313

more pieces than how they were taken. I am not sure as to who else may have been placed in the same situation as we were, but I am sure that there were many. I personally believe that this was and or is much larger than just a few men. No group is that good that they could pull this off with just a few people." He stood there with his head hung low for a moment. "Mr. Myers and I were able to save some of the children that were being held in this region. Like I said, I do not know if there were others, so I do not know if what we did here has affected the safety or the wellbeing of other families. Only time and a lot of footwork will tell."

The general stood up. "Okay Lieutenant, I have a few questions for you."

Larry nodded his head in agreement. "Fire away Sir."

The general had a stern expression on his face. "Lieutenant, just how did you get involved and how did it all begin? Did you just get up one morning and decide that you wanted to ruin America?" Nicholas thought that statement was uncalled for, and he chastised the general for doing so.

Larry gathered his thoughts in order. "I was stationed at Fort Benning. One day, after my daily run, there was knock at the door and two men showed up in uniform sporting captain bars and an insignia that I have never seen. They informed me that their organization needed me and my specialty of explosives. They wanted me to acquire five thousand pounds of Semtex."

The general jumped up. "Five thousand pounds?! Is that what you got for them? Five thousand pounds?"

Larry took a deep breath. "Yes Sir, five thousand pounds."

"At the meeting, I was informed that they already had my daughter, Bella Marie."

"And what gave you that idea Lieutenant?"

Larry had the same feeling of rage come back to him when he was in that meeting. "Because Sir, they made a call and allowed me to see my daughter wherever the fuck it was they had her! That is how I Knew. Sir!"

Nicholas intervened. "Alright, everyone just calm down. Let's hear what the Lieutenant has." Nicholas turned to Jerry. "Think we can get those cuffs off him? I do not think that they are necessary."

Larry looked to Nicholas. "Thank you, Sir." One of the agents removed the cuffs and Larry rubbed his wrists. "Thank you."

Larry looked to Nicholas. "May I continue Sir?" He nodded yes. "I have devoted most of my life to the military. I love this country and I love what I do, but...I love my daughter even more. So, when it came to her life, I put my life, my career and all my morals on the line. I did what I had to do to protect and save my daughter. And General, as you saw firsthand, I was able to rescue and save my daughter."

The general nodded. "I did at that, continue."

Nicholas spoke up. "Lieutenant, if you do not mind me asking, just how in the world were you able to track the terrorist down?"

The general spoke up. "Yeah, me too, I want to hear this." Nicholas gave him the evil eye again. The general shrugged.

"That was not an easy feat, but I was able to do most of the preliminary work before everything went down."

Nicholas looked puzzled. "How so Lieutenant."

Larry smiled. "Well Sir, it was Deval himself that helped with that."

"How so?"

"Well Sir, the day that I was placing the explosives."

The general added. "So, you did that all by yourself?"

Larry looked a little annoyed about being interrupted again. "No, Deval had Mr. Meyers pilot the boat that we used to ferry the explosives out to the pilings so that I could place the explosives at the exact support that was called out by Deval." Larry waited for a response, but none came.

"While we were at a pier, the DNR Police came upon us." Larry chuckled. "Mr. Meyers and I were calling Deval '*George*'. Mainly because we did not know his name at the time. But." He chuckled again. "When the officers asked for ID, he handed it over and they referred to him as *Mr. Bloom* with Homeland. Boy, Deval almost shit himself at that moment."

Larry repositioned and cleared his throat. "Hell, Deval gave me enough to bite on. Knowing who he was supposed to be gave me enough to start digging." He smiled again. "With the connections that I have acquired over the years as an Army officer, I was able to get a few addresses that he had over the years. With all that information, it was just a process of elimination. That is how I tracked him to a residence in Zooks Corner, Pennsylvania. And that is also where Mr. Myers, along with the assistance of some of his family members, we were able to free the children and neutralize the terrorist at that residence." He looked to the general. "Sir, I do believe that you have also met some of Mr. Meyers' family and you were able to witness their abilities."

The general gave a snarl and looked towards Nicholas. "Yes, that I did also." Nicholas smiled at him.

The general looked at Larry. "Okay, you found his residence. Just how did you wind up at the airport?"

Larry stood and proudly exclaimed. "Second Seventy Fifth, Sir! I specialize in extraction, Sir."

Nicholas smiled. "Well Lieutenant, it appears that you were trained and learned well."

Larry smiled. "That I did, Sir. I was able to get the information that I required to track Deval to the airport and catch him and his two-man crew before they were able to escape and take my daughter and Mr. Meyers' son with them."

No one said a word for a moment. Finally, one man raised his hand and looked at Nicholas. "May I ask a question?"

Nicholas smiled. "Sure Rodney." Nicholas looked around the table. "Look, if anyone has any questions for Lieutenant Rollins, then now is the time. Let's get everything out and on the table before the media gets here." About ten hands went up. Nicholas chuckled. "Okay now. We will start with Rod and then go around to his right. Go ahead Rod."

"Thank you, Sir." He cleared his throat. "Lieutenant, you said that other children were there and that they too were freed. Correct?"

"Yes. Sir that they were."

Rodney hesitated a second. "I was wondering...where are the children now? Are they back with their families?"

Larry sat up straight. "Sir that is not an answer that I have. Like I stated, Mr. Meyers and I left the residence in search of Deval that had just left a few minutes before us. I am afraid that you would have to get someone to Mr. Meyers' residence and ask his family." Larry sat there a second. "Sad to say, but I did see a few children there that would be too small to inform the authorities as to who they may be, let alone where they lived and with whom." All was silent for a few minutes. "Also, as I stated early on, we have not a clue as to how big this actually is or was. As far as we know, some of these children could be from a far western state. I do not know."

Nicholas stood up. "Why don't we all take fifteen and stretch our legs. Besides, I would like to speak with General Seltzer privately for a few minutes." Everyone agreed and rose from their seats.

Larry sat there for a moment. "Sir, may I go also?"

Nicholas smiled. "Of course, Lieutenant. You are free to travel with the rest. I just need a few minutes with the general. Thanks."

CHAPTER TWENTY-SEVEN

Colonel Corde approached the lock-up and after some convincing, was allowed past the two guards outside and inside the lobby of the lock-up building. "Soldier, I need a few minutes with these men, alone please."

"Sir, I am not sure if I can allow that. I was given strict orders that no one comes in and no one goes out."

"Sergeant, in case you have not noticed, I outrank you considerably. So, please open that door and allow me in. Then, once I am in, I need you to step outside. I need a few minutes to interrogate these men."

The guard stood his ground. "Sir, I am at orders to let no one in, Sir. I cannot allow that."

The colonel smiled. "Soldier, I respect your dedication to duty, but..." He placed an arm around his shoulder and started to walk him out. "I need to speak to these men, and I do not need anyone to be eaves dropping. Do you understand?"

The sergeant twisted to get the colonel's hand off his shoulder. "Sir, I understand completely. Do you understand my position? I cannot let you in."

The colonel asked for the sergeant's id. As he was getting his wallet out, the colonel reached into his pocket and removed a syringe. He popped the cap as he was pulling it out and went for the sergeant's neck. The sergeant saw his hand coming up and he made a move to defend himself. The colonel was bigger and stronger which gave him the advantage. After a brief struggle, the colonel was able to stick the sergeant and administer the drug.

In the matter of a few seconds, the sergeant started to lose his fight. Slowly, he slid down the wall until his backside hit the floor. The colonel threw the syringe and began looking for the keys to the cell. He searched every pocket. In a low gruff tone. "Fuck! Where the fuck is the keys?"

He had to think quickly. Here, he had a dead soldier on one side of the door and two armed guards on the other side that he had to contend with in order to get out of the building. "Think. Serg! Think!" Never since childhood, has he ever felt so trapped.

He tapped on the door in code. Billy came to the door. "Serg, get us out and we can finish this."

The colonel hesitated at first. "Just hang on a little bit longer. I need to find a way to get this door open. Apparently, the keys are on the other side of this outer door that is in the hands of two armed guards."

"Can't you get them? What is the problem?" The colonel did not like being questioned. He harshly spoke something in Arabic and then Billy answered in English. "Yes Sir, we will wait for your arrival back here."

The colonel never felt so trapped and helpless. Here, he has one guard dead in a room with only one way out and he has two armed guards stationed on the other side of a locked door at adjacent ends of the room for safety. His mind was racing a million miles a minute.

He quickly laid the dead guard near the door, ripped open his shirt and banged on the door. As loud as he could, he called out. "Need help in here! Need help!" The guard nearest the door opened the flap and peered in and saw the colonel performing CPR. He looked up. "This man has apparently had a heart attack. We need to get him to medical fast!"

The guard on the far side was curious. "What's up?"

The first guard started to explain when the colonel called out again. "Soldier, get in here! This man needs help!"

"Colonel, I can call help and they could be here in a short time. But I cannot open that door unless the guard inside there tells me that it is okay or the general orders me to open it."

The colonel got up into the opening. "If you don't open this fuckin' door, this man will die and so will you. I will make sure that the cause of his death is solely on your shoulders and that you will face a firing squad for your lack of action. Now, open this door and the two of you help get this man out of here and straight to medical. That is a direct order."

The guard looked at the colonel with uncertainty in his face. "But Sir."

The colonel yelled out. "NOW!"

The guard called the other over to help him with the downed guard. As the first guard started through the door, the colonel grabbed him by his head and quickly snapped his neck. The other guard attempted to grab his side arm. Before he could get it all the way up and out of the holster, the colonel grabbed for his arm. As they wrestled for the firearm, the colonel kept one hand on the hand with the weapon and reached up with the other arm, got it wrapped around the soldier's neck from the front, bent him backwards and snapped his neck. But, before the instant death came upon him, the guard was able to get a shot off.

The colonel dropped the soldier and stood there in fear. It took a few seconds before he realized that there was a warm feeling running down over his hip and on towards his thigh. The dead soldier was able to at least score a hit before death set in. If the colonel wasn't worried two minutes ago, he sure was now.

It was not but mere seconds before a banging came upon the door. "This is Colonel Samson, Delta Force Commander. Is anyone in there able to hear me?" He received no response, so he repeated himself once more. "This is Colonel Samson, Delta Force Commander. Is anyone in there able to hear me?" When he received no response again, he had one of his men retrieve a scope and slowly raise it to the ledge of a tall window and he moved it around to scan the room.

The man looked at the monitor. In a low tone. "Sir, I am able to see two down, presumed dead. One standing facing the door with side arm, Sir."

Colonel Samson and General Seltzer looked at the monitor. The general spoke up. "What the fuck? That's Colonel Corde."

Larry spoke up. "General, remember what I told you about the lump that I thought that I saw on his neck?"

The general looked at him. "Sorry Lieutenant, but it appears that you may be right. Thinking about it, I do distinctly remember feeling something when I patted him on the back as we left the office."

The general looked towards the colonel. "So, Colonel, what is the game plan? How do we get him out?"

The colonel had an idea. He sent one of his men to Nicholas to retrieve the remote that President Beard had in his possession.

322

When the man arrived back with the device, Colonel Samson had his best techie take a look at the device. "Adams, I need you to make an assessment and I need it quick. We have about two minutes."

Adams unzipped a small pouch in his vest and folded down a small tray. He flipped up a small screen, placed the device on the tray and watched a series of numbers changing on the screen. The colonel was switching his sight back and forth from the monitor looking in the room and Adams working the device. "Adams, any time now."

"Working on it, Sir, working on it." The numbers continued to spin until each one eventually locked on a number. "Almost there, Sir. One more number and we…" He paused, "Got it! I have control Sir. What is your command?"

The colonel looked at the room monitor. "Start the device Adams."

He pressed a few buttons and they watched as Colonel Corde jumped when the device started beeping. "What the fuck?" He grabbed the back of his neck and started spinning in different directions in an attempt to remove it.

"Stop the device Adams." He did as he was told, but Colonel Corde continued in his attempt to remove the device.

General Seltzer yelled in. "Colonel, if you want to walk out of there all in one piece, then I suggest that you unlock this door, step back five steps and then lie on the floor." He waited for a response. "Colonel, if you do not comply, then you will leave me no alternative than to have the device started and let it end this bulllshit." No response. "Colonel Corde, I am ordering you to respond to me!"

Colonel Samson called over. "General. He just went back into lock up. We have an ear open, but we cannot make out what they are saying. We can give them a moment to come out, then after that, I will have my man start the device and we walk away."

General Seltzer looked around. "I find anyone else involved in this shit and will shoot you in your fuckin' head myself. Anyone desire to step forward?" He continued to scan the surroundings.

Colonel Samson called out. "General, get ready, they just came out of lock up." He listened to their conversation.

"General, come on over here." The general made it to the screen just in time to see Billy place a sidearm in his waist band in the back. "General, from what we just heard, they are going to try a 'Butch Cassidy and the Sundance Kid' move."

The trio started to the door. The general softly called out. "Jiggle the doorknob. We need another minute." One of his men reached over and jiggled the knob. They watched as the trio stopped and then began to back up.

The general asked to speak to Colonel Samson alone for a moment. They stepped back about twenty feet. "Colonel, I have a game plan that I believe could end this here and now."

The colonel was game. "Okay General, run it by me." The general spilled his plan and the colonel agreed to it.

The colonel had a man place three small charges at the location of each hinge on the door. They watched the monitor as each charge went off about five seconds apart. The first two charges startled the trio and as each one blew, they moved closer to the door of the lock up. Right before the last charge went off, the power to the building was severed. They watched as the trio fumbled to take cover inside the lock up.

A flashbang was tossed into the room and a squad moved in. They tossed a second flashbang into the lock up. One of the squad quickly, and quietly made his way into the lock up. He could see through his visor that the trio had made it into the open cell. He quickly slammed the door closed.

He gave a thumbs up sign to another that was in the main room and that man in turn looked at the monitor and he also gave the sign. General Seltzer extended a hand. "Colonel, success. You and your squad did great."

The colonel accepted his hand "I can't take full credit; it was your idea." He patted the general on the shoulder. "How about we go in and you finish this up."

The general smiled. "Great idea Colonel."

They played it safe as they entered the holding area. The colonel had eyes placed on the wall so that they could observe the situation in the cell. General Seltzer called out. "Colonel Corde... Billy, it's me, Leon." He hesitated a moment. "Colonel, I know that we do not know each other, then again, that apparently goes for you too Billy." He collected his thoughts. "Gentlemen, as Army Chief of Staff, I am authorized to hold the three of you for many, many charges ranging from conspiracy to treason to terroristic actions." He looked to Colonel Samson. "It also authorizes me to pass sentence upon you."

He motioned for the techie to come over. "Billy, I do not know why, and I guess that I never will know why. But as Army Chief of Staff, I pass the sentence of death unto all three of you. The action will be carried out immediately and without ado."

Colonel Corde slammed the back side of the door. "You smug, arrogant, self-centered bastard. Open this fuckin' door and release me or you will all suffer a fate worse than what you think that you have now." No one flinched. The colonel continued to bang on the door and scream out.

The general motioned for everyone to leave but him and Colonel Samson. "Colonel Bradley Corde, William Dennis Allen..." He thought for a second, then whispered to the colonel. "I really do not know the other assholes real name."

The colonel cocked his head. "For the record, asshole will be fine."

The general continued. "Colonel Bradley Corde, William Dennis Allen and Asshole. I hereby pass the sentence of death onto the three of you that will be carried out immediately."

He looked out into the main room at the techie standing there with the shelf folded down and screen tilted up. "Hit it Lieutenant." The techie pressed a few buttons and the colonel and general heard the device start to beep. They exited the lock up area and secured the door. As they were all slowly exiting the building, they heard the screaming and the banging on the cell door before they heard one final bang. The general stopped. "Colonel, shall we go brief the president?"

The colonel nodded. "By all means General." He extended a hand. "After you Sir."

Everyone was brought into the meeting room. The general and colonel laid everything on the table. Nicholas was still baffled that Billy was a part of it all. He had a seat. "You know, it is rather unique that one can work with someone day in and day out for years, be a part of their family gatherings and in the end, it appears that the whole time, you were breaking bread with a total stranger. I am still blown away..." He paused a second. "Sorry, no pun intended." That did get a few smiles. "I am lost with the words to say."

He stood up and walked to the window. "Sadly, his wife and children are gone. Then again, on a plus side, with them gone, I do not have to face them and tell them that the man that they thought that they knew and loved was not who they thought that he was. Honestly, I am not sure that I would have had the courage to deliver that speech."

There came a knock at the door and Jerry answered it. A few words were exchanged, then Jerry shut the door. Nicholas looked over at Jerry and Jerry raised a finger indicting that he needed a second or two. Nicholas nodded. "Sir, I was just informed that the media is here and set up. Should I give them a time frame?"

Nicholas thought for a second. "Send word that fifteen minutes will be a go. Thanks."

Nicholas went back to the head of the table. He waited until Jerry was done and the door was closed. He leaned in on the table. "I really have no order of thoughts at this moment. So, I will just throw them out there and allow you all to piece them together in the proper order as you see fit." He scanned to see that everyone was paying attention.

"A few hours ago, we all gathered here to hear what Lieutenant Rollins had to say. I am not a judge nor jury and I do not know how each and every one of you feel about the situation. But, at this time, I would like to express my opinion and I would like to go around the room and hear everyone else's opinion. Please, do not feel that you have to agree with me, speak your own mind."

Nicholas said that he was a little torn between what was supposed to be right and what actually happened. "Lieutenant Rollins did play a major part in what happened, but then again, for my children, I probably would have done the same thing. I hope and pray that I am never put in that position. Honestly, I do not know what I would do."

He began to pace. "You all are as much aware as I am that Lieutenant Rollins did not have to say a word about what he was forced to do. He could have remained quiet and none of us would have been the wiser, but...he decided to stand up and admit his part. I am sure that he was fully aware that by doing so, he knew that he faced a good chance of standing before a firing squad." He hesitated a second. "But, Lieutenant Rollins, has integrity and honesty in his blood. By him coming forward, those two qualities shine forth."

He spoke for about another ten minutes before he started around the table. He looked at Jerry. "Oh, Jer, mind passing word that we may be a little longer?"

Jerry smiled. "Will do, Sir, a little more time." He went to the door and passed the information along and closed the door. He took his position against the door and nodded to Nicholas.

Nicholas went one by one until everyone said what they had to say. There were some that showed more emotion than the others. Some stated that they did not hate, nor did they hold the circumstances against Larry that he was presented. Most also stated that if they were thrown into that position, that at this time, they feel as though that they would have done the same thing. There were a few tears as some spoke of not knowing that the last time that they hugged their family that it would have been the last time for eternity.

After the last person spoke, Nicholas looked over the crowd and asked if that was everyone. "I didn't intend to leave anyone out, so, if I did miss you, I do apologize, and you will get a raise."

A few chuckles went around and about ten people put their hands up with smiles on their faces. One called out. "Sir, I think you skipped me twice."

Nicholas smiled. "Good try Marty. Just for that, your raise goes on freeze until the next administration comes in." They all laughed.

"Okay, on a serious note, I would like to say something that is both a personal request and an executive order." He took a deep breath before he began. "We have all heard some pretty graphic and disturbing information in this room in the last few hours. With my whole being, I want you all to know that I trust you all deeply. So, with that thought in mind, I would like to ask you all to do me and all the rest of us a favor." He looked at the group. "What has come out in this room stays in this room. As far as I am concerned, this incident is behind us. We got the bad guys and they got what they deserved. There is no need for anyone outside of this room to know all the details. Any objections?" No one said a word, most shook their head *no*. "Good, let's go introduce the new cabinet to the world."

The new Speaker of the House stepped outside the double doors and stepped off to the side. In a loud voice. "May I have your attention please. I would like to introduce someone." He cleared his throat and belted out. "Ladies and Gentlemen, introducing the President of the United States, Nicholas Lenwood Mitchell." The crowd was in a roar as Nicholas emerged from inside. He stepped right up to the podium and motioned for the cheers and clapping to subside.

"Good afternoon, I apologize for the major delay in getting out here. First off, I thank you all for taking the time and the journey to be here today." Applause was deafening. Nicholas smiled and motioned for stillness again. "Please hold any and all applause until this is over. Okay?" No one responded, he looked around and smiled. "Cool."

He collected his thoughts. "Wow...there is so much to cover, and I apologize that this will be quite a while getting it all out. It has been quite a phenomenal emotional ride these past few days here that I myself am still attempting to piece together. I have so much to share and please bear with me if I seem to drift out of sequence."

He collected his thoughts for a moment. "As most of you already know, a few days ago, our infrastructure was attacked from the inside. Sad to announce, but President Wolford and his family never made it to safety, they perished in the attack on the White House." He felt tears welling up in his eyes. He made a sweeping motion towards his cabinet. "Along with countless thousands of innocents, all of our cabinet members lost their families on that day too. I too did not escape that fate either." He had to stop for a moment in order to regain his composure.

"I know that some of you are wondering how I am here as president and not President Beard. That is another tragic story in its own." He paused and looked at his cabinet. "Sad to announce, but President Beard was fatally injured in an attempt to do what he believed in. So please, keep him in your prayers as well." After that statement, he looked back at Jerry and Jerry nodded in approval.

"But, on a positive note, I would like to recognize and bring forward a few people that due to their actions, made it possible for us to be here today speaking with you. There are many that played an important part in all of this that I cannot just recognize one single person." He stepped off to the side of the podium and leaned in at the mic. "To begin with, here are two major players in the apprehension and elimination of some of the terrorist. May I introduce Major Lawrence Joseph Rollins and John Robert Meyers. Gentlemen, please step forward." Larry almost did not move. All that went through his mind was 'Major'? Nicholas motioned for them to step forward. Larry let John go first.

When they arrived at the podium, Nicholas introduced them. "I want you all to take a good look at these two gentlemen. They are what you would call a true American hero. Major Rollins..." Larry looked at him and Nicholas smiled. "Oh, sorry folks, but before all of this happened, this soldier was addressed as Lieutenant, but due to his heroics, he has been commissioned to Major." The crowd let out a standing applause that lasted a few minutes.

"Major Rollins, along with Mr. Meyers joined forces. They..." Larry tapped Nicholas on the shoulder and whispered in his ear. Nicholas continued. "Forgive me, Major Rollins and John Meyers along with the assistance of a number of Mr. Meyers' family members were able to eliminate a small band of terrorist that are related to this incident. Many are in custody and will be sent to trial for their part in all of this. For Mr. Meyers, he, along with some family members will receive a presidential citation along with other perks that come with what they all heroically did."

Larry said a few words as well as John. After that, General Seltzer spoke of the dedication and the bravery of all the ones involved in this matter. Not one time did it ever come up nor was the idea put out there that John Beard was the head of the terrorist organization.

Even after Nicholas ran down what he thought was everything that everyone needed to know, he opened for questions and boy, did the questions flood in. The questions bounced around to Nicholas, General Seltzer, Colonel Samson, Larry and John. Each one carefully pieced together their answers before speaking them. Sometimes, the questions were directed at the operation that led them to the airport. Larry and John took turns answering them. The press conference had no limit on questions or time. It was almost five hours before things settled down.

The following day, everyone departed Camp David minus the minimum required to get the government back up and running at full speed. Lieutenant McMasters was also promoted. He was brought up to captain and given command of the unit from Hagerstown that Colonel Corde once commanded.

Larry stayed on with the Army for just another six months before he decided to retire and devote his time to his daughter. It was a hard pill to swallow, but Larry passed the promise of tracking down Deval's family to some private groups. They made sure that the message of coming here to the United States and doing something again like we all just went through would never happen again. Just the few days that Bella and Larry were taken away from each other was more than he desired to bear. So, he spent as much time with her as he possibly could. Bella eventually went on to join the military. Due to her father's intervention in apprehending the terrorist, President Mitchell made sure that if she ever desired to do so, that she would be appointed to West Point without having to apply for acceptance.

Years later, with Bella Marie now away at West Point and Larry having no one else to attend to, he went on to live not too far from his sister just outside the Army base in Aberdeen, Maryland. He eventually settled into a small inn with just one room and a bath. After the attacks, he realized that he did not require much outside of the acceptance of Bella Marie.

Not too long after settling in, Larry was diagnosed with congestive heart failure. His sister Judy was close enough by that she would visit him and tended to his needs daily. He remained in his little one room abode until he succumbed to his disease on a warm, sunny day on Sunday, July 29, 2018.

Made in the USA
Monee, IL
26 January 2023

d959d06e-7b2a-4291-a802-c130ed67d472R01